4

DEATH
IN
DAMASCUS

Karen Baugh
MENUHIN

Front cover:
Artefact/Alamy Stock Photo Street-scene
Damascus Bauernfeind Gustav

First paperback and ebook edition March 2020

ISBN: 979-8-6183975-4-4

For
Sam and Wendy,
Charlie, Joshua and Isabella-Rose.

CHAPTER 1

December 1921

'I said, 'your girlfriend's fiancé is in jail. He's been accused of attempted murder and she's asked for help'.' Swift eyed me from beneath a rain-drenched fedora.

'Swift,' I began again, as he stood on my doorstep in the dark, letting the freezing wind and rain blow into my home. 'Will you come inside and tell me what the devil you are talking about?'

He marched into the hallway, wearing a tightly belted trench coat and proper trousers rather than the kilt he'd recently taken to sporting, and placed his rain-spattered suitcase down on the worn mat by the boot room.

'I left a message with Greggs to tell you I was coming.' He tugged off his sodden coat and hat and handed them to me as if I were the butler. I tossed them over the stair post to drip onto the stone-flagged floor and followed him into my library.

I imagine the warmth drew him to the room as Swift had never visited The Manor at Ashton Steeple before. My

little golden spaniel, Mr Fogg, had enthusiastically welcomed the ex-Chief Inspector when he'd knocked on my
door, but quickly returned to his cozy basket by the hearth.

'I haven't seen Greggs,' I said, rather piqued by the
absence of my butler. 'And what do you mean by 'fiancé'?'

'Give me a minute, would you,' he headed for a wing
chair beside the blazing fire and sat down to rub his hands
together in front of the flames. The cold had sharpened
his face, accentuating his angular features below damp
dark hair. Swift and I had first met when he'd accused me
of murder. He'd have had my neck in a noose if I hadn't
taken a hand at detecting and uncovered the culprit
myself. Since then, through circumstance and adventure,
we'd formed something approaching a friendship.

I dropped into the chair opposite. 'Right, so tell me.
I'd really like to hear why Persi Carruthers has a fiancé,
because I was under the impression that she and I had an
understanding.'

'Well, it obviously wasn't the same understanding, was
it!' he replied, then moderated his tone when he saw my
expression. 'Look, Lennox, I'm sorry, but I've come all
the way from the Highlands for this. The man's called
Charles Langton and he's actually her ex-fiancé. Florence
and I received a letter from Persi, she was distraught and
begged me for help. She sent a couple of telegrams too.'

That was another bolt out of the blue. 'Well, where is
she?'

'Damascus.'

'Damascus! You mean the place in the Bible?'

'Yes, Lennox.' He frowned. 'Where have you been? I've been trying to contact you.'

'Melrose Court. Went to see my uncle, he's become rather decrepit poor chap, and… never mind that, Swift. Who is this damn fiancé?'

'Ex-fiancé. I already told you, Charles Langton. He's being held in a Syrian jail and she needs help to get him out. The country was at war and now the French have moved in. Nobody will help and the jail is appalling. She thinks he won't last much longer.'

'But…' I stuttered to a halt, trying to take it all in. I hadn't seen Persephone Carruthers since we met at Braeburn Castle, the clan home of Swift's wife. He had managed to unearth an ancient skeleton and a secret curse and then there were a couple of murders. I had become close to the archaeologist, Persephone, or Persi for short, during the investigations.

'The French have policemen, and they're supposed to be our allies.' I said. 'Why on earth would they allow Persi's ex-fiancé to rot in a foreign jail?'

'Because the lady he is accused of trying to murder is French,' Swift replied.

'But, surely the British authorities are helping?'

'No.'

'Why?'

'Because he's a spy.'

'Really?' That raised my brows. 'Who for?'

His dark eyes regarded me steadily. 'The British, and from what I understand that is part of the problem.'

Well, that was as clear as mud, I thought, although I wasn't entirely listening because my mind kept returning to the word 'fiancé'. Why hadn't Persi mentioned his existence? Surely it was the sort of information girlfriends were supposed to disclose? Admittedly I hadn't really had much time to get to know her whilst tracking down a murderer, but a fiancé, or even an ex-fiancé, was a fairly significant fact. And, why hadn't she contacted me rather than Swift? Did she think I'd refuse? I confess I had always found the fair sex to be a bit of a mystery and it occurred to me that perhaps I hadn't asked the right questions.

My butler entered at a stately pace.

'Greggs!' I exclaimed. 'Where have you been?'

'At our local theatre, sir.' He took on the po-faced look he acquired whenever he was on the defensive. 'We are rehearsing a production of Mr Dickens.'

'Ah, The Pickwick Papers – I rather like that. Dickens wrote some jolly amusing stuff.'

'Actually, it is a Christmas Carol, sir. I am playing the lead role, Mr Scrooge.'

'Hum, well don't take the part to heart, Greggs,' I said, because he was apt to be close in the pocket. 'Anyway, you were supposed to be back before I was and I've been home for a couple of hours now.'

'I was, sir. I have been upstairs unpacking your trunk and re-ordering your rooms. They were in disarray.' He stood upright in his butlering uniform, paunch straining a starched shirt under black waistcoat, drooping chins supported by a white dickie over a stiff collar.

'Right... erm.' I switched tack as he may have had a point about the mess in my rooms. 'Inspector Swift says he left a message?'

'He did, sir.' He paused to fumble in the pockets of his tailcoat before pulling out a folded note. 'Chief Inspector Swift telephoned and asked you to accompany him to release a pie from a mattress. I'm afraid it didn't make sense, sir.'

His deafness was getting worse, which was probably why he hadn't heard Swift at the front door and I'd had to answer it myself. 'A 'spy from Damascus', Greggs,' I told him. 'Not a pie from a mattress.'

'A spy, sir?' he repeated. 'From... from that place in the Bible?'

'Yes.' I nodded. 'I think a hot toddy is required, Greggs. The Inspector is damp and cold. And a snack wouldn't go amiss.'

'Yes, sir.' I don't think he'd taken much in beyond 'spy' and 'Damascus'.

'Cheese and crackers, a few slices of pork pie, some apple and Cook's best pickle?' I suggested as he remained immobile. 'Please, Greggs?'

'Um...Certainly, sir.' He went off in a bit of a daze.

Fogg had looked up at the mention of crackers and watched me with bright spaniel eyes. I reached down to stroke the golden fur on his head and assured him he wouldn't be forgotten. Mr Tubbs, our rotund black kitten, had been asleep next to him in the basket but now woke up and contemplated the ex-Inspector. The little cat went over and jumped up onto his lap with a determined air. Swift made a fuss of him, rubbing his sooty black ears and letting him settle to purr himself to sleep.

'Swift,' I returned to the peculiar news. 'What exactly are you proposing?'

'That we go to Damascus,' he replied, as though it were merely a trip to the metropolis, 'to try to find a way to have Persi's fiancé released from jail.'

'Ex-fiancé,' I corrected him

'Yes, yes.'

I didn't get the impression he was entirely irrational, in fact, he looked quite serious about the whole enterprise.

'Where on earth is Damascus?' I said at last.

'Here.' He extracted a small, leather-bound book from inside his tweed jacket. It was a miniature map of the world which he unfolded from its complicated pleats. A great deal of the map was pinkish-red, indicating those parts which belonged to the British Empire. He balanced it on his knee and pointed to an area which was coloured creamy-yellow and named 'Syria'. It was next to Mesopotamia and the much larger country of Arabia, and all of them were placed on the far side of the Mediterranean.

'Didn't you do geography at school?' he asked, as if I were some sort of duffer.

'Yes, when I wasn't playing cricket, or rugby or tennis, or some such.' I ran a finger between my home, here in the deepest Cotswolds, and those very distant lands beyond the Lebanon. 'It's miles away, Swift. Hundreds of miles by the looks of it, how do you propose getting there?'

'Aeroplane,' he replied. 'We can fly to Paris and then Constantinople, and from there to Damascus. I've studied it.' He sounded rather proud of himself.

I didn't share his enthusiasm; I'd been a pilot during the war and was all too familiar with the discomforts of modern aircraft. 'Do you have any idea how long it could take?'

He turned defensive. 'Couple of days, more or less. We have to get a move on, the man could be dead before we arrive.'

'Well, there's no point in going in that case.'

'Lennox!'

Greggs arrived with a large tray of steaming hot toddies and served out the goodies.

I inhaled the scent of hot whisky, honey and lemon from my tumbler.

'What about Florence?' I asked, knowing her to have recently fallen in the family way.

'She is blooming, thank you,' he softened at the mention of his young wife. 'And insists we go and help.' He eyed me appraisingly over his drink. 'Look, if you don't want to come, I do understand.'

I didn't reply and he watched me as my mind churned over.

'Just tell me what happened?' I said at last. 'To the lady, I mean. The French one who Charles Langton was supposed to kill.'

That rattled him. 'What do you mean 'supposed to'?'

'Well, if he's a spy, perhaps he was *supposed to* kill her!'

'Assassination, you mean?'

'Yes.'

He frowned.

'Do you know what you're getting us into, Swift?'

He ate a slice of apple before responding. 'Does it make any difference?'

It was my turn to hesitate. I tried to imagine Damascus, a place I'd only seen in picture books. Images of dusty deserts, camels, sun-drenched streets, clamorous souks and dark back-alleys filled my mind.

'What did Persi write in her letter to you?'

'The woman, Josephine Belvoir, was reading in her hotel room, someone stuck a gun through the doorway and pulled the trigger. They missed. The bullet hit the wall behind her.'

'She saw him?' I cut in.

'No, just the gun and gloves. And his shoes,' he replied. 'Apparently she spotted his brogues. When the gendarmes questioned the hotel staff, one of the servants said he saw Charles Langton run away down the stairs.'

'This servant saw his face?'

'No, the figure ran past him before he had the chance, although it was enough to convince the French Chief of Police.'

'What was Langton's response?'

'That it was utter nonsense and he was at the souk at the time.' He picked up a cracker laden with cheese and pickle. 'But when the Gendarmes questioned the stall-holders, they all denied seeing him.'

'Hum.' I mused over the details. 'Did he have any reason to murder this Josephine Belvoir?'

'Possibly. She had been the cause of his split with Persi.'

That made my eyes open. 'Good Lord! And Persi still wants him released from jail?'

'Yes, she thinks this woman is lying and it's some sort of scheme to kill him off.'

'Are the jails really that bad?'

'Notoriously so.'

'Oh.' I digested the news. 'Then why does Josephine Belvoir want to be rid of him?'

'I don't know, but Persi said they'd known each other during the war. I assume that's when their affair took place. Perhaps it turned sour.' He gave a light shrug.

'Right.' I nodded although it wasn't terribly enlightening.

He continued. 'And before you ask, I don't know why Langton is in Damascus. But Josephine Belvoir is an actress, she's with a group of Americans making a moving picture. She's the leading lady.'

'Really? Why the devil are they making a movie in Damascus?'

'Arabia is all the rage, according to my wife. Something to do with a film called 'The Sheik'. It's a romance in the desert or some such nonsense and it's sparked a trend. Apparently, they're all jumping on the bandwagon.' He put his empty tumbler back on the tray and carefully picked Mr Tubbs off his lap to place him next to Foggy in the basket. 'I need to change, Lennox, my clothes are still damp and I'm weary to the bone.'

'Right, umm, yes.' I crossed to my desk and rang the bell.

'Sir!' Tommy Jenkins, my boot boy came bouncing in. 'Are you that ex-policeman what found the skeleton, sir? Is it still haunting your castle? What's it like to live in a castle? Did you hang a lot of murderers when you was a detective?'

'Tommy,' I interrupted to stop his barrage of questions.

He looked up at me, a scruffy urchin with freckles, untidy hair and an overactive imagination. 'But, sir…'

'I don't mind, Lennox,' Swift said, his voice warming. 'But one question at a time, young man.'

'Tommy, show Inspector Swift to the front guest room, would you?'

'Aye, sir, it's up 'ere.' He skipped off without waiting.

Swift went to follow, but then stopped and turned on the threshold. 'Lennox?'

'What?'

'Damascus? Are you coming or not?'

I thought again of the beguiling Persi Carruthers; intelligent, beautiful, intrepid and in trouble. Even if she wasn't in danger herself, turbulence was swirling around her and that could very easily lead to threat.

'Of course I'm coming, Swift.'

CHAPTER 2

Tommy came back in and frowned up at Swift. 'Sir?'

'Sorry, right behind you, lad.'

'Will you tell me about the curse, sir?' Tommy chattered with excitement as he led Swift from the room. 'And the treasure, and...'

Their voices echoed from the hall and stairs until I closed the door against the draught. I returned to my chair and mulled Swift's news over in my mind. He was a methodical man, but his story raised more questions than answers. If this ex-fiancé was a spy, what was he spying on in Damascus? And why was Persi there? Was she spying with him? No, she was far more interested in old bones from antiquity, I couldn't imagine her as a spy.

Aimless musings didn't help, so I decided I'd better bone up on some history, or geography, or what have you. The light of flames from the fire glimmered along my books, lined haphazardly on polished shelves set against oak panelling. I paused to gaze at the leather-bound volumes in age-darkened reds, browns, and greens, gold lettering stamped onto their spines. It was an eclectic mix, added to at the whim of the Lennox line over generations and was sure to hold something about the history of Damascus.

Tubbs jumped onto my lap as I was leafing through the Bible. The kitten had been abandoned before he was weaned and it seemed to have stunted his growth. He had stubby legs, a bottle-brush tail and a rotund body that closely resembled a fluffy cannonball. I rubbed his ears as he curled up next to the good book on my lap and settled to sleep. We would have to leave him at home, I mused, although I knew Foggy would miss him. Actually I would too, but we couldn't risk such a small cat in an unknown land and, besides, he'd be company for Tommy while we were away.

Greggs returned to collect the tray.

'Dinner will be served in one hour, sir.'

'Yes, excellent. Need to pack, Greggs.'

'Pack, sir?'

'For the desert.' I looked at him, he had frozen to the spot.

'You mean… you mean, you're going to that place, sir?'

You'd think I'd announced we were going to the moon. 'Yes, Greggs, Damascus.'

'I… I don't think that's wise, sir. It's foreign, very foreign. With a lot of foreigners. It will probably be worse than France, sir.' His old face filled with consternation.

'Damsel in distress, Greggs,' I reminded him. 'Duty calls and all that. Going by aeroplane, so there's no room for the trunk. Carpetbag only and um… a linen suit, I suppose.'

He dithered, opened and closed his mouth, then went off muttering to himself.

Tommy Jenkins bounced back into the library.

"E told me all about the dungeons and the walled-up skeleton with the gold crown and everything!' His excited enthusiasm suddenly faded. 'Sir, the Inspector says you're going off to that foreign place. It's a long way away and it might be like the war again, you could get shot and not come back home.'

I could see anxiety in the lad's eyes below a tousled fringe. His father hadn't returned from the war and his mother had been taken by the epidemic of Spanish flu that had followed. His Aunt, my cook, had taken him in and this house was the only refuge he knew.

'It's all perfectly civilised, Tommy. We're just going to ask the French why they have locked a man in jail and try to persuade them to release him.' Even I didn't think that sounded convincing, so I tried to add a confident tone. 'And Inspector Swift knows all about policing and detecting.'

'I thought he'd given up bein' a policeman.'

'Yes, but they're all foreigners in Damascus, so they won't know the inspector isn't an inspector anymore.'

That didn't seem to reassure him.

'There must be some British people there, sir? Do you think there might be?'

'I'm pretty sure there's an ambassador and Swift said something about people making a moving picture. Americans I think. So, if there are Americans making movies and British ambassadors, you can be certain there will be no danger whatsoever.'

'Making moving pictures, sir! Really? Truly?' All concern evaporated and he jumped into the chair vacated by Swift. 'Gosh, that's smashing, sir. It's… it's… stupendous.' His eyes brightened in eagerness. 'They might ask you to be in it. You're dead tall and Auntie says you're handsome when you bother to tidy yourself up. You can change your name to something dashing, like that Rudolf Valentino. I saw him on the Pathé news at the moving picture house, it was all about the new film, he was a Sheik in the desert and…'

'Tommy, will you go and help Cook, now,' I told him because he'd sit there all evening chattering away if I let him.

'But, sir. They had big curved swords, and knives. There were exotic dancers too.' He was swinging his legs as he talked.

'Dancers?'

'Wearing just a few flimsies, they were, sir.'

Flimsies! No wonder these films were so popular.

'You're too young for dancers, Tommy. Now go and help Cook.'

He didn't move. 'But, but… Can you get an autograph, sir? Of a Star in the moving pictures. Please, sir. No-one else round here has ever met a movie star. Not never.'

'Tommy…' I warned, then softened. 'I'll see what I can do.'

He slipped off the chair, gave me a big grin and went off with a lighter step, leaving the door open to let a winter draught whistle through. I closed it again and poured myself a snifter before settling back in my favourite chair to contemplate the strange story and wonder how on earth we were going to persuade Greggs to come.

He refused point-blank, of course.

'But it will be like a holiday, Greggs. With sun, and sand and…'

Dinner was over and we were in my dressing room where he was folding socks into my carpetbag. 'I am not in need of a holiday, thank you, sir.'

'Well, what about Miss Carruthers? She could be in peril. There are foreigners, and probably snakes and scorpions, and who knows what.'

'I thought you said it would be like a holiday, sir.'

'Yes, right, erm…' I attempted a different tactic. 'Look, we can't just leave her to it, can we? Anything could happen and Damascus is a long way away. Hundreds of miles, actually.'

He paused, mid-fold. 'If you recollect, sir, you promised that once the war was over we would never go abroad again. And that promise has already been broken.'

'You can hardly count Scotland as abroad, Greggs,' I told him, although that didn't cut any ice either. 'Look, she's all alone, or pretty much anyway. We have to go and help.'

He wasn't ready to concede. 'This precipitousness seems quite out of character for the Inspector, sir, and he has only recently married.' He finished with the socks and moved on to shirts, which were already neatly folded and placed on shelves in the wardrobe by someone or other.

'I know, but it's softened him, Greggs.'

'From my observation, sir, Chief Inspector Swift retains his policeman's carapace.'

'Yes, but beneath the scratchy exterior lies a chap with an excess of gallantry.'

'In which he is not alone,' he added dryly as he shook mothballs out of my linen suit.

'Greggs!' I protested, for all the good it did. 'Look, it's up to you, but… it's Miss Carruthers, you see, I'm… well, I'm rather fond of her.'

'But Damascus, sir… it's… it's…'

I could tell he was weakening. 'And someone has to take care of Fogg. We need you, old chap.'

He fidgeted around, picking up ties and whatnots, then he stopped and puffed out his chest. 'Very well, sir, for Mr Fogg and Miss Carruthers.'

'Excellent!' I clapped my hands and turned to survey the room. 'Right, what are we taking with us?'

We packed Fogg's blanket, but had to leave his basket, Greggs argued against taking my tweed suit and woollens and vetoed my small hand pistol, insisting that it was bound to be confiscated or stolen. Swift backed him up despite my entirely rational and logical arguments – I went to bed in a bit of a huff.

The next morning we gathered our bags, left the house

and travelled to London under icy grey skies. Sleet had begun to fall as we arrived at Croydon airfield and we had to hold onto our hats as we boarded an old DeHavilland heading for Paris.

We spent the next couple of days being deafened on aeroplanes, which were actually poorly disguised ex-bombers from the war. The French Government had decided to blaze a trail for the unsuspecting tourist by offering international air travel crossing continents.

Passengers in their most elegant togs were wined and dined at spruced-up airfields as freshly painted aircraft roared outside. All semblance of glamour melted away upon boarding. Weight saving was paramount; the seats were basket chairs strapped to the floor, and there was barely a smattering of sound-proofing. We passengers sat mute, deaf and shaken to the core as we flew from Paris to Constantinople with numerous fuel stops in-between. French champagne was plied in copious amounts at every halt. I don't think any of us drew a sober breath throughout the entire journey, which was just as well because we'd never have got back on board without it.

'Greggs, this is as sophisticated as modern travel gets.' I told him as we were herded back onto a roaring Bleriot-Spad for the final flight to Damascus.

'And it's really quite quick,' Swift added although I think even his enthusiasm for the trip had been dented by the reality.

Greggs remained unconvinced and went to sit at the rear in mute reproach, clutching Fogg to his chest. He had placed cotton wool in his and the little dog's ears, then tied one scarf about his head and another around Fogg's. I'd have been inclined to do the same if the champagne hadn't numbed the nerves.

We stepped into the late afternoon sunshine of Damascus in a collective daze. It was dry, dusty and hot. My linen suit, the only one I owned, looked like I'd slept in it for a week. Swift wore his usual trench coat over a light suit and what little I could see of Greggs, between his heavy black overcoat, bowler hat and scarf, was red and glowing from the heat.

'Vite, vite,' a short chap in a khaki suit and kepi shouted at us. His get-up verged on the military, complete with leather cross-strap and belt with a revolver on his hip. He was French, so I ignored him. A man draped in faded sheets with a cloth wrapped around his head held a camel at the edge of the runway. It had a large hump.

'Lennox,' Swift shouted above the noise of the aircraft engine. 'Will you please hurry up!'

Greggs was clutching Fogg beside me. He stared at the camel, then turned to head back towards the aeroplane on the sand-blown runway. Its propellor raced as the roaring churn of the engine, typical of the Bleriot-Spad, picked up pace.

'Greggs,' I shouted after him.

Just as he approached the plane, someone leaned down and yanked the steps up. The metal door shut with a clang and his shoulders sagged.

The officious French chap came back. 'Vite, vite.' Having harried the other passengers into waiting cars, he waved his arms about and shouted more French at me. I looked over at Swift who was standing near the rutted road, peering into the distance.

Greggs returned slowly to my side and we stopped to take in our surroundings. Jagged mountains broke the far horizon against a bright blue sky. Palm trees dotted the desert plain where a group of camels, ridden by men in black robes, were crossing in an unhurried manner. The men had rifles slung across their backs. Greggs hugged Fogg closer to his chest.

'I'm sure they're perfectly friendly, Greggs.'

He sniffed in disdain. We went to join Swift with the Frenchman at our heels.

'Why the rush, Swift?' I asked.

'The travel representative promised the hotel would send transport. The city is over that hill.' Swift nodded towards a rising crest of sand and rock, shimmering under a haze of heat.

A car drew up, it was an old white Rolls Royce, polished to gleaming with a thin layer of sand clinging to its surface. Sunlight glinted off the silver lady on the radiator, a comforting reminder of home, although in a damn peculiar setting.

The driver jumped out and opened the doors with a bow. He was terribly smart, wearing a uniform of maroon turban and matching jacket over black trousers tucked into half-boots.

'Al Shami, at your service,' he said with a wide grin on his plump Arab face.

'Erm, thank you, Shami, old chap,' I said, handing him my carpet bag.

'Not Shami, effendi. That is hotel. It is 'Hotel Al Shami'. I am Jamal,' he was a cheerful fellow with wrinkles etched around nut-brown eyes.

'We need to get in,' Swift said. 'It will be dark soon and they'll close the gates.'

I climbed in the back with Swift. Greggs went in the front and sat stiffly staring out of the windscreen. Fogg looked forlorn. He still had the scarf wrapped around his head and cotton wool in his ears.

'Which gates?' I asked.

'The city gates,' Swift said. 'They close them at dusk.'

'Why?' I suspected I could guess the answer.

'Because there are enemies everywhere and it's safer that way.'

CHAPTER 3

The journey was stately and slow. No-one spoke as we gazed about in something close to awe. The buildings were mostly sandstone, some with colourful tiled facades, others sported ornate wooden fretwork and shutters. Tall and narrow, the jumble of houses and shops threw dark shadows across roads lit by the late afternoon sunshine.

Jamal, in the driver's seat, nosed the Rolls into increasingly crowded streets. Locals with olive faces and hooded eyes watched from beneath black turbans, red fezzes or white scarves held with corded rope around their heads. Snaggle-toothed merchants thrust woven baskets toward the car from stone-laid pavements. Hustling traders held up intricately patterned rugs, shouting out their prices and the bargains to be had. Shopkeepers stood in hopeful anticipation below gleaming brassware, strung over narrow store-fronts. A rich display of scent, sound and colour met us at every corner.

My senses were reeling by the time we drove through a huge entrance on a broad street within the old town. Jamal slowed the car to a stop.

'We arrive, effendis,' he shouted with enthusiasm. 'This is our much magnificent hotel. You are most warmly welcomed.'

More staff appeared, the doors were opened, gloved hands were offered to help us from the car and carry our bags. I clambered out and found myself surrounded by a group of smiling attendants, uniformed in the same smart maroon and black Jamal wore.

We were escorted into a large internal courtyard of extraordinary beauty. I stopped in my tracks, surprised by the tinkling fountain in the centre of a spacious open-air enclosure, surrounded by high walls. I looked up at tiers of open walkways, protected by exquisitely carved balustrades, overgrown with lush greenery and colourful flowers. Above the walls I could see the cloudless blue sky. I stood transfixed.

A man in a red fez and pristine butlering outfit greeted us with a bow. 'Welcome. I am Hamid, at your humble service. May I offer tea or coffee, most honoured effendis?'

'What?'

'Coffee for all of us, thank you,' Swift told him as he turned to me. 'Lennox, will you stop staring and try to concentrate.'

'I thought we were staying in a tent.'

'But they'll think we're tourists,' he hissed.

'We are!'

Three tiny cups were produced on a gleaming brass tray and placed on the marble-topped reception counter.

We drank the coffee, which was sweetly bitter and very strong. It snapped me awake and cured my hangover in an instant. It even enticed Greggs to relent. He removed the scarf from around Fogg's head and unplugged his ears. Then he did the same for himself.

'See Greggs, it isn't at all like France,' I told him.

'Except for the officious bureaucracy, the police and the military,' Swift said, which almost caused Greggs to replace the scarf.

'May I gather your passports, please, effendis?' Hamid bowed again, his fez nodding. He had placed himself at the reception desk and awaited us with a large register open in front of him. 'And Jamal will escort you to your suites. He is factotum and we offer him to you as your personal guide and taker of care,' he added with an elegant wave of his hand.

Jamal grinned. 'I am yours, effendis. I speak English most excellent.'

Each of us passed over our papers and signed the book before following Jamal up a marble staircase. Everywhere was carved, tiled or painted in rich hues with delicate designs. As we climbed the stairs a vivid green lizard ran across a step in front of me and scrambled onto the thick trunk of a vine woven through the ornate spindles.

We tried to maintain the air of sophisticated travellers but the veneer cracked as soon as we were shown our suites. Greggs' jaw dropped in incredulity.

'For me?' He almost gasped as he stared around the magnificent room.

'Well, there you are, old chap,' I said as Jamal pointed out the fret-work shutters, huge wardrobes and adjoining bathroom. 'Told you abroad wasn't so bad, didn't I.'

He nodded dumbly and finally let me take Fogg from his arms.

'Would you like to take a bath, sir? I will have it drawn for you. Very quick,' Jamal offered.

Greggs nodded again, round-eyed and warming to the idea.

'And bathing lady?' Jamal added. 'For perfect gentleman's washing, effendi.'

'What?' We all said at once.

'Bathing…'

'No,' I cut him off. 'No bathing lady.'

Greggs let out a strangled sigh.

'Greggs!' I eyed him from a very short distance.

'As you say, sir.' Disappointment flitted across his face.

'Good, because I'll tell Cook if you do,' I warned him, knowing that once home, Cook would tell the whole household and anyone else who would listen.

Jamal rang a brass handbell on a low table set before two satin sofas beyond the silk-hung bed.

'I am bath-draw boy, effendis,' a middle-aged fellow with a large, hairy mole between thick, dark brows announced. He wore the same uniform and turban that Jamal sported, although this chap was a good deal shorter, stouter and bandier of legs. He hovered in the doorway, holding a stack of pristine white towels until Jamal waved him toward the bathroom.

'Come, come, effendis.' Jamal requested Swift and me to follow him and we were each shown to our own extraordinary rooms.

Mine was lofty and light and quite frankly I'd never seen anything like it. My eyes widened as I viewed its silken opulence. It was huge! I walked to the window, past the massive bed and collection of sofas, and looked down onto the bustling street below. The rooms spanned the depth of the hotel and went from the courtyard walk-way all the way through to the hotel exterior.

Jamal had been trying to display the dressing room and wardrobes, but I'd been too absorbed by all the luxury to listen. He opened another door and revealed a huge bathroom with a tiled shower, the comforts of which I'd never properly experienced. We'd had a holed bucket hanging from a tree during the war, but that hardly counted. Jamal escorted Swift to his quarters and I shut the door and headed off for some much-needed ablutions.

I emerged shortly after to discover my linen suit had been refreshed and ironed, my carpetbag unpacked and all my kit stowed away. I must say, the Al Shami was a miracle of plumbing and pressing! Actually, the whole place was considerably better kitted out than some of the grandest country houses I'd ever stayed in.

Clean and suitably togged, I set off to explore. I called Fogg, who had already been fed succulent scraps, and we trotted downstairs. The courtyard was almost deserted, apart from men with long tapers, busily lighting numerous oil lamps hanging about the place. I strolled through the entrance archway to reach the teeming streets of Damascus, where babbling chatter, sun-bright colour and the promise of exotic delights beckoned.

Jamal caught me as I stood in the gateway wondering which way to go. 'Effendi, I come with you.'

'No need, old chap. Just taking Mr Fogg for a walk.'

'You will be lost in crowd, effendi,' he pleaded. 'Better to bring guide, if you please.'

He struck me as an older version of Tommy Jenkins with his mixture of enthusiasm and anxiety. I looked down at his plumply earnest features.

I sighed, it seemed the delights would have to wait. 'Oh, very well.'

He gave a gap-toothed grin. 'There is garden. Mr Fogg will like very much. Come, come.'

I had picked Foggy up and put him under my arm because there was not only a milling crowd, there were also donkeys, goats and chickens running free in the street and Fogg was particularly fond of chasing chickens. We wound our way through to a side road which backed onto the Hotel Al Shami.

A pair of heavy wooden gates opened onto a walled garden. The sun was dropping and pale light washed the expanse of earthly paradise as the day fell into dusk. A chap with a turban and what appeared to be a long curved sword sat motionless in a cubby hole half-hidden in the shadows. I assumed him to be a guard and paused for an instant to consider the armed men in the desert – it may look like paradise, but danger, it seemed, rippled not far beneath the surface. I put my little dog down onto the immaculate lawn and he raced off to bark joyously, his ears flapping in his wake.

'You like flowers, effendi? There are many roses. Damascus roses, see.' He pointed to rambling briers clinging to old stone walls surrounding the peaceful garden. 'And jasmine and gardenia, and more roses around the pavilion.' He indicated a pretty domed folly in the centre of the garden. 'Also hibiscus and bougainvillaea by the terrace.' He waved a hand toward a quiet spot where wicker chairs and circular tables were arranged. 'And the yellow...'

'Yes, *thank* you, Jamal,' I interrupted the botanical litany. 'Don't happen to know Miss Persephone Carruthers do you?'

'Ah, the English pearl. A lady of distinguished beauty,' he said. 'If I may so express, effendi.'

'Yes, well, of course. Is she staying here?'

He bowed. 'Indeed. But lady's quarters are top floor, it is Ladies Row. No men allowed. No sir.' He shook his head. 'Only for ladies.'

'But you could give her a note from me?' I asked.

'I will do my most excellent best, effendi.'

'Where is she?'

'She is making movie today, with the Americans. Very fine peoples Americans. Give dollars. Very fine, sir.'

'Ah, yes, of course.' That gave me pause. Perhaps I was supposed to give dollars for tips and whatnot? Where would I get some? 'Erm, well never mind that. Who exactly are these Americans?'

'They are loud mens and beautiful ladies. They have camera and shout with cone. It is all very fine.'

I can't say that was very illuminating.

'Lennox,' Swift called as he strode into the garden from the same gate by which I'd arrived. Fogg barked and ran to him, his bottom wagging with his tail. 'I saw you leave. We should find Persi.'

'She's filming, apparently.' I noted that he too was considerably more neat in his cream suit and without his trench coat.

'What time is it?'

'Almost six,' he replied. 'Where are they filming?'

'No idea. When is dinner served, Jamal?'

'When you wish for it, sir.'

'Really?' This place was improving all the time. 'Well, I think I'll take a snifter first.'

'Lennox, we need to contact the Chief of Police. We should put in a request to see Charles Langton immediately.' Swift said as we followed Jamal back into the hotel through the deserted terrace, passing wicker tables and chairs as we went.

'They're hardly likely to be open at this time of night,' I admit to being keen to sample the hotel's selection of brandy.

'But if he's dying…'

'Well, just one drink first.' I quickened my pace before he could change my mind.

We arrived at the central courtyard from an entirely different direction than Fogg and I had left. I spotted the bar, complete with mahogany counter and barman, behind a small jungle of greenery on one side of the courtyard.

Suddenly, a slim lady with long blonde hair ran from a distant archway and looked about her. She stopped in front of the low wall of the fountain and desperately turned this way and that. Her chiffon dress fluttered as she clasped her hands to her bosom in obvious distress.

At that moment, a man in a smart tuxedo appeared, his face dark and brooding. His arm was outstretched and, even at a distance, I could see he was holding a gun.

'No, no,' the woman shouted, flinging out her arms as though to implore him.

'I can endure it no longer, Beryl, I am in torment, you have brought me to this,' her pursuer replied in dramatic fashion.

His hand shaking, he pointed the gun and pulled the trigger. In a flash, a loud shot ran out and his victim crumpled to the floor, her hands once more clutching her chest.

CHAPTER 4

That stopped us in our tracks. Fogg sniffed the air, paused for a heartbeat then raced off up the stairs toward the bedrooms. Swift was almost as quick to move, he ran toward the woman and I made a dash for the man with the pistol.

'And now, I will bring an end to my misery.' He aimed the muzzle at his temple with another dramatic flourish. I barrelled into him with a rugby-tackle while grabbing the gun, which fired with a bang into the air as we crashed to the tiles in a heap.

'Oomph,' the man cushioning my fall grunted.

A shriek rang out from above. 'Aargh.'

'Cut, cut,' an angry voice bellowed from behind. 'What the hell do you think you're doing you pair of dumbbells?'

'Ow, you oaf, get off,' the man I'd flattened complained.

I climbed to my feet, keeping a grip on the pistol, then looked up for the source of the 'aargh' I'd heard. I couldn't see anyone so I turned back to the man now rising to stand. Apart from a squashed suit, he appeared unharmed and was already smoothing himself down. I left him to it and strode over to join Swift who was kneeling beside the woman. He was feeling her neck for a pulse.

'You just ruined my big scene.' A squat chap bounded up, practically bouncing with rage. He wore a checked shirt, braces and oversized trousers. He stabbed a finger up at me as he spoke in a brash American accent. 'You got any idea what this costs? You bulldoze in here, like a pair of big lummoxes, knocking over my stars, what the...'

'She's dead,' I interrupted him.

'She's acting!' he blazed. 'It's a movie!'

'She's dead,' Swift pronounced firmly as he stood up.

'Don't be ridiculous,' the dapper man, who I now assumed to be an actor, came over to stand beside the stocky chap. He was quite short too. Perhaps they had to use small people so they would fit into the camera frame.

'She's been shot,' I said. 'She's bleeding. Look at her.'

The stocky American didn't look. He wasn't listening to a damn word I said. 'We're using blanks you block-head. What do you take us for? Idiots?'

I eyed him more closely, he'd insulted me three times now and it was becoming annoying. I was still holding the pistol, I put it to his forehead.

'I'll shoot you, shall I? Shouldn't be a problem if they're blanks.'

He stopped shouting. Actually he stopped doing anything. He just stared up at me in piggy-eyed fury.

'Lennox,' Swift reproved.

I lowered the gun.

All attention switched to the lady at our feet, as our words finally struck home. A red stain had started to seep from under her clutched hands and she was lying very, very still.

'She's dead?' The actor's face paled.

'Of course she's dead. You just shot her,' Swift said.

'Good Lord, she's dead?' He dragged his eyes from the body toward me, then back to the bleeding lady. 'But, how... you mean the gun? I shot her? My God!'

The stocky man in the checked shirt bent over for a closer look, then suddenly straightened up. 'Mammie,' he yelled. 'Mammie. Where's the lawyer?'

He trotted at a half run in the direction he'd come from.

I turned to see a man in overalls handling a large camera on a tripod. It was positioned in front of a group of people gathered in the far corner of the courtyard. They looked on goggle-eyed, as though transfixed, and at the front of the pack was Persi Carruthers.

Dressed in lavender-blue, her blonde hair coiled into a neat bun, she looked as stunningly lovely as I remembered her. Her expression was one of astonishment, then, as if woken from a daze, she leapt to her feet and ran towards me.

'Heathcliff! You came!'

'Persi,' I reached out my arms and she launched herself into them.

'Oh, it's been ghastly.' She stifled a sob as she buried her face in my chest.

I patted her shoulder, then placed an arm around her slim waist but decided against a kiss as things were rather confused. The gun was a bit of an impediment, too.

I tried some soft words. 'Erm, well, no need for tears, old stick. And I should be helping Swift with this dead woman.'

'What?' She suddenly released me. 'You mean she's actually dead?' Her focus switched to Swift and the woman on the floor, who was still bleeding and looked more dead as the minutes ticked by.

Swift attempted a reassuring grin. 'Good evening, Persi. We came as quickly as we could.'

'Oh heavens!' Persi clasped both hands to her face. 'She's truly dead?'

'Yes, she's dead!' I repeated, why on earth don't people listen?

'I couldn't hear from over there,' she explained. 'We're not allowed to move or make a sound when the camera is rolling. The director, Mr Vincent, gets terribly angry if so much as a pin drops.' She turned to look back at the spot she'd come from. The man with the camera had stopped gaping and was now rapidly removing a large film container from the contraption. The stocky American, who I assumed to be Vincent, had vanished.

'Who is she?' Swift indicated the expired actress.

'That chap said she was called Beryl.' I pointed to the actor who had left us for the comforts of the bar and was even now downing a large whisky.

'No, that was part of the script, Heathcliff.' Persi

lowered her hands and attempted to pull herself together. 'Her real name is Josephine Belvoir.'

That gave us a jolt.

'This is the lady your ex-fiancé was accused of trying to kill?' Swift asked, the surprise apparent on his face.

Persi nodded, a blush rising over her high cheekbones.

I glanced down at the corpse. I hadn't observed her closely amid the drama. Long blond hair the colour of spun gold had fallen back from her heart-shaped face. There was a trace of pink lipstick on her cupid's-bow lips and her mouth was slightly parted, as though a faint gasp of surprise had escaped her. Wide eyes, flecked with green and gold, stared into the distance — her gaze must have been mesmerising in life. It remained so in death — although it probably wouldn't for much longer.

I turned to take a better look and my heart suddenly lurched.

'She had the most extraordinary effect on men,' Persi was saying. 'The more susceptible kind, anyway. She brought out the Sir Galahad in them.'

'Well, she won't anymore,' Swift replied.

'No...' Persi paused again to stare at the lifeless body. 'What happened?'

'The gun must have been loaded with live ammunition.' Swift turned to me. 'Lennox, check the magazine would you. I'll be back in a minute.'

He strode toward the reception desk, where a number of waiters were peering over the top of the counter.

'What?' I was mesmerised by the body at our feet, her

slim wrist extended to reveal a gold and diamond bracelet, glittering in the lamplight. The clasp had a curious engraving of a galleon or some such thing. Her pink and blue chiffon frock was spread about her, a glossy confection of gauze and silk. She reminded me of Ophelia lying in the lake, I felt tears prick my eye and I...

'Heathcliff?' Persi was staring up at me.

'Um... What?'

'Did you hear what Inspector Swift said?'

'Um, no... yes. I... erm.'

Persi put a hand on my arm. 'Heathcliff, are you all right?'

I looked down into her blue eyes. 'Persi?'

'Yes?'

'Not Heathcliff, old thing. Never liked it.'

'Sorry. But Swift said...'

'Right.'

I focused back on the gun. I'd taken it for a Colt 45, but on closer examination I saw it was actually a Kongsberg-Colt. I popped out the magazine and pulled back the slide to eject the round in the chamber and gave her the emptied pistol. 'These are all live. Here, hold this.'

I emptied the magazine into my palm, examined the bullets, then pocketed the lot before retrieving the gun from Persi and slotting the magazine back in place. It was only then that I remembered I was supposed to be careful about fingerprints.

'Someone exchanged the bullets!' Persi exclaimed.

'Yes, who?'

She paused for a moment. 'I don't know.'

'Well, who supplied it?' I asked.

'It… it was being used as a prop in the film. It's rather strange because the gun they'd brought with them disappeared a few days ago and then Vincent produced this one today and said it should be used instead and… and…'

I could see she was flustered and tried a softer tone. 'Come on old girl, try to spit it out.'

She took a breath and pulled herself together. 'Right, yes. The bullets were checked this morning, they were definitely blanks. I saw them myself. And Harry Bing loaded it into the magazine. Harry is the actor you flattened,' she explained then faltered again. 'I… I don't understand how this could happen.'

I thought perhaps this was an occasion where I should hug her or some such thing, but I wanted some answers first. 'Persi, who does this gun belong to?'

'Heathcliff… I…'

Swift returned to interrupt. 'I told Hamid to call the police. He hadn't moved from reception, I suppose they're used to shooting around here. Were they live rounds, Lennox?'

'Yes.' I nodded.

'Who's the actor?' Swift asked, glancing toward Bing at the bar.

Persi didn't answer, so I told him.

'Harry Bing?' Swift repeated.

'Yes,' Persi found her voice. 'He's the second lead.'

'Not the star?' Swift asked.

'No, that's Dick Dreadnaught.'

'Dick Dreadnaught?' Swift and I both repeated in incredulity.

'It's his stage name, he wanted something memorable,' she explained.

'Well, he certainly succeeded in that,' Swift remarked.

'Never mind all that, Swift. Persi just said something significant.' I told him about the incident of the missing gun and the blanks.

'Do you know who the gun belonged too, Miss Carruthers?' Swift asked.

Her lips trembled.

I sighed, feeling like a heel and wrapped an arm around her shoulders. 'Come along, I'll find you a drink, a snifter will buck you up.' I led her in the direction of the jungle camouflaging the bar.

Half-way across the courtyard she suddenly stopped. 'Wait, Heathcliff. There's something I must tell the Inspector.' She turned before I could utter another word and dashed back to where Swift was standing guard over the corpse. I stared after her, sighed in exasperation, shoved my hands in my pockets and carried on.

Harry Bing was halfway through a bottle of whisky and had the look of someone who was in for the night.

The bartender took one glance at me and poured a large brandy. I downed it. He replaced it with another on the polished counter.

'I didn't do it.' Bing leaned on the bar, clutching a crystal tumbler of amber liquid in one hand and a damp handkerchief in the other. His voice was well enunciated with a polished accent. I assumed he was English.

'Yes, you did. I saw you.'

'Well, it was hardly on purpose. Someone must have switched the gun, or bullets, or something.' He sniffed.

'Really?' I gave him a hard stare.

He took another drink. 'She was evil, you know.'

'What?'

'Josephine.' He knocked back the whisky, which was instantly refilled. 'Terrifying combination – beauty and evil. And she hid it so well. The evil, I mean.'

'How was she evil?' I wondered if he was a bit unhinged by the shock.

'In so many ways, old boy.'

That begged more questions than I could cudgel so I changed tack. 'You're English. Thought all the movie people were American.'

He gave a grim laugh. 'Vincent and his wife are American, they're the money. The rest of us are a mixed bag.' His shoulders fell. 'Good God, she's dead. She stole my heart, and never gave a damn. What a bloody fool she made of me.' His forced smile faded as his eyes rolled. He hiccupped, then slumped slowly onto the bar.

I regarded him, or the back of his head anyway, and suddenly felt terribly tired, dejected and a long way from home.

'Sir,' Greggs appeared at my elbow, he spoke in a half-whisper. 'Sir?'

'What?'

'There's a body, sir.'

'I know, Swift and Persi are with her.'

'Not the lady, sir,' he hissed. 'Upstairs on the walkway. It's the bath-draw boy. I think you may have shot him.'

CHAPTER 5

'What?'

'I fear so, sir.'

'Good Lord, how?'

He eyed my snifter and cleared his throat.

'I came to my door when I heard shouting. The bath-draw boy was on the walkway and he leaned over the railing to see the cause of the commotion and then a shot was fired and he collapsed to the floor.'

'And you are sure he's dead?' I asked, realising it was probably the cause of the 'aargh' I'd heard.

'I cannot say, sir.' Greggs' face was pale above his but-lering togs. 'Blood ran from his head and as I went to help, two rather large ladies came and dragged him away. I tried to intervene but they were insistent and... and...' He puttered out of words.

The bartender placed a double brandy in front of him. He was probably the best bartender I'd ever encountered.

'Where did they take him?'

'I'm afraid I don't know, sir.' He took a swig of his snifter.

'Where's Fogg?'

'He ran into my room when I opened the door. I have now placed him in your suite with his blanket.'

Poor Foggy, he'd always hated anything dead. As soon as I saw his reaction I knew the woman had been killed.

We both drank more brandy, which was excellent actually and almost made up for the appalling contretemps.

'Could we go home, sir?' Greggs asked in a heartfelt tone.

I sighed in sympathy. Just as I was coming round to the idea of enjoying the comforts of foreign parts it had all erupted into chaos.

I glanced across at Persi, or rather her back – she was still in close conversation with Swift, who was listening intently with a crease between dark brows.

A loud whistle suddenly interrupted. It came from the direction of the entrance and was immediately followed by the pounding of boots. A group of gendarmes raced into the courtyard with revolvers drawn, gesticulating and generally making a racket.

'Arret. Arret. Mains a l'air.'

They surrounded Swift, Persi and the corpse. The khaki-uniformed men ran through doorways and archways. It wouldn't be long before they found us behind the jungle surrounding the bar.

'Greggs, go and find Jamal. I think he's hiding behind the reception desk.'

'Pssst. Hello, effendis. I am not there, I am here.' A voice came from among the greenery. 'I have heard all. I go with old chap and uncover the fate of the bath-draw boy. Come.' Two hands parted a potted palm and Jamal appeared, waved and sank below the foliage again.

A couple of gendarmes were running in our direction.

'Hurry up, Greggs,' I urged.

He drained his brandy, crouched down and entered the greenery. I saw them both emerge from the far side and dash into a shadowy doorway as two Frenchmen skidded to a halt in front of me.

'Mains a l'air,' they shouted.

'Go away, I'm English,' I told them.

That didn't seem to impress them. 'Arms to ze sky,' one said.

'No.'

They could have shot me and I think one of them actively contemplated it, but probably realised it would lead to all sorts of complications.

'Tell me, how are you?' the taller one shouted in mangled English, he wore sergeant's stripes, sewn onto a spotless khaki uniform. The shorter one was scruffy and unkempt and stared at my brandy. The bartender poured him a liberal glass. He didn't move, but his fingers twitched.

'I'm Major Lennox, how are you?' I replied.

'I am not to tell you,' the sergeant continued shouting. 'How shot ze lady?'

I looked at the comatose Harry Bing, face down on the counter, and decided discretion was the better part of valour.

The sergeant prodded Bing, who grunted then slid off his barstool to lay spread-eagle on the floor. 'Do not move.' He pointed his pistol at Bing, who began to snore in reply.

I laughed.

'It iz not funny,' the sergeant snapped. 'Allez,' he ordered his scruffy colleague as he grabbed Bing under one arm.

The short gendarme was still staring at the brandy on the bar and suddenly snatched it, knocked it back in one flash of movement, wiped his lips on his sleeve and took Bing's other arm without drawing a breath. I was quite impressed, actually.

'Vite.' They both dragged Bing over to where their comrades were interrogating Swift and Persi by the fountain. Josephine Belvoir lay staring at the stars, largely ignored.

The two Frenchmen dropped Bing's arms and he came to rest at the edge of the huddle. He started to sing, 'It's a long way to Tipperary, it's a long way to go…'

As crime scenes go, it lacked gravitas.

'Vous! Arret!' Another gendarme emerged from the other side of the bar. He waved his revolver at me and I was marched to the fountain where Swift and Persi were arguing with the sergeant.

I was about to join in when a couple of ladies were escorted over.

'Greetings.'

'Oh, hello! I'm Genevieve Hamilton.' The younger lady regarded me with a bright smile. She was tall and slim and had chestnut hair in a fashionable cut. She turned to gaze at the corpse, where the scruffy gendarme was now kneeling and reverentially holding Josephine's cold hand. It would seem, even in death, she hadn't lost her allure.

'I'm Major Lennox,' I said but the chestnut haired lady wasn't paying much attention, then suddenly she turned toward me.

'I saw it all! Isn't it exciting?' Her dark brown eyes glowed and she clapped her hands together. She wore a modern dress in yellow, with a long string of pearls around her neck in the flapper style.

'Erm… What?'

'She is dead, isn't she? It's not play-acting.'

'No, I mean, yes. Erm, what I mean is…' I stopped because I was babbling; a bad habit when around pretty girls. I was also a bit nonplussed by her enthusiasm for murder.

'Genevieve!' the older one admonished, aiming piercing grey eyes at me. 'You must not talk to strange men.'

'I'm not strange,' I protested.

The steel-haired lady gave a haughty sniff. Dressed in pale puce, she looked every inch the 'Grande Dame' and her thin face was without a hint of humour.

A man's voice caused us to turn around.

'Do not prod me, dumbkopf.' A German, wearing a white bowtie and tuxedo, was being frogmarched toward us. 'Do you not know who I am? I am the film star, Dick Dreadnaught and I vill not tolerate your behaviour,' he shouted, for all the good it did him, a revolver was instantly stuck under his nose.

'Oh, Auntie M!' The young lady, Genevieve, pointed. 'It's Dick Dreadnaught! I would simply adore to have his autograph. I say, Mr Dreadnaught?'

He didn't deign to turn his profile in our direction. A handsome man with classic German colouring – fair hair, blue eyes, square jaw and block-head. He stalked off toward Persi, Swift and the sergeant and joined in the harangue.

The American director, Vincent, had been winkled out and was being herded toward the general throng. A lady of comfortable proportions with greying brown hair and a red flowery dress walked quickly to keep up with him. There were two more gendarmes at their heels.

'Don't answer any question until the lawyer gets here,' Vincent told the lady.

'I will not, dearest. I will not,' she replied in a softer American accent. I assumed her to be Mrs Vincent.

Things were getting colourful in the courtyard and I folded my arms to watch the show. There was a lot of shouting and gesticulating; the sergeant had been at the centre of it all but a tall man in an officer's uniform now arrived to take command. Vincent immediately began berating him.

Swift made his escape and came to join me. 'Absolute bunch of rank amateurs. The murder scene is completely contaminated.'

'Oh, come off it, Swift. She was shot, the only relevance is the gun.'

'Humph.' He wasn't convinced. 'Where is it?'

KAREN BAUGH MENUHIN

'In my belt.'

'You'll have to hand it over. It's evidence.'

'Tell me what Persi wanted to discuss with you first?'

He frowned. 'She told me she had handled the gun. Her prints will be on it.'

'I know.'

'Not just the gun.'

'What?'

'The magazine, too.'

'What?' I repeated. 'But how?' I was quite aware I'd passed her the pistol, but I hadn't given her the magazine.

'No time.' He glanced over his shoulder. 'You'd better give it to me, we must hand it over.'

'No.'

'It's evidence, Lennox, and Persi insists we pass it to the police.'

I regarded his hawkish features, wondering why he was so insistent. The gendarmes were throwing glances at us.

'But I could wipe it clean first,' I hissed.

'No, she specifically told me not to,' he replied sotto voce. 'We shouldn't interfere in a crime scene, and...' he was cut off by a shout from behind.

'He's got it,' Vincent pointed a stubby finger in my direction.

The babble of voices stopped in an instant and all attention turned to me.

The tall gendarme with an air of authority, immaculate uniform and discrete gold braid, marched over and thrust out his gloved palm.

46

'Give it to me,' he ordered in lightly accented English. I hesitated. French revolvers swivelled in my direction so I slowly pulled out the pistol from behind my back and surrendered it.

He popped the magazine. 'I am Colonel Fontaine, where is the ammunition from this weapon?' He demanded in a clipped tone.

I stand at six feet three and he was almost my height. He wore a kepi over sandy hair above sandy brows. His lean face was darkly tanned and creased by deep lines. He was probably about the same age as me, around thirty, with a hard expression in pale blue eyes – I'd say he'd seen a lot of life.

I turned the bullets over in my pocket with my fingers, rubbing them, smearing any prints that may have been left on them, then handed them over.

'You did not wear gloves?' He frowned as he placed a cleanly laundered handkerchief around the bullets and passed it to the sergeant who had come to his side. 'Tell me your names.'

Neither of us spoke, we were weighing up the Colonel, considering how far to co-operate – well I was anyway.

'Names?' he repeated.

'Detective Chief Inspector Jonathan Swift.'

He raised his brows but didn't comment.

'And you?' he demanded.

'Major Heathcliff Lennox.'

'A British detective and an army Major…' Fontaine regarded us appraisingly.

'Royal Air Force, actually,' I corrected him.

The chatter had sprung back up as the group around the fountain watched. They had edged toward us and away from the body, for which I could hardly blame them.

'Quiet.' The Colonel turned to address us all. 'You will have your fingerprints taken and you will make statements.' He rattled off something in French to his sergeant before returning his attention to me and Swift. 'I will be watching you very carefully, gentlemen.'

The gendarmes started to shout orders at the staff, who had gone into hiding on the appearance of the French, but now emerged from various bolt-holes around the courtyard.

'Ladies and gentlemens.' Hamid approached, hands clasped together, to resume his role as Maitre'd. 'Please to follow me to the dining room.' He bowed and led the way in his handsome butler togs and red fez.

Bing had come round and he wobbled to his feet.

'Vite!' A flank of gendarmes formed to herd us all past the bar and the bartender wiping glasses on a tea towel.

We were escorted to a room reminiscent of a grand banqueting hall. Mahogany walls, polished to a deep dark hue, glowed in flickering candle light. Richly coloured rugs covered the tiled floor and potted palms were clustered in corners. The table was laid with a crisp white table-cloth, napkins, cutlery and sparkling crystal glasses. Candelabras shone from the low ceiling, reflecting sheens of silver and gilt from the condiments and silver whatnots lining the centre – it all gleamed and glittered with comforting familiarity. A quartet of musicians arrived and set up in earshot. They tuned their instruments and started playing a melody by Mozart. It was as surreal as it was unexpected.

Hamid was still at our head. 'Please to be seated, most honoured guests of Hotel Al Shami.' He bowed and pulled out a chair for the steely English aunt, who settled herself regally. The rest of us followed in a bit of a daze.

As we were unfolding napkins, another group of staff appeared and drew aside the heavy damask curtains to reveal a range of delicately framed French windows. We fell silent to stare at the lamplit garden where a faint breeze caused flowers and trees to softly stir on slender stems. The scent of jasmine and roses drifted into the room and a bird sang out in the fragrant darkness. One of the ladies gasped in delight because it really was quite exquisite.

Colonel Fontaine arrived to rap out more orders. 'You will be called for questions. Your fingerprints will be taken shortly. During this time, you may eat.' He gave a stiff nod of the head and exited between two of his men who had positioned themselves to guard the entrance.

I was quietly impressed.

I had grabbed a seat next to Persi and took her hand to give it a squeeze. She forced a weak smile.

'Persi,' I began as delicately as I could. 'The woman, Josephine Belvoir, she was… erm… she was your rival in love, wasn't she?'

'Some time ago, yes.' She nodded, then suddenly shifted in her seat to face me. 'Heathcliff, are you asking me if I had a hand in killing her?'

'No, no, nothing like that.' I lowered my voice as attention swivelled our way. 'I just thought it may have been a bit awkward for you.'

'Awkward in which way?' She whispered quite sharply. 'Her death or her attempts to have Charles locked up?'

My efforts at reassurance weren't going well. 'Um…I erm, just meant when you arrived and found her here.'

'I knew she would be here!' she hissed.

'Oh. Well, wasn't there a bit of an atmosphere?' I imagined the two women had been at daggers drawn.

'I am perfectly capable of being polite, Heathcliff. Even to that scheming vixen.' She turned away to talk to Swift who'd been listening, along with everyone else in the room.

I refrained from reminding her not to call me Heathcliff.

Hamid returned to clap his hands, causing a distraction. Waiters filed in, carrying silver trays of decanters and dusty wine bottles. I chose the red and took a deep draught. It was French and a very good vintage.

The sergeant returned with two more men. One held notepaper, the other an ink pad.

Vincent instantly objected. He jabbed his finger in the direction of the French. 'Where's the lawyer? You can't do nothin' unless our lawyer says so.'

He was ignored.

'Make your names at ze top and underneath you place your digits,' the sergeant instructed in an officious tone.

Pages were handed around and everyone started writing. I pulled out my Montblanc pen to scrawl my name but it was leaking. I ended with blue-stained fingers which were then smeared with black fingerprint ink. A waiter came and handed each of us a hot, damp towel to wipe off the mess. Finally the gendarmes gathered up the papers and cleared off, which was a relief as I hadn't been able to touch my wine during the entire process.

'Well, Swift,' I said, 'as far as investigations go, the French gendarmerie knock your bobbies into a cocked hat.'

He frowned at me then shouted at the drunken actor sitting opposite. 'Bing.'

Bing was propped up on an elbow, woozy but conscious.

'What ho, old man.' He raised a glass.

'Explain what happened, will you?' Swift asked.

Bing laughed, knocked his wine back, then let out a strangled groan. 'I shot Josephine. I can't believe it. She's gone.' His voice broke over the last words and he dragged his crumpled handkerchief from his pocket and blew into it loudly.

Genevieve Hamilton was sitting one side of him and her Aunt was seated on the other, they both shifted away.

'Pull yourself together, young man,' the Aunt told him.

'Leave him be, the poor boy.' The American lady, who I'd assumed to be Mrs Vincent, tried to reach a plump hand over to him around Genevieve. 'Harry, my dear, we know you didn't do it on purpose.' She spoke with a soft southern accent. 'We will have our lawyer look after you. You will be exonerated.'

'Unless he did it on purpose,' I remarked.

I received frowns all round for that one.

The aunt rapped a spoon on the table. 'This is really too confusing. Will you please introduce yourselves?'

'Yeah, the lady's right, you need to know who I am. Dino Vincent.' The director had placed himself at the head of the table. 'I'm in charge here. We're making a movie. It's big business now. Lotsa money involved.'

His wife laid a hand on his arm and he suddenly remembered his manners. 'And this is Mammie – Mrs Vincent.' He forced his features into a smile resembling a smirk.

'Hello, my dears.' Mammie Vincent smiled kindly, her round face creased with wrinkles. 'Do please call me Mammie, everyone does.' She turned to the Aunt. 'And I do hope we will be friends.'

The Aunt's expression remained basilisk. 'I am Lady Margaret Maitland. It suffices to call me Lady Maitland.' She turned to her young companion. 'And this is my niece, Genevieve Hamilton. We are travelling home from India and exploring ancient historical cities on our way.'

Harry Bing hiccuped.

Persi had calmed down and smiled over to Genevieve who was probably only marginally younger than her twenty-eight years. 'Persephone Carruthers,' she said.

'But, please call me Persi. I'm sorry I haven't had time to say hello. You arrived yesterday, didn't you?'

Yes, we did,' Genevieve replied, with a bright smile. 'But it was quite late and we were terribly tired so we didn't speak to a soul. Today has been,' she paused and giggled, 'really rather exciting!'

'Exciting?' Persi's brows raised a notch. 'That's not quite...' she stuttered to a stop. 'Anyway, if you're exploring historical sites, I can show you some of the local digs.'

'Persi is an archaeologist,' I said, reaching for her hand again.

I must have been forgiven because she tightened her fingers around mine.

Genevieve laughed. 'Oh quite! Ancient stones and bones are absolutely my favourite! Isn't that so, Auntie M?'

Lady Maitland gave the faintest of haughty nods.

Swift took a turn. 'May I introduce myself? I am Detective Chief Inspector Swift.' He paused and I waited to hear what came next. 'Of Scotland Yard.'

I hid a grin.

The German was seated at the other end of the table. He stood up, made a sharp bow and clicked his heels. 'My true title is Baron Wilhelm Grunberg. But I am now a movie star and you may call me Dick Dreadnaught.'

'Ohhhh, Dick Dreadnaught,' Genevieve sighed, her Aunt snapped a frown.

The sergeant returned, marched up to the table and stiffened to attention. 'Monsieur 'Arry Bing. You follow with me now.'

'No,' Bing answered back.

The sergeant slapped his hand on his gun holster.

Bing shrugged. 'Oh, if you insist.'

We watched as he staggered to his feet and wobbled off ahead of the Frenchman. It was proving to be the most peculiar dinner I'd ever attended and nobody seemed to be in the least distressed about the cold-blooded murder of Josephine Belvoir.

CHAPTER 6

'He must have done it!' Genevieve declared.

'Nonsense,' Persi snapped, then composed herself. 'I'm sorry, I didn't mean to sound sharp, but I really don't think he would. He has a good heart.'

'When he's sober,' Vincent cut in.

'Even when he's not sober,' Persi retorted with a flash of her eyes.

I'd forgotten how fearless she was and smiled at her, but she wasn't looking at me, she'd fixed a fierce stare at Vincent, who was squaring up for a fight.

'Pappie,' Mrs Vincent quelled him with a word.

'Well, you're a policeman, Inspector Swift?' Genevieve turned toward him. 'Who do you think it was?'

'I don't have the facts, Miss Hamilton.'

'Oh, do call me Genevieve!'

'Yes, erm Genevieve,' he replied, the sharp angles of his face accentuated in the candlelight. 'I would like to hear about the events leading up to the murder.'

Their faces sobered at the mention of the word 'murder'. Fortunately, a waiter appeared and refilled our glasses.

Swift sent a hawkish glance around the table. 'Mrs Vincent, perhaps you could help?'

'Mammie. Please call me Mammie, dear.' She smiled warmly. 'I will tell you whatever I can remember. Wellll...' she lengthened the word. 'The gun we were using went missing a few days ago. It was a big one, wasn't it, Pappie?'

'Yeah,' Vincent replied. 'Colt 45 automatic. I wanted somethin' big enough to be seen by the camera, but that could be hidden under a coat. Some jerk stole it.'

His accent was rough, loud and unpleasant. He was a belligerent blighter and I had taken an instant dislike to the man.

Swift had withdrawn his notebook from his jacket pocket and was now poised with pen. 'When did you notice that the Colt had gone missing?'

'I think maybe it was two days ago,' Mammie replied, with a crease between her plump brows. 'It was in our equipment room, which is next to our suite on the second floor.' Her southern accent grew more pronounced.

'Was it locked away?' Swift asked.

'Yes, most of the time. But whenever we're filming there's always someone running in and out,' Mammie replied. 'We're such busy bees here. No-one knows where anything ever is.' She gave a small trill of laughter.

'Were you filming on the day it went missing?' Swift questioned as he wrote.

'Oh my. Yes, we were. It was the romantic scene where Beryl – that was poor Josephine of course...' She paused, confusion suddenly crossing her face, then shook herself and continued. 'It was when Beryl realises she loves Sheik Omar and must cut all ties with her affianced British Lord. We managed to get the scene in the can in only six takes.' She clapped her hands together as though this were marvellous news.

'I play Sheik Omar,' Dreadnaught put in, then went back to looking bored.

'Harry played the rejected fiancé,' Persi said. 'It's a tragic tale of forbidden love, you see.'

'Right.' I nodded, thinking these movies sounded utterly tedious. 'Were you involved in this 'taking of scenes', Persi?'

She didn't answer as we were interrupted by Hamid, followed by another file of waiters laden with trays. Succulent titbits on gilt-edged dishes were placed in front of us. There were delicate pastries and brightly coloured vegetables in a cream sauce and various whatnots. I had no idea what they were, but they were delicious.

Persi smiled at me, wiping her fingers on a napkin. 'Mammie asked me if I'd like to help behind the scenes and I jumped at it. I had been kicking my heels around here, hoping for news and becoming rather despondent.'

Mammie joined in. 'And the dear girl has been adorable. Our supporting actress became ill and we had to send her home last week. And now we've lost Josephine, too. It is a blessing we have almost finished, or the whole movie would have to be cancelled.'

Swift and I stared at her for a moment but she seemed oblivious to the callousness of the remark.

'But there are not any more ladies now,' Dreadnaught complained. 'We will need ladies to make more movies.'

'Plenty of pretty girls around,' Vincent smirked. 'I can take any one of them and make them a movie star. Wanna be a movie star?' He leaned in the direction of Genevieve with a barely disguised leer.

'She most certainly does not,' Lady Maitland instantly retorted.

Genevieve opened her mouth to object but was quelled by a fierce glare from her aunt.

'What about you, blondie?' Vincent turned toward Persi.

I was watching Mammie Vincent, she had pursed her lips when her husband propositioned Genevieve but now she turned to Persi.

'Oh, do say yes, dear, I think you would be quite divine. I was saying it only this morning to Pappie.'

'I... I...' Persi stuttered to a halt, with a look of surprise on her lovely face.

'Can we please stick to the subject?' Swift asked. 'How did the previous gun go missing?'

'It was simple,' Dreadnaught said. 'Someone entered the room and stole the gun. You must listen. This is not difficult to understand.'

A frown flitted across Swift's face then he wrote a rapid note before returning to the fray. 'What happened today?'

Another round of waiters arrived to exchange the

dishes for plates of succulent lamb cutlets accompanied by something like ground rice with sultanas and spices in. I must say the food here was far better than I'd expected. I'd have to get Greggs to ask for the recipe.

'Vincent supplied the new gun,' Dreadnaught answered.

We looked down the table to Vincent who was picking his teeth with his nails. 'It was in the props box. I ain't noticed it before, but that don't mean nothing. We got spares for everything here and there's two warehouses full back in the States. I got more stuff than I know what to do with.'

'Yes, and...' Persi began but Swift held up his hand to stop her.

'I'm sorry, but I'd like to hear it from someone else please,' he told her, then carried on note-taking.

I frowned at him as a blush rose to her cheeks.

Genevieve spoke up. 'I saw it all. It was fascinating. I wanted to watch how they made the movie. Rehearsals began around ten this morning. Harry Bing shot Josephine and she fell down, then he pretended to shoot himself. This was the action, you see. They rehearsed it over and over. The bullets were obviously blanks or Josephine would have been killed earlier.' She ended with a nervous giggle.

Mammie added, 'We were all present. It was the 'grande finale' of the movie, so everyone wanted to watch.'

'I assume Bing pretended the shot to the temple because of the deafening noise?' Swift was making careful notes as people spoke.

'And the risk of powder burns,' Mammie answered. 'Pappie angled the camera so that Harry only appeared to shoot himself.' She laughed lightly. 'We wouldn't want dear Harry to be harmed by powder burns.'

'Where is your cameraman?' I asked, wondering where he'd disappeared to.

'That's Bruce,' Vincent cut in. 'He took off with the camera as soon as he saw what was happening. He's no fool, he'll be hiding out somewhere.'

'He never leaves the camera alone for one minute,' Mammie said. 'There's only one and we simply cannot make movies without it.'

I wondered why they only had one but I'd heard such equipment was extraordinarily expensive, so imagined that to be the reason.

'But why use blanks at all?' Swift asked. 'It's a silent film.'

'Gun smoke,' Vincent replied. 'The audience loves to see the action and there's always gun smoke. Got to show the action, they want their ten cents worth.' He laughed harshly.

The door banged open and Harry Bing was brought back into the room by a couple of gendarmes. We paused, expecting them to take someone else but they went off alone. Bing grinned at everyone and downed the glass of wine in front of him, which was instantly refilled by a hovering waiter.

Swift asked, 'Where was the gun kept during these rehearsals?'

'What gun?' Harry Bing swayed in his seat.

Genevieve ignored him and turned back to Swift. 'Harry left it on the wall of the fountain just as lunch was being served. I noticed it was there when Auntie M and I went by on the way to the terrace.'

'Where was Bing?' Swift asked.

'Takin' his lunch at the bar,' Vincent cut in. 'And you ain't doing no more movies with me unless you sober up, Bing.'

Bing laughed, which probably didn't help his career prospects.

Mammie smiled and leaned forward, her plump cheeks pink from the wine. 'Pappie picked up the gun and took it to our rooms. We wanted a certain light for the big scene and decided to wait until the lamps were lit in the court-yard. So we went to rest while Bruce set up the camera. We didn't come down until everything was ready, which was just before six o'clock. Pappie called for quiet like he always does. Harry picked up the gun, he and Josephine took their places, and then Pappie shouted for the camera to roll. They played the scene beautifully. Josephine ran out, spoke her lines, Harry responded and… and that's when you arrived…' she stuttered to a halt and put a hand to her lips. After all the drama and noise, I think the real-ity of the murder was finally beginning to sink in. 'Oh, Pappie.' She whimpered and held out a hand.

He patted it awkwardly.

'Bing,' Swift had to shout at the man as he was now almost comatose. 'Was there a spare magazine?'

'Possibly, old man, no use asking me about it.' His voice was slurred. He giggled, sank below the table and fell with a thud to the floor.

The sergeant returned. 'Inspector Swift. You come.'

'Blast it. Lennox, take notes, would you.' Swift shoved his pen and notebook in my direction.

I watched him leave, took another quaff of wine, then eyed the faces around the table.

'Right. Why did you all hate Josephine Belvoir?'

That rattled them.

'What the devil do you mean?' Dreadnaught demanded in Teutonic tone.

I regarded him quietly. 'What did she do to you?'

His eyes darkened. 'Nothing, she did nothing to me. You are barking at the wrong tree, my friend.'

I looked at each of them.

'Hate is a very strong word, Major,' Mammie said in soft reprimand.

My gaze shifted to Genevieve.

'Did you know her?'

She laughed awkwardly. 'No, don't be silly, we only arrived yesterday. We have never met anyone here before.'

'Who are you to ask impertinent questions, young man?' Lady Maitland sought to deflect my attention from her niece and I briefly wondered why.

'Yeah, who the hell are you?' Vincent joined the attack.

'Major Heathcliff Lennox,' I said. 'I'm helping Chief Inspector Swift with his inquiries.'

'Why?' Vincent demanded.

'Because... because we've come here to get my girl-friend's fiancé out of jail,' I retorted.

Lady Maitland's thin brows rose.

Actually that hadn't come out quite as I'd intended.

'Ex-fiancé,' Persi corrected.

'Yes! Ex-fiancé,' I shouted.

'Charles Langton? He's in jail,' Vincent interrupted. 'He deserves it. He tried to shoot Josephine, the sap. We already know all about it.'

'That's not true,' Persi argued. 'He was set up and nobody has done anything to help.'

'Well, we did offer our lawyer's services,' Mammie protested. 'Really, dear child, what else could we do?'

'So, Major, you have come to help a criminal.' Lady Maitland eyed me frostily. 'Do you intend digging him out of his cell? Or perhaps you have brought a gang of desperados to enable a jailbreak!' She ended with a cold smile. I assume this was her idea of amusement.

'We will prove his innocence.' Persi rallied.

Vincent jumped into the fray. 'Yeah, by shooting his victim.'

'I did not shoot her!' Her eyes flashed.

'This is correct, it was Harry.' Dreadnaught joined in. 'Though you may have provided the bullets.'

'Nonsense.' I slammed my hand on the table. Most of them shut up and looked at me. 'She didn't shoot anyone or provide any bullets and we are going to find out who did.'

Lady Maitland turned acerbic. 'How ridiculous. Let me remind you, that you and Inspector Swift have no jurisdiction here.'

'Yeah, and what qualifies you to investigate us, anyway?' Vincent demanded.

That caused me to stutter. I was beginning to wish Swift were here. 'I've... erm. I have helped with a few murders. To uncover them, I mean, with Inspector Swift.'

'You said you were in the Royal Air Force,' Dreadnaught rejoined. 'I heard you tell the Colonel. You are not a detective.' He stood up and pointed a manicured finger at me. 'You are a charlatan.'

It was delivered with such ludicrous drama that it made me laugh. He continued shouting, then everyone joined in at once. Vincent threw more accusations at Persi, Mammie objected to Genevieve's suspicious stare, Lady Maitland was demanding quiet and I'm pretty sure Bing was singing again.

The French sergeant came back, followed by Swift.

'Lennox, what the hell are you doing?'

'Asking questions,' I had to shout above the noise.

He picked up his notebook which was still open at a blank page. 'You haven't written a word.'

'Well, they haven't answered anything yet,' I retorted, rather stung.

'Mademoiselle Carruthers.' The sergeant ignored the melee and snapped his boots together. 'You come with me.'

'Heathcliff,' Persi called out in appeal as she was marched away.

I swore to myself and strode after her. The two French guards on the door stepped forward.

'You sit,' one ordered.

I glared at them, they glared back, so I gave up and returned to the table.

'Your man was very rude,' Lady Maitland told Swift.

'He's not my… Look,' Swift banged a fist on the table. 'Sit down, and shut up.'

They shut up.

'Lennox,' Swift ordered. 'Carry on.'

'You're lying,' I said quietly. 'Every damn one of you. And we want to know why.'

A heavy silence fell, apart from the musicians playing Mozart from the rear. Calling them all liars may have been a pretty infra dig, but I wanted to knock them off-guard. It didn't work.

Mammie spoke for them. 'Truly, dear boy, we have not lied to you.'

'A woman is dead, so someone is lying,' Swift returned, then sighed as tension once again rippled around the table. 'Charles Langton cannot have killed her and I will not stand by and leave an innocent man to rot in jail.'

'You don't know nothin',' Vincent growled. 'And it ain't nothin' to do with neither of you.'

Swift opened his mouth to argue just as the Colonel entered the room, followed by a number of his men.

'Ladies and gentlemen.' He paused to ensure he had our attention. 'We have completed our enquiries for tonight. You will go to your rooms. But…' His cool gaze swept our faces. 'Our inquiry is not complete. Indeed, it is only commencing.'

'Where is Miss Carruthers?' I demanded.

He looked at me. 'She is detained in her rooms. She is not allowed to leave this hotel.' He moved to turn away.

'What the devil does that mean?'

He stopped, observed me for a moment. 'It means she is under arrest for the murder of Mademoiselle Josephine Belvoir.'

CHAPTER 7

Fontaine exited, ignoring our cries of protest before we were herded out. The two English ladies went first. Lady Maitland, slim and straight-backed as she walked briskly alongside Genevieve, who flowed with a sinuous gait. Harry was prodded into tottering along by a couple of gendarmes, followed by Vincent and Mammie. Swift and I brought up the rear behind Dreadnaught.

Everyone was escorted to their respective suites. As we passed Greggs' room, I could hear him snoring through the locked door. Mine was next and Swift halted to talk, but the gendarme behind us stepped forward.

'Allez,' he shouted.

'I will see you at breakfast, Lennox,' Swift said, stifling a yawn.

I nodded, being as weary as he sounded.

Foggy greeted me ecstatically. Poor little dog, he'd been left in a foreign place, surrounded by strangers and without his little cat, whom we both missed. I ruffled his fur and ears as he jumped around my knees, then placed him on the bed. He fell asleep as quickly as I did, among silken sheets and soft damask covers.

Swift didn't arrive with the dawn.

Filtered sunlight threw lattice patterns onto the wall. Muted voices rose from the crowded streets below and, in the distance, I could hear some sort of singing call, rising and falling in quavering cadence. Dust floated upwards, caught in the spinning draught of a fan rotating in the centre of the ceiling. The warmth of the dawning day seeped into the room and I lay in soft comfort, my head resting on my folded arms on feather-filled pillows, reluctant to move, or even think – apart from wondering where breakfast was.

A hesitant knock sounded at my door, Fogg gave a small bark in reply.

'Come in.'

Jamal peered into the room, turban first.

'Effendi.' He saw me and grinned. 'You wake! It is a glorious morning.' He went over to open the shutters and a blazing shaft of sunshine lit up the room. 'Is it your wish to breakfast in your bed or on the garden terrace, effendi? It is most beautiful in the garden and not a person is yet present.'

'Erm, no. I'll take breakfast here please, old chap.' I indicated an ornately carved red and gilt dressing table.

'At your wishes, effendi.' He made to bow out.

'Jamal?' I'd thought of something. 'The bath-draw boy. What happened to him?'

'Ah, I am most sorry for the inconvenience. Bath-draw boy interrupted his duties to watch the proceedings below and he suffered an injurious blow. His family removed him instantly to attend his affliction, but they inform me it was too late. His inopportune action has led to his demise.' He shook his head in momentary sorrow. 'But it must not hinder your enjoyment of Hotel Al Shami, effendi, we can most quickly find a new bath-draw boy.'

'So he is dead then?'

'Indeed, this was confirmed to me.' Jamal tried to escape the room again.

'Wait. Did he have any children?'

'He did, effendi. He was head of numerous progeny and two wives.'

'Two wives?' My brows shot up.

'It is the custom. One may take four, if one has the resources.'

'Good Lord, four!' What on earth were they thinking? Four women in the same house! 'Erm, I assume there must be some sort of legal situation, Jamal. Compensation, perhaps?'

'No, no, it is not necessary, effendi. We care for such unfortunate peoples as widows and orphans. It is our custom.'

'Yes, but I really must contribute something to their futures,' I told him.

He opened his mouth to argue but I held up my hand. 'I insist.'

He nodded and put his hands together as though at prayer. 'Inshallah.'

'Right, and erm… has anyone mentioned this to Colonel Fontaine?'

'Oh, no, effendi. That would not be well advised.'

'Hum… well, excellent. Thank you, Jamal.'

'American dollars are preferred.' He smiled again and made a rapid exit.

I stared at the closed door and wondered once more where American dollars were to be found – probably from Americans, I concluded. Foggy reminded me, with a woof, that he would like breakfast and a walk in that order.

I threw back the covers, strode into the adjoining bathroom and made use of the steaming shower. Fifteen minutes later, I emerged fully dressed to find a splendid array of food waiting on the table. Fogg was seated on the chair, eyeing the feast with spaniel eyes like chocolate saucers.

I placed him on the rug and tucked in.

We shared the goodies. There were lashings of cream cheese, scrambled eggs with tomatoes and tasty herbs, and another plate of flatbread with honey and dark balls of doughnuts, all washed down with many glasses of mint tea. It was excellent and put a bit of a spring back in my step.

Swift still hadn't shown up and neither had Greggs. I put Foggy under my arm and made for the stairs, pausing on a step halfway down to wonder how Persi was and when I would be able to talk to her.

The courtyard was quiet and now entirely free of any trace of the unfortunate Josephine Belvoir. My footsteps echoed as I bypassed the dining room and unoccupied terrace to wander onto the dew laden grass for Foggy to run around gaily. It was a haven of peace, hidden behind high walls and allowed my mind to unravel a few thoughts.

Most of them spun around the singular events of the previous evening and the other hotel guests. My knowledge of America was pretty sketchy, but I knew there were deserts in Texas. The film crew could have gone there with a lot more ease than trailing all the way to Damascus. I also found it hard to believe Lady Maitland and Genevieve were here by chance and thought Genevieve was trying too hard at playing the ingenue. So, what had drawn them all to this particular spot?

Dick Dreadnaught came out onto the terrace to break into my musings. He was dressed in an immaculate pale tan suit, I felt rather a scruff in my linen, despite it having been pressed overnight by the hotel staff. The German gave a curt nod, then sat down as a waiter arrived to serve him. I'd no desire to talk to the block-head, so I scooped Fogg up and carried him off in search of Swift.

I got as far as the fountain.

'Good morning, Major Lennox. Oh my! Pappie, the doggie! Just look at that adorable little doggie.' The effusive tones of Mammie Vincent rung in my ears.

'Yeah, very nice, dear,' Vincent's voice growled back.

There was a great bustle in process. The cameraman, the tall and lanky Bruce in overalls, was carrying the heavy camera in his arms, heading towards the arched gateway. He was followed by a stream of uniformed

Arabs, laden with various boxes, tripods, lights and the essential whatnots needed for movie making.

'Are you leaving?' I asked as I came to a halt beside Mammie.

Vincent was dressed, as yesterday, in check shirt and braces. His forehead was damp with beads of sweat, he was red in the face and shouting out orders.

'No, of course not, dear Heathcliff. We are going to film around the city,' Mammie replied.

I could see she was tired, her cheeks creased with wrinkles in the bright sunlight. The flowery green dress she wore did little to enhance her colour.

'Urm, it's Lennox. Not keen on Heathcliff. My mother, you know, romantic...' I tailed off and changed tack. 'I thought you took the last scene yesterday?'

For some reason she found this terribly amusing. 'Oh no, dear. We do not film in sequence. We have completed all the interior and close-up shots. Now we are going to take clips of the desert with palm trees and scenes of camels crossing sand dunes. It's all about atmosphere!'

I nodded, trying to appear as fascinated as she patently was. 'Marvellous. Very erm...'

She wasn't listening. 'And our lawyer, Mr Midhurst, has not returned. It is most inconvenient. We sent him to find suitable locations but now we must do it ourselves. And after last evening...' She sighed. 'May I pet your doggie?'

'Yes, yes. Why did you send your lawyer to find filming locations?'

'Oh, we all do many jobs here.' She was ruffling the fur on Foggy's head with red, painted nails. 'Making movies in foreign climes is terribly expensive, so we hire locals on the spot and restrict our own crew to just the most experienced hands.' She laughed, her curls bobbing. 'We all throw ourselves into it.'

'Hey, Lennox,' Vincent waddled over to his wife's side. 'I got an idea. We can do a short. People love dogs, and yours is kinda cute. We can make a short movie. 'Delilah of the Desert', I can see it now. What d'ya think, Mammie?' He was holding his hands up in a sort of square as he spoke to her.

'Oh, my dearest, yes. It sounds perfect! You are so clever with ideas.' She turned to me. 'How much for the doggie?'

'What?' I stepped back, clutching Fogg closer to my chest.

'What d'ya want for the mutt?' Vincent asked.

'My dog is not for sale,' I told them, in no uncertain terms, wondering what sort of people ask to buy someone's dog.

'Oh, no, we mean how much would you like for him to star in the movie?' Mammie assured me with a tinkle of laughter. 'It will only take one or two days. And we will make it while we're filming locations.'

'He can't stay out overnight,' I said, taking another step backwards because I wasn't sure about this new enthusiasm.

'We don't never stay out at night,' Vincent said. 'Twenty dollars a day, plus twenty more when it's in the can.'

I blinked. That seemed quite generous and I was in need of dollars. I tried to calculate how much a dead bath-draw boy might be worth.

'Thirty,' I said.

'Done,' Vincent snapped. 'Give him to one of the boys.' He pointed toward the bevy of hotel staff still carrying out the equipment.

'Absolutely not.' I replied. 'My butler will go with him.'

Their jaws dropped.

'A butler,' Mammie uttered. 'Did you hear that, Pappie. A real butler!'

'You have a butler?' Vincent said with a tone verging on awe.

Well, at last I'd finally impressed somebody.

'Yes, he's here somewhere.' I turned to look around and spied him returning from the direction of the dining room. 'Greggs.'

He arrived in unhurried fashion, sporting pristine butlering togs and a trace of egg on his chin. 'Sir?'

'Where have you been?' I asked.

'Taking breakfast,' he informed me in stately fashion. 'You did say that I should treat this trip as a holiday, sir.'

'Did I?'

'Indeed, sir.'

'Well, they're going to make a movie with Fogg, Greggs. He's a girl; 'Delilah of the Desert'.'

He leaned forward a touch, possibly to check if I'd been drinking. 'Pardon, sir?'

'It won't take long, only a day or so,' I continued before he could object. 'And not overnight. They will bring you back later today so you won't miss anything.'

'Sir, I don't... I...' he stuttered.

'It'll give you a chance to see the place,' I offered in persuasion.

'You can be in a movie.' Mammie smiled at him. 'Just imagine telling everyone you've been in one of Pappie's shorts.'

He blanched and gazed at the lady wide-eyed.

'Mrs Vincent means a short film. Greggs,' I explained. 'And they'll pay you in American dollars.'

'Indeed?' That diverted his mind. He turned to me. 'Sir, may I have quiet word?'

'Certainly, Greggs.'

We stepped out of earshot.

'Um, sir. About the unfortunate deaths last evening...'

'Ah, yes, old chap. Don't worry about it, I'm pretty certain neither of these two was involved,' I assured him. 'Particularly not with the bath-draw boy.'

'No, sir, but somebody did kill the lady on purpose.'

'Yes, Greggs, but from what I understand she probably deserved it.' I realised that sounded rather heartless and re-grouped. 'And I wouldn't let Fogg go if I thought there was any danger.'

He frowned at me.

'And there's thirty dollars a day in it.'

He leaned in. 'For each of us?'

'Absolutely.'

'Erm,' he thought about it for a second. 'Very well, sir.'

Behind his customary hangdog expression I could detect a glimmer of excitement. I knew he'd revel in the telling of his movie experience once we returned home, not to mention the princely sum of thirty dollars a day.

'Right.' I handed Foggy over. 'And look after him, Greggs.'

'Sir,' he replied loftily. 'You may be certain I will protect Mr Fogg from all peril.'

'Excellent, old chap.'

We returned to Vincent, who was pulling dollar bills from a fat roll as we spoke.

'That's thirty a-piece and you make damn sure not a hair on their heads is harmed,' I warned him.

'Yeah, sure.' He thrust a bundle of dollars into my hand and waddled off, followed by my old retainer clutching Fogg.

I stood with hands in pockets for a moment, dithering and concerned that perhaps I'd been a bit hasty in letting them go. As the last Arab bag-carrier filed out, I decided to see them off.

A crowd had gathered at the hotel entrance and formed a semi-circle around the Rolls Royce which had brought us from the airport. Greggs had got into the front seat with Fogg on his lap. The little dog was staring around with his ears perked up and tongue hanging out. Mammie and Vincent had just climbed in the back. I didn't recognise their driver, it wasn't Jamal.

Behind the car were three camels, each held by a turbaned Arab in flowing robes of bleached linen. Perched upon the first was Bruce, the cameraman, on a tasselled saddle clasping the camera to his chest. The second and third animals were laden with more movie making gear. Chickens pecked around their cloven feet and a small phalanx of uniformed Arabs, presumably borrowed from the hotel, brought up the rear.

The Rolls set off at a dignified pace; one of the camels bellowed, causing the crowd to take a step backwards. With assorted grunts and snorts, the caravan trundled off, followed by the paid help. I watched as they disappeared down the dust-hazed street, then wandered back into the courtyard.

Swift was talking to Hamid at the reception desk, but called out when he saw me. 'Lennox, where have you been?'

'I could ask you the same thing,' I replied. 'Thought you said you were coming to see me at breakfast.'

'You didn't come to the dining room.' He too looked tired, but his cream suit was immaculate.

'I ate in my room and you said…'

'Yes, well… Actually, I overslept.' He looked a bit sheepish. 'Anyway, Colonel Fontaine is here. He's been questioning the staff and he said he wants to talk to us. They're going to interview Persi.'

'When?'

'Now.'

'Why?' I asked.

'Because he thinks we're involved.'

'What? You mean we're suspects?'

'Yes. Come on.' He headed off.

CHAPTER 8

We passed the terrace and crossed the lawn to the folly in the centre of the garden. It had an elegant facade built of eight columns with walls of white stone and black wrought-iron grills for windows. Actually, it was hard to see much detail because most of the building was smothered in roses, climbing up and over the domed roof.

Fontaine was seated at a teak table, pen in hand, the sergeant hovering behind him. They were both uniformed, although Fontaine had removed his kepi and placed it next to an open notebook on the table. He motioned for us to sit.

The place was furnished with a couple of chairs, two white couches covered in pastel cushions and a rug on the stone floor which was scattered with rose petals. It would have been rather romantic in different circumstances.

Persi was already seated on a sofa, she gave me a wan smile as we entered. Her blonde hair was again caught in a bun, she wore a peach dress which looked as washed-out as she did.

'Hello, old stick.' I sat next to her, placing an arm around her shoulders to give her a comforting hug.

'Move away from the prisoner,' Fontaine ordered. 'Do not touch her.'

'Why the devil shouldn't I?'

Persi reached out her hand, and in so doing, dropped something into my pocket.

'Major Lennox,' Fontaine insisted as the sergeant stepped forward.

I got up and moved to a chair, wondering what Persi had slipped to me. Swift was watching from the other chair.

'Major Lennox, Chief Inspector Swift.' The Colonel wrote both our names in his book. 'You gentlemen have come here all the way from England to aid this lady?' Fontaine started without preamble.

We nodded.

'By helping her kill her rival, Josephine Belvoir?'

'Don't be ridiculous,' Swift replied.

Fontaine's pale blue eyes narrowed. 'Mademoiselle Carruthers has been most active in her attempts to have Monsieur Langton released.'

'Not to the point of murder,' Swift said.

'And how do you know this?' Fontaine snapped.

Swift hesitated and countered. 'What evidence do you have to justify holding Miss Carruthers?'

'Her fingerprints were on the weapon.'

'Among others.' Swift remained calm, although I could hear anger rising in his voice.

I jumped in. 'I gave her the gun to hold when I emptied the magazine.' I turned towards her. 'Isn't that right, Persi?'

She nodded, tension etched on her face.

'Her prints were also on the magazine,' Fontaine continued.

I glanced at Persi again, but she had shifted her gaze to her hands clasped in her lap.

'What of it?' I asked.

'There were two magazines. We found another one in a plant pot by the bar.'

Swift leaned forward. 'Loaded with blanks or live ammunition?'

'Blanks. It was evidently discarded,' Fontaine replied. 'The magazines were switched, it would have been quite simple.' He paused to scrawl a brief note, then looked up again. 'Did you supply the weapon and magazines?'

Swift bristled. 'I told you last evening. Lennox and I didn't arrive until around four in the afternoon. That gun had been used in the rehearsals the same morning. There are witnesses who can attest to it.'

Fontaine didn't respond, he made more notes in his book. I thought it was a bit of an act because he would have known about the rehearsal already.

'Were there any prints on the hidden magazine you found?' Swift demanded.

'No, it had been made clean.' Fontaine didn't glance up from writing. 'But there were two sets of fingerprints on the magazine loaded with live rounds.' He stopped and fixed me narrowly. 'One was yours, Major Lennox, and the others belonged to Miss Carruthers.'

That put me on the back foot and I paused for a second, then retaliated. 'That doesn't mean a damn thing. A murderer would wear gloves, or wipe it clean. Your accusations are ridiculous.'

'Mademoiselle Carruthers, what is your explanation?' He turned to stare at her, his tanned face hard and cold.

She remained silent as moments ticked by. A bird sang in the garden.

'Persi?' I said.

'I recognised the gun,' she replied at last.

'And who did it belong to?' Fontaine nodded, the ghost of a smile crossed his lips.

'Charles Langton,' she whispered.

That was a jolt. I glanced at Swift, thinking that he could have told me. Damn it. It was probably what they were talking about while I was at the bar.

Fontaine muttered something in French to the sergeant and was handed the Kongsberg-Colt. He ejected the magazine and laid both items on the table, then the sergeant placed another magazine beside it.

'This is an unusual gun, made in Europe under licence from Colt. It's almost an exact replication, except for the imprint here.' He ran a finger along the slide where the lettering had been impressed into the metal. 'It was known Langton carried one, but it was not in his possession when he was arrested for attempting to murder Mademoiselle Belvoir,' Fontaine stated, then stared in accusation at Persi. 'Did you have it? Was it you who made the first attack on the lady?'

'No, don't be ridiculous,' Persi retorted. 'I wasn't here, which you are quite aware of. I don't think anyone attacked her, I think she made the whole thing up and you know it!' Her eyes suddenly flashed and she leaned forward to shout at him. 'You're holding Charles under false pretences because he has information you want and he won't give it to you.'

He glared back, anger in his eyes. 'There was a witness. The bath-draw boy, he was guarding Ladies Row at the moment of the attempt. He attested to seeing Langton leave the Ladies floor and run down the stairs.'

I shifted in my seat and wondered if I should admit to his untimely demise, but decided it probably wasn't a good moment.

'Bribed or coerced!' Persi fought back. 'You and Josephine Belvoir set this up from the beginning.'

Fontaine pointed a finger. 'Is that why you arranged for her to be shot? Because you thought she had set up your fiancé?'

'That's a lie! Your accusations are absurd,' she retaliated.

'Wait.' Swift interrupted. 'This isn't helping.' He waved his hand in a placatory manner, trying to calm the argument. 'Miss Persi, your fingerprints were only on the loaded magazine because you ejected it from the gun. Could you explain how this happened, please?'

Persi sat back in her seat, a flush on her cheeks. She closed her eyes for a second before turning to

Swift. 'Bing had the gun all morning during rehearsals, then he left it on the fountain wall at lunch time. Vincent saw it, he was angry because he'd already had one stolen. He took it away with him.' She paused to gather her thoughts then carried on. 'After the afternoon break, as the camera was about to roll for the final scene, Vincent handed the gun to me, telling me to give it to Bing when he arrived. That's when I noticed the imprint, it looked like the one Charles used to own but I couldn't understand what it was doing there.' She gave a slight shake of her head, the light glinting off strands of blonde hair. 'I checked to see if it was scratched. You see, Charles puts the letter 'C' on his possessions, I think it was a habit from his school days. It was utterly stupid of him.' She paused to shrug away her anger. 'Anyway, there wasn't anything on the gun, so I popped the magazine.'

'And was there a letter 'C' on it?' Swift asked a leading question.

'Yes, and I realised it was his gun. I... I was so surprised,' she stuttered.

'Did you see the bullets?' Swift asked.

'No, I didn't have time, and it didn't even occur to me. Why would it?' Her voice rose and she took a breath to calm herself. 'Harry arrived as Vincent called for everyone to take their places. I closed the magazine and handed it to Bing. Then we were told to keep quiet because of the filming. They started the scene and... and Josephine was shot.' She looked at me. 'And that's when you came in.'

My shoulders slumped. I understood her reaction; I'd have done the same. It was instinctive and she could never have imagined it would be used as a murder weapon. I stifled a groan, because it was still a bloody disaster.

Swift was talking. 'And you are certain you didn't see, or touch the bullets, did you?'

'No.' Persi shook her head. 'I told you, everything happened at once and I was terribly flustered. You can check the casings, my prints won't be on them.'

'They had all been smeared, Miss Carruthers, so we cannot verify this,' Fontaine replied.

I shifted in my seat again. I'd rubbed the prints off the bullets, but I needed to see how this would play out before saying anything else.

'Were both magazines marked with a letter 'C'?' Swift asked. He'd taken his notebook out and was making rapid notes in his precise hand.

Fontaine answered. 'No.'

'And the magazines between Colt 45 automatics are interchangeable?' Swift continued although he would have known as well as the rest of us that they were. We were a generation deeply conversant with weaponry of all kinds after experiencing the war. He was just being his usual pedantic self.

Fontaine nodded dismissively. 'These weapons are very common. Even we use them.'

'So you could have done it,' I put in.

He ignored me.

'Is it true you are holding Langton to obtain information from him?' Swift asked. 'Because that's against the Geneva Convention and it is my intention to call on the British Ambassador this afternoon.'

'There is no British Ambassador, Inspector.' Fontaine smiled coldly. 'He and his entourage have departed. You are all alone here.'

That gave us pause and a bit of a cold shock.

Persi broke in, 'You must release Charles Langton. He patently did not kill Josephine Belvoir yesterday and he did not make the attempt on her life earlier.'

'Enough!' Fontaine slammed his hand on the table. 'You have made your representations.'

Swift jumped to his feet. 'Fontaine, you have nothing but circumstantial evidence. You cannot hold Miss Carruthers.'

'Ha!' He laughed harshly. 'Did you know she is a spy? Even your famous Geneva Convention does not protect spies.'

'I am not a spy,' Persi shouted at him.

Fontaine ignored Persi's outburst. 'As is her fiancé.'

'Ex-fiancé,' I corrected him.

'That is not the story Charles Langton or Mademoiselle Carruthers has supplied to me.' He sat back to watch my reaction.

I glanced at Persi, expecting another eruption of fury, but she bit her lip and didn't move. I'd had enough and stood up, kicking my chair backwards to fall with a bang on the floor.

I leaned over the colonel's desk. 'You believe what you bloody well like, Fontaine. But Miss Carruthers didn't kill anyone. Leave her out of your games. And if Charles Langton is innocent, you have no right to keep him locked up either. We may be a long way from France, but your famous justice system is just as applicable here as it is in Paris.'

He was unimpressed. 'Venez.' He waved a hand at his sergeant and they both escorted Persi out. We stood in impotent silence as she was marched across the garden and into the hotel.

'They're being held to bloody ransom, aren't they?' I swore as we left the folly. 'That whole show was nothing but a damn charade.'

'Well, I hope it was a charade, because it's serious if it isn't.' Swift replied.

We reached the terrace, where wicker chairs were arranged around circular tables. Simple terracotta tiles covered the floor and the usual plethora of potted plants were spread throughout. I yanked a chair out and dropped into it.

'Lennox, calm down,' Swift told me. 'Acting like a bull in a china shop isn't going to help anyone.'

'Fine, but Persi is being held for murder and there's a lot more to this than we're being told.'

'I've asked Harry Bing to meet us here at ten o'clock. We might get something out of him.'

'If we pour enough whisky into him first,' I retorted.

A waiter arrived. 'Coffee, sirs?'

We both nodded and the sweet, bitter brew was served with small biscuits of crisped honey and nuts.

We waited for him to leave, then Swift asked quietly, 'What did she pass to you?'

I gave a half grin, he always was sharp. 'Tell me what Persi told you while I was at the bar first.'

'She disclosed nothing more than she just told Fontaine in the interview.'

'Why didn't you let me wipe the magazine?' I wanted to know.

'Because we didn't know if any other prints were on it. Lennox, you haven't learned even the most basic principles of detecting. You must NEVER interfere with evidence,' he raised his voice. 'And you handled the bullets!'

Really, he could become ridiculously overexcited about the most trivial of things. 'But she knew the gun belonged to Langton.'

'Yes, but not how it came to be there. It was obviously a ploy.'

'To what end?' I demanded, which shut him up because he didn't know.

Arguing didn't help so I dug in my pocket and pulled out a tightly folded piece of paper. I unwrapped it to drop the contents onto the glass-topped wicker table. It fell with a clunk, rolled briefly on its thick edge and rattled to land on one side of its flat surface.

It was a bronze medallion, about two inches across and coated with grime. It had the appearance of something from antiquity. There was a hole punched through the top sector, as though it had once hung on a chain. We could make out squiggly lines engraved across the surface, enclosed within a circle of raised dots, blackened with age. I picked it up and held it to the light.

'Keep it hidden, Lennox. Here…' Swift handed me a small magnifying glass. 'Use this.'

We both leaned in to peer at it.

'That could be a house with a dome on it,' Swift said, pointing to an etched shape in the centre.

'It could be a dead camel for all we know,' I remarked.

'Has she ever said anything about this?' Swift asked.

'No,' I replied.

'Was there anything written on the paper?'

I gave it to him.

He turned it around. 'It looks to be hastily written. It's says, 'Find the tomb-robber; exchange this for the house of Hanno the Navigator. Keep it on the QT. Yours as ever, C. L. xx'.'

'What?'

'Langton must have passed it to Persi. It's a secret.'

'Yes, I know what QT means, Swift.'

He carried on. 'The tomb-robber and Hanno the Navigator? Has she said anything to you about them?'

'No,' I replied. 'Was that it?'

He turned the paper over. 'Yes.'

I cursed to myself – damn Charles bloody Langton, he was responsible for dragging Persi into this.

I picked the medallion up and turned it over. 'Look!'

Swift looked. 'It's the same as on Josephine's bracelet!'

'Yes.' I could see the pattern more clearly now. I'd noticed the clasp on Josephine Belvoir's bracelet as she'd lain by the fountain, but it had been too small to see the 'galleon' clearly. The engraving on the medallion was larger. It was a stylised ship with a single square sail and a cresting horse's head on the bow.

'There's a connection,' Swift stated the obvious as we peered through the magnifier. 'We need to talk to Persi.'

'Um.' I nodded, and wrapped the paper back around the medallion to shove it into my top pocket.

He continued. 'And I think we need to question the bath-draw boy too.'

'Erm, there could be a bit of a problem there, Swift.'

He raised his brows.

'I might have accidentally shot him.'

'You did what?' He almost choked on his coffee.

'It wasn't on purpose,' I protested. 'The gun went off when I tackled Harry Bing and he got in the way of the bullet.'

'You shot the bath-draw boy?'

Really! Swift was so excitable at times.

'Yes, I just explained, it's not that difficult to understand.'

'Damn it, he was the only witness we had.'

'Well, he can't testify now, can he.' I brushed crumbs off my lap. 'Anyway, we'd better go and find out about this house of Hanno.'

'For heaven's sake, Lennox. Langton is rotting away, we must find a way to have him released.'

89

'Are you sure about that?' I argued. 'It's obvious Langton is being held because the French want to prise information out of him. Fontaine's hardly going to let him die before he's got it.'

Swift considered that. 'But once the secret is uncovered, there's a risk Fontaine will leave Langton locked up in that hell hole.'

'True,' I replied, although it was a risk I was willing to take. 'Anyway, we need to clear Persi's name first.'

'She's not in any danger, Lennox.'

'You don't know that,' I argued. 'We can't leave her at the mercy of the French.'

I could see he was wavering.

I pressed home the point. 'And we need her to find out who this Hanno is.'

'Do you think this could be the key to why they're all here?' He asked.

'Yes, I just said so!'

'Well, it wasn't very clear,' he complained.

'Nonsense, Swift, you just weren't listening.'

'For heaven's sake, Lennox,' he was about to argue when he paused. 'I suppose we may be able to use the secret to negotiate his release.'

'Yes, and we need to find the murderer and clear Persi's name.'

'So, we need to find the murderer and this Hanno?' Swift said. 'Or, find the secret and then…'

'Swift.' I interrupted.

'What?'

'It's rather confusing.'

'Yes.'

Well, at least we were agreed on something.

CHAPTER 9

Harry Bing arrived with an amiable grin and slipped into a wicker chair opposite us.

'I say, old chaps, how about a drink.' His eyes were puffy, as were his cheeks, but his dark hair was neatly combed and he was dressed in a well-tailored suit.

'Let's stick with coffee,' Swift said.

A freshly brewed pot was served by the attentive waiter.

'Spill the beans, Bing,' I told him as he blew on his steaming coffee.

He smiled. 'About my deep dark sins or...' he waved his hand indicating the hotel and inhabitants.

'Just talk,' Swift pulled his notebook from inside his jacket.

'Righty ho.' He leaned back in his chair. 'Josephine Belvoir...' His voice faded across the name. 'The most beautiful woman I've ever encountered. She stole my heart, not that she cared. We met in Paris in the Spring of 1917, when I was sent to work making movies with the Vincents.'

'There were films being made during the war?' I interrupted in surprise.

'Yes.' He nodded. 'When America entered the war, they sent a number of movie-making crews to shoot documentaries. The folks back home were desperate for news about their boys out in foreign fields. Anyway the powers-that-be decided these crews were the perfect cover for some covert activity.'

That made me sit up. 'You mean, you were spies?' I glanced at Swift who had paused taking notes to fix a hawkish gaze on Bing.

'Yes, of course,' Bing replied as casually as a postman might admit to collecting stamps. 'We were all spies, that was our job.'

'But, are you still spying on… well, on…' I tried to form a coherent question without mention of secrets or whatnots.

'Let's not get ahead of ourselves,' Swift cut in. 'Carry on, Bing.'

He'd watched us over his coffee cup and took a sip before replying. 'Wilko! So a few of our finer agents were fingered and sent off to join the moving-picture business. Actually, it was rather a clever move on the bods part, it allowed us access to places we'd never have got into otherwise.'

'Who ordered you to join the Vincents? The Foreign Office?' Swift questioned.

Bing smiled. 'Can't help you there, old boy. Official secrets and all that.'

'But what were you supposed to do?' I asked, rather fascinated by hearing the mysteries of espionage at close quarters. 'As a spy, I mean.'

'Oh, you know,' he waved a hand vaguely. 'Liaise with resistance groups, pick up details about troop movements and numbers, or any build-up in armaments in a new sector. It's not about spying through peep holes, it's about gathering information.'

I opened my mouth to ask more questions but Swift motioned to me to shut up.

'We need to know how it operated, Lennox. Go on, Bing.'

Bing pulled out a solid gold case, extracted a slim cigarette, tapped it twice and lit it with a matching lighter. 'Mammie ran the show. Vincent had been employed as a cameraman in the States and made a few short films of his own on the side. Then he met Mammie and, according to rumour, she fell for him, head over heels,' he said between puffs of smoke. 'She had money and he had ambition, so it was a match made in heaven, you see.' He gave a wry grin. 'Mammie is well-connected in political circles, so I suppose the American Government approached her. Anyway, Vincent promoted himself to director and they headed off to France armed with a camera and oodles of readies.' He fidgeted. 'We could shift to the bar, old chap. Much more convivial, you know.'

'No,' Swift replied sharply. 'Was Bruce with them at that time?'

'No, it was just the two of them.' Bing sighed. 'Although they were under the auspices of the American army, so they were hardly alone.'

Swift glanced up briefly, then continued writing. 'Carry on.'

'As I said, I was sent to meet them in Paris, they were staying at the Ritz. There seemed to be bucket loads of money. Everything was absolutely first rate and Josephine was sitting with them among all the opulence. She was like the jewel in the crown, sparkling, beautiful and utterly entrancing...' His voice faded, then he started up again. 'I'd just come back from the front and suddenly found myself back in the comforts of luxurious civilisation. They were drinking champagne below glittering chandeliers. Vincent looked bored, Mammie was on form, and I couldn't take my eyes off Josephine.' He paused again, letting the cigarette burn to ash between his fingers. He lurched forward to stab it out in the ashtray, which was instantly replaced by the nearest waiter.

Never having seen a moving picture, I was rather confused. 'But if they were making documentary films about real life, surely they wouldn't need actors?'

'Well, yes, you're right. They didn't really, it was just a cover. But the Vincents organised proper jobs for us, and it worked out rather well actually.' Bing straightened up. 'They couldn't film injured men being tended in hospital because the real nurses were covered in blood, so Josephine would don a clean uniform and Vincent would film her bandaging a soldier. It was a proper depiction but without the gore and he'd usually take the shot at an angle so her face wasn't fully visible.'

'And you?' I asked. 'Were you on screen?'

'Yes, at times. I'd be a Tommy leaning over a gate, or a doctor wearing a mask. Once I was an officer on a horse, but I fell off.' He laughed half-heartedly. 'I never was very good at riding.'

'But it was largely real?' I asked.

'As much as possible, yes it was. Vincent has more scruples than you'd imagine,' he said. 'When it comes to filming anyway. He's actually rather good at what he does. At one time he made a short called 'Missing in Action'. He started with a young woman opening a letter, just her hands are visible and there's an engagement ring on her finger. The page is held as though being read, then the hand starts to tremble and, after a few seconds, the letter falls to the floor. Then he cuts to the lady with a tear running down her cheek. She was turned toward the window, so her profile was outlined against the light and her face was in shadow with long auburn curls falling down her back. It was rather beautiful actually.'

'But Josephine was blonde,' I broke in.

'We had another girl with us.' Bing's voice dropped. 'A pretty young thing…'

'Who was she?' Swift asked.

'Beatrice Langton. Charles Langton's sister.'

'Good Lord!' I exclaimed as Swift and I exchanged glances.

'What happened to her?' I asked.

'She was betrayed and captured,' he replied quietly. 'Better not to think about it, really.'

'When was this?' Swift asked.

'September 1918,' Bing said. 'Only a few weeks before the Armistice. Someone reported a rumour that she'd been taken behind German lines.' He sighed. 'Everything had gone swimmingly up until then. We were in Northern France near St Quentin, Beatrice went out one night and didn't come back. We put feelers out, trying to find out where she was and what had happened, but there was a massive offensive going on at the time. You probably remember those battles, the Allies were making the final push forward and they were bombing the place to smithereens.'

Swift and I nodded, his face, and probably mine, sombre with nightmarish memories impossible to erase.

'Carry on, would you.' Swift broke the hush that had fallen.

Bing's dark eyes flicked away, then he resumed his story. 'There was talk that she'd been executed and we were ordered back to Paris. That's where Charles found us. He was in the same business, espionage you know, and he came to find out what happened to his little sister.'

'Did Langton discover anything?' I asked.

He shook his head, his smooth features creased with melancholy. 'No. There was no possibility of going to the front, it was disintegrating by the day, so he spent a couple of weeks in Paris digging for information without getting anywhere.'

'Someone must have known how she was betrayed, or who was responsible,' I suggested.

'It wasn't Josephine, before you ask. I'm sure of it. She and I had been...' He hesitated. 'Very close for a while, when we were in St Quentin. Even after our relationship ended I knew where she was almost by the minute. I was obsessed with her.' He lowered his gaze. 'I never stopped loving her, but… My devotion, you see, she said it was pathetic.' He gave himself a bit of a shake. 'Anyway, Charles was creating the most almighty fuss, he thought his sister may still be alive, and was convinced one of us knew something. But Beatrice had her own contacts, just as we all had. If one of them had been captured and made to talk, or simply sold out, we'd never have known.'

'Was Persi with you? Or around anywhere?' I asked.

'No,' he shook his head. 'I'd never met her, or heard of her, until she turned up here.'

'Hum,' I was relieved to hear that. I focused back on Bing. 'Langton and Josephine were erm…romantically close?'

He laughed hollowly. 'That came later, after the Armistice. Langton went away and then returned once it was signed. As agents of espionage we were effectively redundant and were left to kick our heels in Paris. When Langton returned, Josephine entertained herself by seducing him.'

I had watched the expressions crossing his face. Perhaps he was a good actor, but it seemed to me that he was genuinely cut up by it all.

'Why did you stay?' I asked. 'It must have been torment.'

'Yes, but the Vincents said they'd be returning to Hollywood and I wanted to go with them. Bright lights and all that.' He forced a smile.

'What were they doing during all this?' Swift asked.

'The Vincents? Once we returned to Paris they carried on filming, there was plenty of good footage out on the streets and they made as many shorts as they could. They used us occasionally, just to keep us busy. Mammie is very thoughtful in that way.'

'Did Mammie and Vincent have their own spy network?' Swift asked.

'Yes – us!' Bing grinned. 'We were passing information back to our respective handlers, and we shared it with Mammie. She sent it on to American Intelligence. That was the way it had been organised.'

Swift dashed a few lines, then asked, 'And Dreadnaught, how did he fit into this?'

'He didn't really. He had been captured during the war and was Josephine's contact in the nearby Prisoner of War camp. The Allied camps were much more open than the German equivalents – Gentlemen's honour and all that. They were hotbeds of rumour and gossip – a rich hunting ground for inside information if anyone could access it. Josephine found a way in by recruiting Dreadnaught and he passed on any relevant titbits.'

'So, he was one of Josephine's conquests, too?' I asked.

He nodded. 'She used people. She had the morals of an alley cat, and that's slandering the cat.' He tried another grin but failed and merely looked more miserable.

'Is that why you said she was evil?' I asked.

'Oh, not only that.' He sighed. 'She killed without a thought, I've seen her do it. We were questioning a

Frenchman and realised that he was actually a stooge working for the Germans. She pulled out a stiletto knife and stabbed him through the heart. She remained absolutely expressionless throughout. I'd say she felt nothing at all. That's what made her such a marvellous actress – she'd been acting like a normal human being her whole life.'

I thought of Josephine again, picturing her face as she lay on the floor beside the fountain. It was hard to reconcile Bing's words with the ethereal beauty she had been – assuming he was telling the truth, that is.

Swift asked. 'Did you rekindle your affair with Josephine Belvoir at any time?'

Bing frowned at the indelicate questioning, but Swift had been a Detective Chief Inspector of Scotland Yard and could be coldly logical.

'No, I maintained a professional relationship, but they all knew I carried the torch for her, and she played on it when it suited.'

'She wore a diamond bracelet.' I raised the subject. 'Was it from you?'

'No.' He regarded me. 'I don't know who gave it to her, but she collected wealthy admirers, and pretty baubles.'

'But it was someone here?' I asked.

He nodded.

Swift returned to the questions in point. 'What happened exactly, at the end of the war?'

Bing replied. 'Our respective governments signed us off our duties and Vincent agreed to keep Josephine and me on the acting pay-roll. Charles Langton was recalled to London and Dreadnaught was released from the POW camp. Josephine introduced him to Vincent and with his handsome phizog he was a shoo-in for the leading man. We all headed for the Hollywood hills and had a rare old time.' He grinned. 'The glamour and excitement helped bury the past, you see.'

'So, why are you all here now, reliving that past?' Swift shifted forward in his seat.

'Ah, well, that's where I really can't help you, old chap. I've given up espionage and daring-deeds for the old country. They don't trust me anymore, you see. Taken to the bottle and it's a poor combination, secrets and booze. So they won't let a sniff escape and I don't want to know either.' He stood up abruptly. 'And now if you'll excuse me, gentlemen, I have some sorrows to drown.'

We watched him go, a compact, dapper chap with a straight back, square shoulders and a world of woes in his heart.

CHAPTER 10

'Poor blighter,' Swift put his notebook back in his pocket.

'And poor Beatrice Langton,' I remarked.

'Yes, her last days don't bear thinking about.' His face darkened. 'Not one of them has thought to mention her until now.'

'Or the fact that they're all spies,' I added.

'Were spies,' he corrected.

'Oh, come on, Swift.'

'Yes, you're right,' he conceded. 'It's no great surprise, though, is it?' He yawned and stretched.

'Swift,' I started, then faltered because I was beginning to question everything. 'Persi? She couldn't be involved in murder, or assassinations, could she?'

He shook his head. 'No, she wouldn't have asked us to come all the way here if she were.'

'But she didn't actually know we were coming.' I said.

'Of course she did, I wrote and told her.'

'How did you know I'd agree?'

'Why wouldn't you?'

'Because I do actually have a mind of my own, Swift.'

'Well, why don't you make more use of it?'

'I do make use of it!' I protested.

That fell on deaf ears. 'We need to interview the Vin-cents,' he said

'We can't, they've gone off, they're making a film of Fogg.'

'What?'

I told him about the strangely assorted expedition that had left the hotel this morning.

'Delilah of the Desert?' He found it rather amusing. 'And Greggs!'

'He's had some experience of the stage, you know,' I spoke in defence of my old retainer.

Swift returned to the murder hunt. 'We'd better find a way to speak to Persi. Where are her rooms?'

'Top floor, which is off limits.'

He raised his brows in question.

'Ladies only,' I explained.

'As far as they're concerned I'm still a Chief Inspector of police,' he stated. 'That's all the qualification I need.'

'Swift, not even your kilt qualifies you for Ladies Row.'

He ignored me and walked off, so I followed to find out how far his qualifications got him.

There was a large, bearded Arab sitting on a stool at the entrance to the uppermost walkway. He wore a black tunic, trousers and boots and held a sword across his lap; it was long and curved, with a finely honed blade and a wicked glint. The guard didn't move when he saw us, but his eyes slid in our direction. We took one look and turned around again.

'I'm going to talk to Hamid, he'll gain us entry.' Swift was already half-way down the stairs as he spoke.

I stuck my hands in my pockets and slowed to a meander. Swift had slipped back into his role as a detective but I was in a more meditative mood. I'd found the morning's events a jumble of confusion.

I returned to my rooms and crossed to the ornate red table which I'd nominated as my desk. I was about to sit down when I realised that I didn't know where my notebook was and, after much searching, eventually came across it in the bottom of my carpetbag! It was all very well for Greggs to treat this outing as a holiday, but there were times when I needed him.

My fountain pen still leaked. I cleaned the nib with blotting paper and opened the leather-bound notebook. It was curled and scuffed because I'd used it before at Braeburn Castle and it had become damaged during my adventures.

Despite Swift's nitpicking strictures, I think I had learned something about sleuthing. I'd been swotting too. In the last few weeks I'd read more of Conan Doyle's excellent volumes about Sherlock Holmes. Observation was vital, so was evidence, according to the great man. And motive, and interviewing witnesses, which reminded me about the bath-draw boy, or rather the lack of him.

I sighed and wrote down my first note about the case. *Who murdered Josephine Belvoir?* Then paused because it could have been just about anybody. I mused on the morning's events; I'd found Persi's actions puzzling. Ejecting the magazine was reasonable because she thought she'd recognised the gun, but once she had seen Josephine Belvoir murdered with it, why on earth didn't she wipe it clean when she had the chance? I suppose Swift had a point, it may have had the killer's prints on it. But if she had truly been the killer, she'd have used gloves, in which case her prints were actually evidence of her innocence, or… actually I was becoming muddled now so I turned my mind to the interview.

Langton framed? Persi certainly thought Josephine had set up Langton, and Fontaine could have been involved. They were both French so the idea was perfectly plausible.

My mind wandered back to Harry's tale of espionage during the war. Persi hadn't been involved in those unpleasant events. Actually, I didn't even know where she'd spent the war or when she'd become engaged to Langton. I mulled on that for a while then gave up and turned to the activities of the film crew.

Did the murder of Josephine stem from what happened during the war? I shook my head. If it had, why wait until now? Perhaps it was because they were abroad? Perhaps they arranged to come abroad in order to kill her? In which case, it must be Mammie, or possibly Vincent? No, it seemed implausible, the key must lie here in Damascus.

Who is the tomb-robber, where is he and what is the secret of the house of Hanno the Navigator? I had no idea about that, although I admit to finding it intriguing. I stared at my list of puzzling questions, sighed, blotted the page and put my pen down.

I tugged the medallion out of my pocket and peered at it, turning it over in my fingers. It was obscured by grime so I went and fetched my toothbrush and paste from the bathroom and used them to scrub away the thick layer of dirt.

It worked quite well actually, although now I needed a new toothbrush. The squiggles were more easily discerned in the shining bronze. They had been deeply engraved then filled with black paint or tar. The raised dots framing the centre were far more interesting – they glittered! I held the medallion to the light to better view the gleam of gold I'd uncovered. There were four gold spots dotted about the rim, interspersed with five of silver and the same number of sparkling glass, or perhaps they were diamonds! There were three black gems that could have been onyx, but I didn't take much notice as my mind was racing through visions of diamond mines or perhaps chests of hidden gold.

That's what it must be – a treasure map! No wonder they all wanted it.

A tentative knock sounded at the door and I quickly stuffed the medallion back in my pocket.

'Come in,' I shouted.

It was Jamal. He entered.

'Effendi,' he bowed. 'I have widow.'

'Erm… what?'

'Widow of bath-draw boy, effendi.' He bowed again. 'She awaits. Please to come and follow me.'

He waved an arm in the direction of the walkway, so I tossed my notebook on top of the wardrobe, picked up my cream fedora and followed him up the stairs. We arrived at a roof garden.

It was marvellous, I stopped to contemplate in quiet wonder. Rooftops stretched in every direction, shimmering in bright sunshine over a haze of sultry heat. In the near distance, a slim tower stood beside a rose-hued dome. There were other domes dotted among terracotta roofs and flat topped gardens furnished with curtained day beds, set among flowering plants in pots of every size and shape. The roof garden opposite held a fat man in a pristine white robe, he was reclining on a couch, smoking a long pipe attached to a jar. I looked at him, he looked back.

There was a day bed on our rooftop too, it was hung with light muslin cloth, which wafted in the breeze. Actually the whole place was given over to lounging in general. Wrought-iron sofas were strewn with colourful cushions set in secluded spots. The centre of the rooftop was scattered with circular tables and chairs and, anywhere there was space, pot-plants had been clustered in gaily coloured groups.

Jamal had trotted over to a small jungle while I'd been gazing about. He returned, closely followed by an apparition draped entirely in black.

'Here is number one wife of bath-draw boy.' He smiled.

'Erm… Greetings.' I bowed in the direction of the robes.

'You have dollars?' Jamal asked.

'Yes,' I said, fingering the bills tucked snuggly in my pocket.

There was a lot of huffing and puffing coming from within the drapery. The poor lady must have been extremely hot under the voluminous fabric. I must say, they took mourning very seriously in this country.

'Jamal…' I began. 'Doesn't happen to speak any English does she?'

'Oh no, effendi. And widows must not speak to strange men in any language.'

'Um, right.' Actually given some of the terrifying women I'd come across, that seemed like a jolly good custom.

The widow was broad, short and heavily built. There was a slit cut into the fabric which would have rendered her eyes visible but even this was covered by a veil. She thrust a pudgy hand in my direction.

The dollars were in ones and fives. I tugged two off the roll and placed them in her palm. The palm remained extended, so I added another and carried on. Apparently a dead bath-draw boy is worth twenty American dollars, and that was just for wife number one. I should have demanded a higher day rate for Foggy.

'Jamal,' I called to him, as he was about to follow the widow down the steps.

'Effendi?'

'Could you give a message to Miss Carruthers?'

'Ah, this is not allowed. Expressly ordered from the Colonel. I offer my apologies, effendi, but the Colonel must be obeyed. The French are high and mighty.'

Hum, only according to the French, I thought.

'The bath-draw boy was the same chap who witnessed the first attempt at shooting Miss Belvoir, wasn't he?'

'Indeed, effendi, it was he! He was guard, but he failed in his duty and was made lowly. But, now he cannot be witness, nor tell no tales.' Jamal smiled, then departed in the widow's wake. It all seemed just a little too convenient to my mind.

I gazed into the distance, wondering where Greggs and Fogg would be and how their unlikely movie-making venture was going. Apart from roofs and gardens there wasn't much to see, so I leaned over the parapet to take a look at the stone walls of the hotel. There were rows of windows on each floor. One of them would be Persi's, but it was a sheer drop and impossible to climb either up or down, and it was a damn long way down. I watched the activity on the street below me, where passing locals dodged donkeys, goats and chickens. I sighed and went to find Swift.

I found Hamid instead, he told me Swift had spoken to him earlier but had apparently gone off somewhere and no-one knew where. I walked through the courtyard, where Harry Bing was perched on a barstool working his way through another bottle of whisky. It crossed my mind to join him for a quick snifter, but I decided it was probably a bit early.

A light breeze blew in from the arched tunnel leading to the open gateway, I turned toward it. Perhaps they sold local maps at the souk? If I was right about the medallion being a treasure map, it would seem like a jolly good idea to identify where it was a map of. And besides, I was in need of a new toothbrush.

Outside the hotel, the streets and alleyways twisted and turned, I wandered about until I got my bearings, then made my way in the direction I assumed the souk to be. Every other house was a shop and I was politely harried by merchants in striped tunics and red fezzes offering their wares as I made my way. I was tempted by a monkey in a felted waistcoat, but thought it would probably cause havoc back home and Greggs would be bound to raise objections.

The souk was a jostling throng of buyers and sellers haggling noisily. Souk shopping, it seemed, consisted mostly of shouting. I wove my way through the crowds, searching for stalls selling either maps or toothbrushes. After an hour in the stifling heat and mass of people, I'd had enough. I spotted a well-populated cafe in a leafy arcade and wound my way over. An aproned waiter escorted me to a metal-work table, served coffee then left. I sat back quietly and watched the activity.

The stall opposite me was formed from wonky poles topped with a yellow awning fringed with beads. Under its shade, an array of bowls was set on a rickety table, guarded by a stooped chap with bright eyes and a trusting smile.

A tall thin man in a faded blue tunic approached to examine the wares then began a noisy exchange with the stall-holder. From their jerky gesticulations and furious shouts I expected a fight to break out, but suddenly they both stopped and smiled as though they were the best of friends. An olive-wood bowl changed hands for a fist full of coins and the buyer went off, happy as Larry, while the vendor looked around for more customers to wrangle with.

I realised I hadn't seen any uncloaked ladies among the multitudes of men. There were numerous black-swathed widows, which made me ponder the fate of their husbands. I imagined the wars must have cut a scythe through the tribal warriors as war seemed a perpetual state of affairs here. Having thought about it, if one man had four wives, it meant three-quarters of the male population was surplus to requirement. Or even if they only had two, it was still half. So it was no surprise they spent time waging war, because they can't have had much else to do.

I was mulling the peculiarities of foreign mores when I spotted Dreadnaught making his way in the direction of the cafe. He pulled a chair out and sat opposite me without bothering to ask if I minded.

Now what? I thought.

CHAPTER 11

'Good day, Major Lennox.' Dreadnaught greeted me, a smile on his handsome face.

I frowned at him, he laughed.

'I was a pilot in the war too, you know.' His accent was light, he actually spoke English extremely well when he wanted to.

'Um...' I muttered without encouragement.

'You were in the Royal Air Force. Perhaps we crossed swords in the air.'

Having considered him a block-headed Boche, I was suspicious of the apparently friendly overtones. 'Perhaps,' I replied. 'What colours did you fly?'

'Bavarian blue with a red tail. I was not difficult to spot,' he laughed.

I smiled. Many German pilots were scions of aristocratic families and had decorated their fuselage in heraldic colours. We Brits stuck to dull camouflage and lasted rather longer because of it.

'Yes,' I replied, 'in Northern France, near Amiens. I remember you. You flew close to the wind.'

'Too close, one of your chaps shot my red tail off. The crash landing left me with a broken leg and at the mercy of your Tommies. They carried me to hospital and I was eventually detained at your King's pleasure.' His laughter tailed off and his handsome face turned grim. 'The war was a profanity, it destroyed my family. I was forced to kill my own friends.'

That gave me pause. 'How?'

'I had been sent to school in England, at Rugby. My mother was English, my father was Bavarian.' He sipped his coffee. 'Once my education was complete, I returned to Germany and then the war started. Naturally I joined up.'

'For the Kaiser?' I asked.

'He was a friend of my father so it was expected, old fellow.' Dreadnaught smiled wryly. 'I was not sorry to be captured, despite my broken leg.'

The aproned waiter returned.

'Would you take lunch with me, Major?' Dreadnaught asked.

I realised I was hungry and could smell food cooking in some distant kitchen so I decided I may as well partake. It came very quickly. We were each served with a platter of small dishes filled with pastries, spiced meat and roasted vegetables, which were far tastier than the over-boiled mush we had back at home. It all came with side dishes of fermented cream-dips and sauces accompanied by jugs of mint tea. I must say the food here was marvellous.

We watched the market while we ate. Awnings had been pulled down over narrow alcoves where the vendors kept their jumble of merchandise. A gentle lull fell over the place, as shoppers and sellers alike paused for sustenance.

'You came here to spy, Major,' Dreadnaught turned to the subject that he'd no doubt come to discuss.

'No, I didn't,' I replied between mouthfuls.

'Oh, come along! Your government sent you and the Detective Chief Inspector.'

'Absolute nonsense. Did yours?'

'Ha! I am not welcome in my own country, Major.'

'So, why do you think we're from the British Government?' I asked.

'Because there are so many new Britishers here now. First the spy, Charles Langton, followed by his fiancé, then two English ladies and now you and the Chief Inspector. You secret agents are gathering like bees around a honey pot.'

'I am not a spy,' I said rather too loudly because heads turned to look at me. 'And nor is Swift or Miss...' I spluttered to a stop. 'Look Dreadnaught, Harry Bing has opened up, so you may as well tell me what you know.' I exaggerated a bit but thought I'd get away with it.

He laughed as though I'd said something highly amusing. 'I see my error, Major Lennox, you cannot possibly be a spy. You are an innocent abroad.'

'And you're a traitor,' I snapped back, then felt ashamed of saying it.

Dreadnaught's tone turned cold. 'Nein, I am not, or rather.' He paused, then dropped the indignant tone. 'I am no longer. Please, Major, the war is over. Our activities during that time are finished. Do not rake it over; it will gain you nothing.'

'What happened to Charles Langton's sister?' I wasn't ready to give up. 'She was called Beatrice, wasn't she?'

He sighed in irritation. 'If you spoke to Bing you already know that I was interned in France in one of your prisoner-of-war camps at the time. So why do you ask me this?'

'Because you were one of Josephine Belvoir's informants. You would have heard about it.'

He pushed his lunch aside. 'I met the girl only once.' He frowned and looked away, then continued. 'They came to the camp to film us. We were working in the fields, like happy peasants. It was for propaganda.'

'Did you meet all the film crew? Including the Vincents?'

'No, they made the film from the distance, then took tea with the British commander in charge of the camp. We men spotted the ladies and we called out to them. We had been in captivity for a long time, you can understand we were keen to have a talk with them.'

'And they came over?'

'Yes, both of them. Josephine had the attention, but I liked the little one, Beatrice...' he paused and I saw a cloud pass over his face. 'She was gentle and kind, she reminded me of my mother. I spent a long time talking to her, but then Josephine distracted me and made the pretence she liked me. I was flattered.' He laughed harshly. 'I didn't realise for a long time it was just an act. It was very stupid of me.'

I refrained from nodding agreement. 'Were you well treated in the camp?'

'Ja, although food was scarce,' he replied as a waiter removed his half eaten meal.

I remember how scarce it had been, everything was scarce almost all the damn time. 'What did you hear about the betrayal of Beatrice?'

'Merely that she had been taken.' He suddenly sat back in his chair, as though trying to move away. 'It saddened me, she would have suffered before her execution and it was all for nothing.'

I tried another tack. 'Something happened more recently didn't it?'

He hesitated again, then nodded. 'Very well, Major Lennox. You seem determined to play the sleuth. After we arrived here, Josephine began to send out, how do you say – lures? We'd had a brief affair when we first arrived in Hollywood, but it was not long lasting, and she did not capture my heart, not like the foolish Bing. When she made her eyes at me, I thought it would be a pleasant entertainment. But then…'

'Then…?' I waved my hand in encouragement.

'Mammie had a talk quietly with me. She said she did not want complications.' He looked down at his mani-cured hands. 'She said this movie was important, no time for playing. I laughed her off, but she was most insistent. And then she said to me, 'Josephine betrayed the girl.'

She was most clear. It was Josephine who had placed the information about Beatrice Langton's activities.'

His face was grim and drawn, I suspect mine was too.

'Did Mammie say why?'

He shook his head.

'And you didn't confront Josephine?'

'No, she would only have lied.' He folded his arms. 'It may only be a few years ago, Major, but I am sickened by the past.'

'When did Mammie say it happened?' I persevered, although I could see the tight lines in his face.

'Almost at the end of the war.'

I nodded, that tallied with Bing's account. 'Before the Vincents returned to Paris?'

Dreadnaught shrugged. 'I was not there. I cannot tell you.'

'When did Langton arrive here in Damascus?'

'Shortly after we did,' he replied. 'But you know this already and you have rather spoiled my lunch, old fellow.' He stood up.

'Yes, well it didn't do much for mine either,' I said. 'And I'm sorry, Dreadnaught, for calling you a traitor. It was infra dig.'

'I accept your apologies, Major.' He smiled suddenly. 'You see, I have learned the lesson of humility.'

I didn't think he'd learned it terribly well, but wasn't about to say so.

'Wait,' I called after him. 'Did anyone else know about Josephine's betrayal of Beatrice?'

'I do not know, I have not told anyone.' He bowed with a sharp nod and walked off.

I remained seated for some time, pondering on his disclosure and wondering why he had come to join me. Was it to set me on a trail, or divert me from one?

The market was once more bustling; bargain hunters had returned to the fray, refreshed and ready to hone their bartering skills. I remembered my own quest and launched back into the scrummage. Toothbrushes appeared to be in short supply in Damascus and it didn't help that I couldn't speak a word of the local lingo. My efforts at acting out the desired object were met with laughter and incomprehension. No-one seemed to have any maps either, although there was no shortage of baubles, rugs, curtains, perfume, cushions and domestic whatnots. I was contemplating a prayer mat when I realised I was being followed.

I took a fast paced saunter behind a few stalls, then ducked into a narrow shop selling pointy-toed shoes. A beggar leaning on a crutch had been hobbling in my footsteps since I'd left the cafe. He was the sort who stood out in a crowd – grimy skin stretched over bone, one foot wound in rags, black hair resembling a dead hedgehog, a hooked nose and a toothless grin.

As I waited for him to pass, the shop owner began holding up various cobbled confections for my consideration.

'Try my most beautiful shoes, oh lofty one.' He stroked a red velvet slipper as though trying to entice a genie out of a bottle.

I watched the beggar from behind the door post as he halted to survey the teeming masses then he limped off, his gaze darting this way and that.

'Effendi?'

'What?'

The shoe seller had an armful of shoes.

'Umm... how much?'

'Only one dollar, sometimes two.' His kindly old face smiled up at me with hope in his eyes.

After much haggling I paid him three dollars for a pair of red velvet Turkish slippers that might fit my Uncle Melrose should he shrink any further with age.

I set off to return to the hotel before anyone began to think I was a soft touch.

'Lennox, I've been looking for you.' Swift spotted me as I was depositing my purchases with Hamid.

'Why?'

'Colonel Fontaine asked me to search Josephine Belvoir's rooms and you could have helped.'

'Did you find anything?' I asked.

'No.'

'Well, I wouldn't have been much help, would I.'

'Lennox...'

I cut him off. 'Did he say anything about Persi?'

'Come to the terrace and I'll tell you.'

Gin and tonic with fresh sliced lemons arrived with the next waiter; I realised it was exactly what I needed. There was a low hedge of bougainvillea running alongside the terrace with pink and red blooms on their thorny tips. I eyed the folly as I took a long sip of the ice-cold G&T and wondered if the French Colonel was lurking within its fragrant walls, but couldn't see any signs of life.

I turned back to Swift. 'Why did Fontaine let you into Josephine Belvoir's room?'

'I think he wanted to see what I did,' Swift replied.

'What on earth for?'

'To check if I knew the police routine.'

'Oh.' It seemed rather odd to me. 'What did you do?'

'The usual of course!' He was in a tetchy mood. 'They'd obviously searched it. I carried out the standard procedure, except dusting for fingerprints because I could see it had been done.'

'And there wasn't anything at all?'

'Not of any interest,' he calmed down as he sipped his gin. 'She had all the usual feminine clutter; too many shoes, frocks, handbags, suitcases, scarves, and more cosmetics than I've seen on a pharmacy shelf. But nothing out of the ordinary, apart from the perfume. Someone must have dropped a whole bottle of the stuff on the walkway outside. Everywhere stank of it.'

'And was Fontaine in the room with you?'

'Yes, he watched me at work. I even cleaned out the makeup jars to see if anything had been pushed into them, but there hadn't.'

'Did you find out anything about the bracelet?' I realised that I'd forgotten to ask Dreadnaught the same question.

'Yes, he said it had been returned to its rightful owner.'

'What does that mean?'

'I have no idea. He refused to tell me anything more.'

Hamid arrived with a bow. 'May we offer another refreshing serving, effendis?'

'No, thank you. Just coffee,' Swift ordered before I could even open my mouth. 'Two, please.'

'Swift!' I protested, then gave it up.

A waiter returned on the instant with a tray. The coffee was accompanied by sweet confections of honey and chocolate formed into little balls and encased in crushed nuts.

'Fontaine must be searching for the medallion Persi gave me,' I said.

'Obviously!'

I leaned forward. 'It's a treasure map.'

'Nonsense.'

'Humph.' I straightened up. 'What do you think it is then?'

It was his turn to sigh. 'I don't know. It's just one damn mystery after another.'

CHAPTER 12

'Did you see Persi while you were up on Ladies Row?' I asked.

'No, Fontaine says she's not allowed to leave her room and the Arab guard won't let any man pass without the Colonel being present.'

'Could one of the other women give her a message?'

'Possibly.' Swift paused then added, 'But I don't trust them.'

'Hum.' I sipped my coffee. 'Which room is she in?'

'Fontaine wouldn't tell me that either. Josephine Belvoir's suite is the third door along and it's kept locked. Fontaine has the only key.'

'Talking of lock and key, did you discuss Langton?'

'Yes, the Citadel is guarded by the local militia and if we go near the place we'll excite all sorts of trouble. He said Langton is being held as a foreigner and has certain protections. He implied that his condition may have been exaggerated.'

'What?' That made me sit up. 'You mean we've come all this way to save the man and now he was supposed to be perfectly safe?'

'My reaction was the same as yours, I was furious. Once I'd calmed down he explained that Persi had probably heard the terrible reputation the Citadel has and she assumed the worse.'

'Huh!' I didn't believe a damn word. 'Or he's trying to drive a wedge between us and Persi by implying she's hysterical or lying.'

Swift nodded agreement. 'Possibly, but he sounded sincere.' He sighed. 'Look, his job here is to keep the peace. I think Langton's situation may have actually been over-stated, but he's right about this city – it is a powder keg and we all need to tread carefully.' He turned the subject. 'Anyway, where have you been?'

'The souk.'

That didn't impress him. 'Lennox, we need to concentrate on the murder.'

'I am! I questioned Dreadnaught while I was there,' I retaliated without actually admitting the circumstances. I told him the tale of Beatrice Langton's fate and Josephine's treachery. It brought a crease to his brows.

'Why would Josephine have betrayed her?' He asked.

'He didn't know, but if it's true, it gives Langton an overwhelming motive to murder Josephine Belvoir,' I replied.

'*If* Langton knew what Mammie had said.'

'Agreed, and Bing said he was certain Josephine hadn't betrayed Beatrice.'

'We can't take his word for anything, he's barely sober and his emotions waver one moment to the next.' Swift stated.

'But, if someone did feed the story to Langton, could they have done it in order to use him?' I mooted.

'As a pawn in their game? I suppose it's possible, but we only have Dreadnaught's word for it.' He ate one of the honey and chocolate balls as he thought about it. 'We need to question Mammie as soon as they return from filming.'

I nodded. 'Dreadnaught was pretty cut up, you know.'

'Enough to murder Josephine?' he asked.

That gave me pause. 'No, I don't think so. He only met Beatrice once.'

'Hum.' He seemed lost in thought.

'He's not a bad chap, Swift.'

He snapped out of his reverie. 'It's not a question of good or bad, it's about uncovering their actions. You can't judge their guilt based on how much you like or dislike them. You have to learn to remain detached,' he lectured.

Typical Swift, he was like a damn terrier at a rat when detecting and treated me as if I was some sort of minion. I was half a mind to go to my rooms, but the waiter brought another pot of coffee and more confections, so I stayed.

Swift eyed me while I was licking my fingers. 'Lennox.'

'What?'

'You haven't… ummm.' He cleared his throat. 'You haven't taken advantage of any of the services offered by the Bathing ladies, have you?'

'What?' That made me sit up. 'Why on earth would you ask that?'

'Well… well, I wondered if you could bribe one.'
Colour rose in his lean cheeks.

'To do what?'

'Find the whereabouts of Persi, of course and pass on messages. What else would you do with them?'

'I…' One or two ideas flashed into my mind, but I shook them off. 'Why me? You could do it just as easily.'

'I'm married Lennox. What would Florence think if she heard about it?'

'Don't be ridiculous, who on earth is going to tell her?' I demanded.

'I don't know. Anyway, you could ask Jamal to arrange something,' he insisted. 'It may be our only chance.'

'For heaven's sake, Swift, there must be something better we can come up with.'

'Short of dressing up as a woman, no there isn't. Don't be so damned prissy, man. You're only offering a bribe, it's not as if you're going to make use of them.'

'How do you know?' I retorted. 'I can take up the services of a Bathing lady if I want to!'

That raised his brows.

I heard a giggle behind me and we swung around in our seats.

Genevieve and her Aunt walked in. We scrambled to stand up in greeting.

'I didn't, not that I meant… I wasn't…' I spluttered.

'Really, Major Lennox, you do not need to offer an explanation. No doubt you consider yourself a man of the world,' Lady Maitland remarked haughtily, and sailed off to a table as far away as possible. Genevieve followed, throwing me a sparkling smile as she went.

'I... I... Damn it, Swift,' I cursed.

Swift had the grace to laugh. 'We'd better go.' He set off.

'Where?' I had to put on a quick pace to catch up with him.

'We'll have a look at your medallion against my map,' he told me as we trotted upstairs.

His rooms were orderly and he seemed to know where everything was. He pulled the map from a dresser drawer and unfolded it carefully on his desktop.

I took out the freshly polished medallion and placed it on the out-spread sheet next to Damascus in the creamy-yellow coloured country of Syria. The diamonds around the medallion's rim glinted in the sunlight streaming through the window.

'What have you done to it?'

'Cleaned it!' I remarked, thinking he really did ask the most ridiculous questions.

He shook his head then pointed on the map to the Lebanon and then the medallion. 'Here, look, the etched black line represents the edge of the Mediterranean. See how the coastline is shaped like an inverted 'J'. And these small, red spots look like ports.' He returned his finger to run along the paper. 'Tyre, Byblos, Sidon, they're ancient cities. Perhaps the gems were the items they traded. The star shaped mark by the punched hole is probably the North Star, that's what most seafarers used for navigation.'

'Oh.' I felt rather deflated.

'It's probably a symbolic token worn by ships' Captains or some such.' Swift pulled his magnifying glass from his jacket pocket. 'If it belonged to Hanno the Navigator, it may have been his ports of call.'

'Or where he kept his harems of dancing girls,' I remarked glumly. 'What about the dead camel – it could be Hanno's house? Or Damascus?'

'Ummm… it's the right place for Damascus, but the images on the medallion are far too stylised to be a proper map of any sort.' He handed me the magnifying glass.

I took a closer look, but was losing heart. 'We need to ask Persi.'

'Ummm,' he agreed, his concentration on the medallion.

'We could take a look at the walkway below hers,' I suggested, having given it some thought. 'We might be able to climb up the vine or the supporting pillars, some-where the guard can't see us.'

'It would have to be after dark,' Swift looked dubious.

'Yes, but we could reconnoiter now, then we'll know what we're facing,' I said with growing enthusiasm. 'And surely the guard goes home at some time?'

'I asked Hamid about him. He's got a brother, they take it in turns. Apparently they're newly appointed by Colonel Fontaine, they sacked the old one after Langton's failed attempt to shoot Josephine.'

'The bath-draw boy?'

'Yes,' he replied briskly. 'He was demoted, and now you've shot him. I suppose we may as well take a look at the walkway, there's no-one around to interview. Just a minute.' He turned and walked to a wardrobe, pulled out his trench coat, shrugged himself into it, tightened his belt and said, 'Come on.'

I grinned, tucked the medallion back in my jacket, shoved my hands in my pockets and followed.

We were on the second floor below Ladies Row. Both of us leaned out, backs against the bannister rail to peer up at the floor above. We had advanced as far as we could along the walkway where it ended in what looked like a servants' door. I'd tried it, it was locked.

Creepers and vines clung to the balustrades and pillars which supported each walkway. I tugged on a trunk over two inches thick, causing leaves to fall and flutter away.

'Feels pretty firm,' I said and climbed up onto the bannister rail to balance on top, trying to find a hand hold among the creepers. It worked, so I climbed higher.

'Wait,' Swift hissed. 'We can't go up until nightfall.'

'I know,' I hissed back. 'I'm testing it.' I went up another couple of arm lengths and realised I could reach the tiles of the walkway above with my outstretched hand. I pulled myself up a little further, causing more leaves to rustle and fall away. A head and shoulders appeared over the walkway rail.

'Oh, how daring! What *are* you doing, Major Lennox?' Genevieve smiled down at me.

'I... um.' I gazed up at her. 'I'm looking for Miss Carruthers room, actually. Couldn't help, by any chance?'

'Haha, you are keen, aren't you!' she laughed. 'It's the

fourth from the end, but don't let either of the brothers Grimm catch you. They're a fearsome pair!'

'The guards?'

'Yes,' she giggled. 'Our unlikely guardians. Do be careful, he's watching as I speak.'

Genevieve disappeared and another figure appeared in her place.

'Ah, Major Lennox.' Lady Maitland gazed down at me. 'And what, may I ask, are you doing now?'

'Ermm... I am attempting to reach Miss Carruthers, for... erm, well, I need to talk to her...'

'How very fervent of you, Major Lennox. I really must commend your ardour,' she drawled, then promptly withdrew.

'Raarghhhhh,' a terrible yell bellowed out, followed by the thudding of pounding boots.

I half fell, half clambered down and pushed Swift back against the wall.

'What?'

'Shush.'

There was loud grunting and slashing of foliage to be heard, then the stamping of feet and sabre rattling.

'Lennox, you idiot,' Swift hissed.

We waited while the boots tramped around and eventually went off.

'Not sure that's going to work,' I said, brushing myself down. 'I think he's gone, now.' I stepped back into the light.

'Why must you be so damn...?'

'Oh, give it up, Swift!'

'Who were you talking to?'

'Genevieve. She told me Persi's rooms are fourth from the end.'

'Humm.' He calmed down and looked along the passage. 'Isn't this the floor the Vincents are housed on?'

'Yes, along with their equipment room.'

'We could have a look around,' he suggested.

I stared at him. 'Seriously, Swift? You are actually proposing that we sneak around their rooms without permission?'

'Sometimes it's necessary to break umm… bend the rules,' he muttered.

'Fine.' I stepped over to the nearest door and tried it. It was locked, but I had with me my favourite detecting device, a set of lock picks I'd confiscated from a petty thief at Bloxford Hall. I'd spent quite some time in the interim mastering the art of their application; the lock turned as I fiddled about on my second attempt. I could see Swift was impressed.

Beyond the door was a sumptuous set of suites, it made even my rooms look insignificant. Huge mirrors were set in gilded frames above spindly legged sofas, upholstered in yellow satin. The bedroom was stately, with green silk hangings falling from a centre point to frame the huge bed. More chairs and sofas of similar hue were arranged in a group before the window. We picked through cupboards and drawers, finding all the usual outfits and geegaws everybody takes along whilst travelling. There were two handheld still cameras and rolls of film and whatnots of that sort as well.

I found a stack of photographs in a briefcase stamped with Vincent's initials. The top set were of Josephine, she was posing in various diaphanous frocks and in one picture she was wearing a rather fetching bathing suit. She had signed them all in a scrawled hand. Dreadnaught and Bing made up a tidy handful and there were half a dozen of a lady I didn't recognise. She'd been photographed in poses similar to Belvoir's, her name was written neatly at the base; 'Maria Finch'. I assumed her to be the actress sent home after succumbing to some illness or other.

There were some older photos underneath, slightly dog-eared with their gloss worn off. They were of a pretty girl – large, expressive eyes gazing into the camera, a half-smile playing on her lips, hair gathered up in a loose bun with long curls falling around a gentle face. There was no artifice about these, they were simple, natural images taken with what I'd have guessed was a loving eye. Beatrice Langton's name was written across the bottom-right corner. I passed them to Swift. He gazed at them, a shadow crossing his sharp features, then I put them back and snapped the briefcase closed. We exited feeling rather flat.

'We should search their storeroom too,' Swift told me. 'We may as well be thorough.'

I can't say I was keen and, upon entry, we took one glance around the place and abandoned the plan. It would take a small army to rifle through the trunks, boxes, and bags set haphazardly around that spacious room which was awash with rails of costumes, feather boas, hats and props of unlikely sorts.

Swift picked up a coil of rope and stared at it. He tugged on one section, as though testing its strength, then looked at me.

'Lennox,' he said. 'I have an idea…'

It was a ridiculous idea. We argued about it all the way up the stairs, giving the guard a wide berth, and crossed the roof garden from the walkway to the outer wall.

'Swift we should wait until dark.' I said.

'Then we won't be able to see anything,' he replied. 'And it's dangerous enough as it is.'

'Exactly. I really, really think you shouldn't do this,' I repeated firmly. We were standing next to the ledge which ran around the perimeter of the roof garden, scrutinising the drop to the nearest windows against the length of rope. The street below was teeming.

'It's quite simple.' Swift sounded determined but unconvincing. 'We'll tie the rope to this seat, you sit on it to make sure it doesn't move, and I'll climb down and knock on Miss Persi's window.'

'It's suicide, Swift. If you fall, it's a forty foot drop to the pavement.'

'Nonsense, I can do it,' he had knotted the rope to a wrought-iron couch and was even now wrapping the other end around his waist. He leaned over the wall then suddenly stepped back. He swayed and fell onto the seat, white as a sheet.

I peered at him. 'No head for heights?' I remarked.

He spluttered a bit then said. 'Not really, not that sort of drop anyway.'

I sighed. I hated heights too, which was always a bit of an impediment for a pilot. 'I'll do it.'

'No, it's my responsibility.'

'You're about to be a father, Swift. Breaking your neck isn't going to help your wife or child. Just give me the damn rope.'

It took further persuading but he finally handed it over. I tied a series of knots along its length before looping it around my waist. I'd been forced to do some mountain climbing by my school and knew roughly how it worked. I gazed down the wall to the ground again, felt dizzy, perched on the ledge and took a deep breath.

CHAPTER 13

'Swift?' My eyes were fixed on the crowded street below.

'What?' he replied from the iron-framed couch.

'I forgot to ask which end.'

'What are you talking about?'

'Persi's room – it's the fourth window from which end?'

'For heaven's sake Lennox, you should have thought about that before.'

I noticed the fat chap in white robes on the roof opposite take the pipe from his mouth and lean forward to gaze at me.

I ignored him and shuffled closer to the precipice.

'No, effendi, no! Don't do it,' Jamal suddenly called out from somewhere behind me. I twisted around. He appeared from the stairs and was now dodging around tables, chairs and potted palms to rush in my direction.

'Don't be ridiculous, Jamal, he's got a rope,' Swift told him. 'Come and sit on this seat.'

Jamal paused to stare open-mouthed and realised I was indeed secured to the end of a tether.

'Jamal, come and sit down and don't move,' I ordered. Then I took a deep breath, turned round and lowered myself over the side.

The rope swayed and I swung like a pendulum for a couple of seconds, my heart racing. I clung to one of the knots I'd tied as my knuckles turned white. The parapet jutted out about a foot which was enough of a gap to allow me to rotate slowly on the rope without actually touching the stone wall. I looked down as I swivelled 360 degrees and realised the window was only about three feet below me. I lowered myself down the next two knots and, still spinning, tapped the glass with my left foot as I arrived level with the top of the frame.

Nothing happened.

'Damn it, Persi. Come on,' I cursed aloud.

I went a few inches further down and could see some sort of shadow in the window, which I now realised was opaque with a layer of grime. I kicked again as the gentle spinning of the rope brought me back to face the glass.

Still no response. 'Persi,' I tried yelling.

That didn't work either. I lowered myself to the next knot in the rope, waited until I'd rotated level with the window, raised my fist to rap on the pane then let out a shout. 'Hell!'

'What?' Swift called out.

I didn't answer.

There was a face pushed up against the glass. A shadowy grey face with a slack jaw and wide, open eyes staring out at me.

A window opened further along the row, it was Lady Maitland. Why the devil did she always appear at the most inopportune moments?

'Major Lennox! What, pray, are you doing now?'

'I... I...'

The window on the other side opened. Persi put her head out and shouted. 'Heathcliff! What on earth are you doing out there?'

I was still spinning slowly and had involuntarily turned to face out over the rooftops at the fat man in white, who was now gaping at us.

'I have to see you, Persi,' I told her as I rotated in her direction.

She held her hands to her cheeks. 'Heathcliff, do be careful! There's a forty foot drop below.'

'I know! And will you please stop calling me Heathcliff.'

'Miss Carruthers,' Lady Maitland said cooly, 'I suggest you inform your Romeo on a rope that there are easier means of access than this desperate escapade.' She slammed her window shut on her words.

'Persi,' I gasped. 'I'll be back,' and hauled myself up knot by bloody knot.

'Body, Swift.' I could barely catch my breath. 'In the window. Dead body.'

'What sort of body? Whose?' He rattled questions off at me as I sat wheezing on the parapet. I'd untied the rope and flung it onto the tiles. Jamal was peering over the edge, down at the windows, as I told Swift what I'd seen.

'I don't know. A man.' I was still trying to catch my breath.

'The perfume!' he exclaimed. 'It wasn't spilled, it was dropped deliberately to cover up the smell of a body.'

'Effendi,' Jamal returned, 'effendi, you must not go on rope. It is too dangerous. Not to go again, sir. Be a good fellow now.'

'Have to, Jamal.' My breath had almost returned. 'No choice.'

'Please. If I help you, please not to tell anyone.'

Swift and I turned our gaze on him. 'How?'

'There is stairs for use by servants. I can show you, if you promise no more ropes.'

I grabbed the end of the cord nearest to me, coiled the damn thing up and tossed it over the parapet. 'Agreed, Jamal. Now lead the way.'

'First, you must take note of my words, effendi.' He held a finger up as he spoke. 'Doorway to inner stairs is behind reception desk and Master Hamid will prevent your entry. It is not a worthy place for honoured guests.'

'Then you will have to distract him,' Swift ordered.

'Ah, yes, be certain that I will do this, effendi. But this new guard for the ladies is not so easy. He will observe you along the walkway before your goal is reached.'

This gave us pause for thought. An arm suddenly pushed aside the curtained day bed in a far corner. Harry Bing leaned out from between the posts – we hadn't even noticed he was there.

'I say, you there. Couldn't keep the noise down, could you? Trying to have a doze, you know.'

'Bing! Just the man,' I called to him. 'Come over here.'

'No.'

'Bing,' Swift shouted.

'Oh, very well.' Harry rose to his feet, swayed a little and tottered over, circumnavigating chairs and shrubs as he went.

'Came up for some fresh air.' He wafted a hand in the direction of the bed. 'What are you up to?' He brought us into focus with blood-shot eyes.

'Umm, never mind,' I said. 'Listen, Bing, we need a bit of a favour. You couldn't distract the guard on Ladies Row, could you?'

'Why?' He frowned.

'I want to see Persi. Miss Carruthers, you know. She's my girlfriend.'

'Thought she was engaged to Langton?'

'Well, she isn't,' I told him firmly. 'Anyway, could you do something?'

He blinked a bit. 'Well, I can do magic, but I'd need a rabbit and top hat for that. I can mime!' he exclaimed. 'Do you think that would distract him? I used to be awfully good at it in my schooldays.' He grinned suddenly. 'It helped get me into show business, miming.' He suddenly stopped as still as a statue and then started to pretend there was a solid wall in front of him, hands outsplayed as though pushing against it. It was quite funny, actually.

Swift frowned. 'I can't see the guard being amused by that.'

'It doesn't matter,' I replied. 'As long as he's distracted.'

'Right, come on,' Swift tightened the belt of his trench coat and headed for the stairs.

We pushed Harry ahead of us when we reached Ladies Row and waited to watch what happened.

Utter bemusement was the reaction. The guard sat open-mouthed clutching his glinting sword across his lap as Harry started an impromptu performance. We silently filed down the stairs while Bing mimed himself out of an invisible box, quite obviously enjoying himself.

Hamid was easier to distract. Jamal simply led him to the fountain and began some lengthy explanation about something or other.

We spotted the staircase in a corner behind the reception desk, made a dash for it and raced up the stairs. Taking the steps two at a time, we passed linen cupboards and dimly lit corridors, not stopping until we reached the very top floor. The door to the outside was locked, but there was a large metal key hanging on a hook next to it.

We stepped out onto a shaded alcove at the very end of Ladies Row. Harry was performing at the other extremity, with the guard still turned in his direction.

'We need to examine the corpse,' Swift insisted.

I hesitated, keen to see Persi, but realised he was probably right.

'Fine,' I whispered back, 'it's the fourth one down.'

We crept along, Swift was right about the perfume, it

was sickly sweet and only made bearable by the breeze wafting up from the courtyard and through the open walkway.

I tried the handle on the door, it was locked so I pulled out my lock picks.

'Hurry up,' Swift hissed.

I fiddled with a long, hooked tine then heard the satisfying 'click' as the levers sprung. As we opened the door, a different sort of stench hit us. I took a step backwards, Swift had a stronger stomach and shoved me inside, pulling the door behind him.

'The perfume isn't going to smother this any longer,' Swift said as he eyed the deceased.

I gave a muffled reply through my handkerchief.

The man was a ghastly grey with green overtones and purplish in parts. He wore an expensive suit, well-cut and western in style. His face was long and thin to the point of cadaverous, which wasn't surprising really.

We were in a cupboard of sorts, it held mops and brooms, buckets and domestic whatnots. It was quite narrow, the corpse was propped on a stool by the grimy window through which I'd seen him. Swift turned him around so that he ended up staring glassy-eyed at the unpainted ceiling. I hung back.

'Look,' Swift said.

'I'd rather not, actually, old chap.'

He ignored my squeamishness and pointed to a purplish red cut under the dead man's chin. 'He was killed with a stiletto knife.' He leaned in more closely and pointed. 'It would have been a quick upwards stab, probably took him unaware as there are no signs of a struggle.'

'Bing said he'd seen Josephine use one during the war.'

'And she was carrying a stiletto when she was killed.'

'Really?' I stared at him. 'How do you know?'

'I found it strapped to her inner thigh.'

I stepped backwards. 'You found it on her thigh? What were you doing searching her thigh...'

'Lennox, will you stop being so damn prudish. She was dead!'

'That's worse, probably... but... well, what happened to the knife?'

'I left it there and Fontaine found it. He questioned me about it later.'

'Hum, I still don't think you should have...'

'I think it's the lawyer,' he cut in.

Yes.' I was still talking through the handkerchief. 'Midhurst, I think he was called.'

'Wait!' Swift exclaimed. 'There's something here.' He bent over the corpse, trying to open the right-hand fist. He unlocked the stiff fingers, held in a claw-like grasp, to reveal something written on the dead man's palm.

'He was hiding this.' Swift was fond of stating the obvious.

I moved closer, despite the stink.

'Raqisa,' he read out, then looked at me.

'Who?'

'Or what?' He read it again, then shrugged.

'We should go. Bing will be running out of mimes.' Actually, I was keen to get away from the corpse.

'Yes, just a minute.' He searched the clothes further but found nothing and the stench was truly overpowering. He gave up and we cleared out.

We trod quietly along the corridor, close to the wall, staying in the deep shadows, away from the bright, warm sunlight. We halted and I rapped quietly on the next door along. It opened.

'Oh, at last!' Persi smiled at us both and opened the door wide. 'What's that awful smell?'

'We think it's the lawyer.' I was about to offer a peck on the cheek, but she froze and stared up at me.

Swift closed the door and came into the room, which was really very pleasant, although not as large as the Vincents', nor mine actually.

I managed to gather her into my arms and cleared my throat to indicate to Swift that he should give us a moment. He didn't take the hint.

'You mean… Mr Midhurst?' Persi said as I scowled at Swift. 'But…?'

'Yes, he must have been in the cupboard a couple of days,' I said.

'You don't mean…?' Her hands shot to her lips as she realised the implications. 'He's dead?'

'Yes, he's been stabbed with a stiletto,' Swift told her, rather brutally to my mind.

'We think Josephine did it,' I said as she turned pale and went to sit on one of the sofas by the window.

'But, why would she do that?' Persi uttered.

I went to sit beside her.

'We don't know. Look old thing,' I said as kindly as I could. 'You must tell us as much as you can, we're totally in the dark here.'

'Yes, of course,' she said. 'It's just been so…'

She was interrupted by the sound of the door opening. We swung around to see Lady Maitland standing in the doorway with a gun pointed straight at us.

CHAPTER 14

It seemed to be another day for surprises. Our reactions must have shown on our faces as a smile flicked across Lady Maitland's thin lips. The door opened again and Genevieve slipped through – she was only armed with a handbag so we were probably safe from her.

'Stay where you are,' Lady Maitland ordered.

'You're British secret agents, aren't you,' I said rather loudly.

I received a cold glare in response.

'Where is the house?' Lady Maitland advanced on Persi.

'You should be helping Charles Langton. He's one of your men, isn't he?' Persi retorted, her eyes flashing. 'You've left him to die.'

'We have very little time, Miss Carruthers.' Her Ladyship ignored the outburst. 'I saw the corpse. Your misdirected Gallahads have allowed a stench to escape that will very shortly attract the guard's attention. Tell me where the house of Hanno is.'

'I can't because I don't know,' Persi snapped back.

'If you truly want to help your fiancé, I suggest you co-operate,' Lady Maitland replied.

'He's not my fiancé,' Persi retorted.

'I do not like repeating myself, Miss Carruthers. Where is the house of Hanno the Navigator?'

Persi glared, she looked magnificent when she was angry, but then she hesitated. 'I haven't been able to contact the tomb-robber.'

Lady Maitland raised her brows. 'So the exchange has not taken place?'

'No,' Persi replied. 'Not as far as I know.' She glanced at me with a questioning look.

I shook my head and shrugged.

'Have you found the tomb-robber?' Lady Maitland demanded of Persi.

'No.'

'Does Langton know how to contact him?'

'Why don't you ask him?' Persi retaliated.

'Do not test my patience,' Lady Maitland glowered. 'If you really want to help, tell me how to contact the tomb-robber.'

Persi stared in anger then dropped her eyes.

Genevieve had remained with her ear next to the door, listening for any noises outside. 'I can hear the guard, he's moving towards the cupboard. He'll find the corpse,' she called out.

Lady Maitland suddenly turned on me. 'You have it, don't you? That's why you're here.'

'No,' I replied, taken unawares by the sudden shift.

'Give me the medallion,' she demanded, the gun now aimed at Swift and I.

'What are you going to do, kill us?' I retorted.

'No, Major Lennox, but I will damage you.'

Genevieve called out, 'I can hear a commotion downstairs. I think the guard has gone for the gendarmes.'

'Miss Carruthers,' Lady Maitland turned her attention back to Persi. 'Without the information from the tomb-robber, the French will not release you, or Langton. If they find the information before we do, we will have nothing to negotiate with.'

'Why should I trust you?' Persi sounded uncertain.

Lady Maitland turned and held her hand out toward me. 'Give it to me, or I will be forced to act.'

I took a step back.

Swift stepped in. 'Raqisa.'

'Swift!' I protested.

'It's an impasse, and I believe she is telling the truth,' Swift was looking at Lady Maitland as he spoke.

She turned toward him. 'How do you know it's the Raqisa?'

I realised Swift was fishing for information and had thrown her the bait. He continued. 'The lawyer had it written on his hand, I think he was killed because he'd found out about it.'

Genevieve turned around to call out, 'I can hear shouting. You must hurry.'

'Leave,' Lady Maitland ordered Swift and me. 'Both of you go to the terrace. I will meet you there shortly. Do not forget what is at stake.'

Swift turned to me. 'Come on, Lennox.'

I paused to give Persi a quick, but heartfelt kiss then dashed after Swift.

We reached the door to the servant's staircase just as the guard, followed by Colonel Fontaine, the sergeant and a number of soldiers, reached the top steps of the walkway. They didn't see us as we slipped through to race down.

We came out behind the reception desk before pausing to catch our breath. There was a group gathered at the fountain so we casually sauntered over to look up at the commotion high on Ladies Row.

'What's happening, Hamid?' I asked the Maitre'd who was standing nearest to me, wringing his hands.

'Ah, effendi,' he replied, without taking his eyes from the top floor, 'there is something very terrible occurring. It is the mystery of the locked cupboard. I cannot understand it, the key was lost for two days and now the door is unlocked and it has revealed a tragedy. And yet, still, the key is missing.'

'Ah, right, yes. A great mystery,' I muttered and retreated to the rear where Swift had gone to stand out of earshot of the servants.

'Fontaine will realise Josephine did it,' he said.

'Yes, I suppose so,' I replied. 'There are some damn strange women about the place.'

His hawkish look was more pronounced. 'I suspect her Ladyship's quite ruthless.'

'Yes, do you think she killed Josephine?'

'It's possible,' his face hardened. 'We'd better go and hear what she has to say.'

I was about to follow when I was hailed by Bing. He was back at the bar, indulging in its delights.

'What-ho, old bean.' He raised a glass in my direction with a grin. 'He loved the show. Haha.'

'Well done, Bing, but don't broadcast it, there's a good chap.'

He replied with a shaky salute.

We reached the terrace and were almost instantly supplied with a gin and tonic apiece. I'd barely taken a sip when Lady Maitland and Genevieve arrived to sit on the other wicker chairs at our table. Neither of them accepted the waiter's offer to bring them a drink.

'Miss Carruthers has confirmed that you have the medallion, Major Lennox,' Lady Maitland said.

I regarded her in silence.

'Who is this tomb-robber, and Hanno the Navigator?' Swift leaned in. 'And why are you looking for his house?'

'Chief Inspector.' Lady Maitland paused in her reply. 'I do not take you for a fool. You must realise this situation is of national importance. I am not at liberty to tell you any more than you need to know. Do you understand?'

'Would it make any difference if we knew who Hanno the Navigator was?' I asked.

'I don't see why they shouldn't know,' Genevieve said to her Aunt.

The lady conceded. 'Very well. He was a Phoenician from Carthage. I assume you know their history.'

'Not in detail,' I said – actually I'd only vaguely heard of them.

'The Phoenicians were the most prolific sea-traders in the ancient world. Hanno was their greatest explorer and he retired here, to Damascus. His house is said to depict his accumulated knowledge of the Phoenician world and their craft.' She finished her potted lecture. 'Now do you understand?'

'So it is treasure?' Swift said.

'Ha!' I exclaimed. 'Told you so, Swift.'

'Not as such,' she replied.

'Oh, well, what is it then?' I asked in exasperation.

'Major Lennox, I assume you received a good education,' came the haughty reply. 'You should be quite capable of devising the reason yourself.'

I thought she was being deliberately obtuse.

I opened my mouth to ask if she knew anything about Josephine's bracelet, but then decided against it. Swift held his tongue, too.

'Now,' she continued. 'I have need of your services.'

'To do what?' I enquired.

'To meet the tomb-robber and exchange the medallion for the whereabouts of the house.'

'Why us?' Swift demanded.

Genevieve leaned forward. 'Because the Raqisa is a nightclub. It's men only.'

'What sort of nightclub only permits men?' I asked, then realised it was probably a stupid question.

Genevieve laughed. 'A club with dancing girls, of course.'

'Right. In that case, we'll go,' I decided on behalf of us both.

Swift turned his hawkish gaze on Lady Maitland. 'Why have you left Miss Carruthers at the mercy of the French police?'

'Because it is quite possible she murdered Josephine Belvoir.'

'Of course she didn't,' I protested.

'Can you prove that?' She regarded me.

'Yes.'

They all looked at me in surprise. 'Well, not right at this very moment. And… and anyway…' I was becoming a bit flustered, 'anyway, there's no proof she did it. In fact anyone could have done. Including you.' I finished on a note of retaliation.

It didn't garner me much. Lady Maitland merely laughed. 'Why would I do that?'

'Because Josephine Belvoir betrayed Beatrice Langton. And Beatrice was one of your agents.' It was a stab in the dark, because I had no idea if she even knew Beatrice.

She blanched. Her thin lips trembled briefly. 'How do you know that?'

'I'm not at liberty to tell you.' I threw her words back at her.

Genevieve had been watching me, but her eyes sharpened on her Aunt. Well, I assumed she was her Aunt. Frankly, I wasn't too sure about anything now.

Lady Maitland took a breath, pulled herself together, then fixed us both with cold eyes.

'I will make a pact with you gentlemen, you will cooperate with us and we will keep you informed, where necessary.'

'Very well,' Swift agreed.

'Good,' she nodded. 'Go to the Raqisa club. Exchange the medallion for the directions to Hanno's house and return with it to me. Do you agree?'

'We agree.' Swift spoke. My mind was still fixed on the previous conversation.

'Very well.' She turned toward me. 'Major Lennox, tell me how you knew Beatrice Langton was my agent.'

'I didn't, but it seemed logical and you've just confirmed it.'

She looked furious, rose to her feet and stalked off with Genevieve in her wake.

We stood as they departed, before dropping back into our chairs. I was glad to see them go. I stretched, being somewhat stiff after the rope climbing exertions.

'If that's an example of our secret service at work, we can all rest easy in our beds,' I remarked while looking around for another gin and tonic.

'I assume that was meant as sarcasm,' Swift replied dryly.

Hamid came in with a silver tray supporting two glasses, a small dish of sliced lemons and some crunchy cheese things.

'What news from the courtyard, Hamid?' I asked.

'Ah, effendi, it is as feared, another tragedy. We suffer war beyond our city walls and now death sneaks like a thief into our haven. I am a man distraught,' he said in mordant tones. 'And the Al Shami is once more overrun by our Lordly Masters, the French.'

Poor chap, seemed like we were all having a difficult day.

We drank in silence, both of us deep in thought.

I churned events in my mind. After that whole damn palaver, I thought, all Lady Maitland wanted us to do was go to a nightclub and watch dancing girls. Quite frankly I'd have gone anyway.

'Our lady spies didn't murder Josephine,' Swift said at last.

'No,' I agreed. 'They're here to rescue Langton.'

'They're here to rescue Langton's mission,' Swift corrected.

'These Phoenicians – I thought they were some sort of myth. Don't happen to know who they were, do you?'

'No, but then I haven't had the benefit of your expensive education.'

'Hum.' Can't say I'd made much use of it either. 'Persi will be able to tell us all about it.'

'Once we manage to talk to her. Look, I need a shower.' He stood up.

'Um.' So did I after all that rope climbing.

'We'll meet at dusk.'

I nodded and followed him through to the courtyard. It was as busy as a train station with Gendarmes firing questions at the staff and anyone else they'd been able to corner. The sergeant tried to intercept us but Fontaine was there; he knew we couldn't have been involved in the lawyer's murder and waved us away.

'Swift,' I said as I was about to enter my rooms.

'What?'

'Where is the Raqisa?'

He paused for a moment. 'We will have to find out. But Lennox,' he warned, 'don't tell anyone, it must be absolutely hush-hush.'

'Yes, of course!' I replied. 'I'm perfectly capable of keeping secrets, Swift.'

CHAPTER 15

I emerged from the shower in my dressing gown to discover my little dog had returned. He greeted me ecstatically and I gave his ears a good ruffle as he leapt about my knees. Greggs was still wearing his butlering togs with a smidgeon of sand about his person. He was fidgeting about my room, picking up towels and socks and what have you.

'Greetings, old chap.'

'Good evening, sir,' he intoned. 'There were a number of Frenchmen in the courtyard.'

'Yes, another body, Greggs,' I told him.

'Another, sir?'

'Um, the lawyer, Midhurst, I think.'

'Dead, sir?' His brows had shot up.

'Yes, that's the nature of bodies, Greggs.'

His mouth opened and closed. I gave him a moment but he just stared, so I began donning my linen suit.

'How went Fogg's foray into films?' I asked while buttoning up my shirt.

'Erm... Mr Fogg wore a ribbon, sir. It was pink.'

'Good Lord!' I picked the little dog up to give him a reassuring cuddle. 'Where?'

'On his topknot, sir.' Greggs reached a hand above his head as though pinching some hair, he looked like a ponderous ballerina.

'Ah.' I hid a smile. 'And the movie making?'

'It was… singular, sir.'

'Singular?'

'Indeed, sir. The cameraman, Mr Bruce, first recorded various shots of the city and the desert under the direction of Mrs Vincent and then Mr Vincent began the 'short'. He directed the hired hands to race from one side of an area to the other, and then they had to hold up their arms in fear and run through a gate.'

'And this was outside of the city walls?' I asked.

'It was, sir. I assumed you would have understood that to be the case.'

'Yes, thank you, Greggs. Carry on.'

He sniffed. 'Mr Vincent had devised a story, 'Delilah of the Desert'. Mr Fogg was lost in the desert when the aeroplane he and his owners were travelling in crashed. Mr Fogg was the only survivor.'

'And did the Vincents have an aeroplane?'

'No, sir. The opening scene was written on a board called an 'inter-title' and held before the camera. With this being merely a short movie, there is no need for extravagance.'

'Oh.' Obviously he was an expert now. 'Well, carry on.'

'A local boy was used for the role of the shepherd boy. He found Mr Fogg and carried him to a tribal group, seated about a fire.'

'And these were also locals?'

'Yes, sir, there was nowhere else they could have come from.' He sounded a tad testy. 'The chieftain snatched Mr Fogg from the arms of the boy, knocking him into the sand to crawl away. Then the chieftain tied Mr Fogg up and placed him next to another boy who was already tied up.'

He paused to wait for me to say something, but I refrained from comment. 'The next scene was explained by another inter-title board. These ruffians had kidnapped a young Prince from a neighbouring tribe and were holding him to ransom. But, the shepherd boy had a good and brave heart, sir. So he sneaked into the camp while the tribe was carousing around the fire and attempted to cut through the ropes.'

'And he released them?'

'Unhappily, he was discovered and he too was made a prisoner.'

'Oh!' I exclaimed. It sounded like quite a good story, actually.

'And then Mr Fogg chewed through the ropes – it was part of the movie.'

'Really?'

'No, it was 'staged', sir, I gave him a sausage which looked like a rope.'

'Ah, excellent, Greggs. Well done, old chap!'

He puffed out his chest. 'But just at the very moment of their freedom, warriors from a warring tribe appeared on the horizon galloping on horses and waving swords.'

'Good Lord! And this was the Prince's father?'

'Alas no, sir. It was indeed a warring tribe and we had to gather ourselves, the equipment and camels and make haste for the safety of the city. I saved Mr Fogg, sir.'

'Marvellous! So you are the hero of the day?'

'Oh,' he demurred, 'I would not go so far as to say that, sir.' He smiled, making his chins wobble.

'Greggs, you are too modest.'

'Thank you, sir.' He gave a small bow.

'And is the movie making finished now?'

'No, sir, Mrs Vincent has informed me we will be venturing out again tomorrow.'

'Ah, well there's no need to hand over the dibs until it's all over, is there,' I told him, because I only had a few dollars of my own left and I had no idea what expenses would be required at the Raqisa.

He frowned.

'Don't worry, you will get it!'

'Humm, very well, sir. May I enquire of your day?'

'Erm...' I thought of Persi, the souk, the rope, the corpse, Lady Maitland holding a gun and said, 'This and that, you know.'

'Ah, in that case, sir, do you mind if I retire early? It has been a somewhat adventurous day.'

'Certainly, Greggs. I'm just going to, erm... have a drink, early dinner and all that. Goodnight.'

'Goodnight, sir.'

'Fogg?' I called. 'Foggy?' He had burrowed under the bed covers, but he raised his head when I called, yawned, stretched, wagged his tail and jumped down to the floor. He was a game little dog.

I picked him up and carried him to the roof garden, which he hadn't explored yet. He found a nest of mice in one of the pots which was terribly exciting. While he yapped and raced around the urn, I sat on a wicker chair in contemplation. The sun was dropping below the distant mountains, sending pastel colours to play along low strung clouds. A camel bellowed somewhere in the city, followed by a braying donkey.

What time was it at home? I wondered. Tea-time probably. Cook would be taking hot scones from the oven, Tommy would be sitting on the rocking chair near the stove with Tubbs curled snuggly on his lap. There would be a kettle on the boil and steam rising to mist the windows. Snow was probably piling on the sills as winter set in and down in the village, they would be hanging Christmas wreathes and candle lanterns. I sighed.

'Come on Foggy,' I called and we made our way back to my rooms.

I settled at my desk with my dog at my feet, opened my notebook on a blank page and started to write. *Did Josephine truly betray Beatrice?* Then added, *Lady Maitland knew Beatrice Langton,* and paused again before jotting down, *Lawyer most probably killed by Josephine. Were Fontaine and Josephine working together? If so, Fontaine could have killed Josephine?* I struck a line through the last sentence because I couldn't imagine why he would have done. I paused to consider Lady Maitland's entirely inadequate history lesson. *Hanno was a Phoenician, his house contains a map, or something, which is of national interest – beyond gold and riches. What could an ancient house contain that is of interest to a modern-day government?*

I paused to stare at the page a few seconds and then stopped because no amount of thinking on my part was making matters any clearer. I blotted the page, tossed my book back on top of a wardrobe and went off in search of a drink and Swift in that order.

Bing was still at the bar, he waved.

'Lennox, all hail, old bean.' His words were slightly slurred.

'Greetings, Bing.' I slid onto a stool next to him as the excellent bartender placed a snifter in front of me.

'They found the lawyer,' he confided. 'Someone stabbed him with a stiletto. No prizes for guessing who did it, eh?' He ended on a laugh devoid of all humour.

'She wasn't worth the heartache, Harry. Cut out the booze, it's not helping.'

He was propped up by the elbows on the mahogany counter. 'Become a bit of a habit.'

'Haven't seen Swift or Mrs Vincent, have you?' I asked as I took an appreciative sip of excellent brandy.

'No idea where Sherlock is, but Mammie was being interrogated by the French fuzz. They found her lawyer

– he's dead you know. Getting bally dangerous around here!' He hiccupped and reached for the bottle of whisky next to his glass but the barman beat him to it.

I held my hand up. 'Put it away. Mr Bing has had enough.'

'No, I haven't.'

'Yes, you have.' And I was right because he gave a groan and slumped to the bar.

The bartender and I looked at him and shrugged, then I thought of something and leaned in.

'Don't happen to know the whereabouts of the Raqisa, do you?' I asked the man quietly.

He shook his head.

'Doesn't speak English,' Harry whispered loudly.

'Thought you were out of it?' I frowned at him, he was still face down on the woodwork.

'Fooled you, haha.' He gave a drunken giggle.

'Bing,' I warned, although there wasn't much I could do to the damn sot.

'Wait.' He sat up. 'I know where it is.'

'What?'

'The Raqisa. I've been there.'

'Where is it?'

'I can't tell you.' He pushed his empty glass aside. 'But I can show you.'

'You're not coming.'

'You won't find it on your own.' He smoothed his tie down and then his hair.

'I'll ask the staff.'

'Fontaine's got them lined up for questioning too.'

I looked around. He was right, apart from the barman there was no-one else to be seen.

'I promise not to drink.' Bing held a hand up. 'Scouts' honour!'

I let loose a quiet curse as Swift came down the stairs.

'Ready, Lennox?' He was wearing his trench coat over cream slacks and a white shirt and tie, hardly the sort of attire for an evening watching dancing girls.

'I'm taking you to the Raqisa,' Bing called.

'What?' Swift glared at me. 'You told him! Good God, Lennox, what the devil did you do that for?'

'I didn't,' I protested. 'Well, not on purpose. Anyway, there was no one else to ask.'

'Hamid will know,' he marched off before I had a chance to tell him about Fontaine and the staff.

He came back after a fruitless circuit. 'Where is everyone?'

'Being questioned. Now look, Swift. We can trust Harry, and I won't let him touch another drop.'

'Dyb dyb dyb.' Bing held his fingers in the Scouting salute then struggled to his feet. He wavered a little then set off in the direction of the street. 'Follow me.'

'Lennox,' a voice hailed me from the stairs. It was Dreadnaught. 'Are you fellows going out? I'll join you.'

'No,' Swift replied. 'You can't.'

'We're going to the Raqisa,' Harry called out. 'Dancing girls, you know.' He swung around with his arms extended, giggling.

'Ha, excellent! I like that place very much,' the German replied as he caught us up.

'No, no. Now look, you can't,' Swift started but was interrupted.

'You guys going to that joint with dancing girls?' Vincent called out as he too came trotting downstairs. 'Great idea!' He grinned. 'Mammie's lyin' down with a headache and I gotta get outta here. They found our lawyer dead in a cupboard. That Frenchie's been giving us a hard time ever since we got back. Hey, Lennox, your mutt's gonna be a star. And as for your butler, if he ever wants a job…' He slapped me on the back.

Swift was almost hopping. 'No. No-one's coming!'

He held up his hand for all the good it did, they laughed in good humour, walked around him and strolled out into the street.

It was cool under a moonlit night. I gazed up at the sky, now a deep blue with countless sparkling stars. Damascus was different after dark; the chattering crowds had dispersed and the streets were mostly silent. The stones retained the day's heat, but the air was chill. Dark alleys dipped away from lamplit streets, muffled voices and suppressed stirrings escaped the shadows, suffusing the city with a sense of menace. The smell of beasts and spices hung heavily and we weaved through twisting cobbled streets, before turning into a deserted square.

Bing paved the way, the night air having blown some of the alcohol from his fuddled mind. He stopped and looked around as we caught up with him.

'Down there.' Vincent pointed to a dimly lit passage,

his voice bouncing off the walls and shuttered houses that surrounded the yard.

'No, it was this one.' Dreadnaught motioned to an arched alley.

'I distinctly remember it being this one.' Bing went toward another gateway.

'How did you find it last time?' I asked, rather losing confidence in our companions.

'Guide,' Bing replied.

'Wasn't the bath-draw boy, was it?' I asked.

'Yes,' Dreadnaught replied. 'You know, old fellow, I haven't seen him around recently.'

I decided not to say anything.

'This is ridiculous,' Swift snapped. He'd been stalking behind us, hands thrust deep in the pockets of his tightly belted trench coat. The evening walk didn't seem to have improved his mood.

'Pssst, effendi,' a voice hissed from the shadows. 'It is I, Jamal.' He emerged, peered about carefully then trotted across to join us.

'Greetings.' I was relieved to see him. 'Just the chap we need!'

'I escaped the French and followed, effendi. I fear for you in the night. This is not a place of safety.'

'Nonsense!' I clapped my hands together, relieved that the evening was not entirely lost. 'Where's this Raqisa place then?'

'I do not know, effendi. I am too lowly for its portals. And it has girls without veils, it is a bad place.'

'Yeah, that's why we're goin' there.' Vincent grinned.

Jamal looked up at our faces as we formed a circle around him. 'I have heard it is to be found in the alley of the donkey, effendi.'

'And where is that?' Swift demanded.

'It is the passageway over there.' Jamal pointed toward the archway.

'Ha, as I said!' Dreadnaught's smile was a flash of white in the darkness.

Swift stalked toward it, muttering under his breath

The narrow road wound steeply downhill. It was evidently well named because there was dung liberally spread along the cobble stones. We turned a corner to find a short man in baggy trousers, shirt and red waist-coat sweeping up the droppings and placing them in a basket. Behind him were a group of tethered donkeys in front of what looked like a stable.

Bing hailed the donkey-minder with a cheery greeting, Swift hissed at him to be quiet.

'Wait! It's here,' Bing shouted suddenly. He walked down some steps leading off the road and into a deeply shaded alcove. It smelled of dank, decay and something of the sinister.

'I remember the head. Look.' Bing pointed at a brass lion's head fixed to a heavy wooden door. He picked up the ring suspended from its mouth and rapped it. The banging reverberated through the empty streets and alley-ways. If everyone in the district hadn't heard us before, they certainly had now.

CHAPTER 16

A small metal grill opened in the door, barely visible in the darkness, and a voice rapped out something incomprehensible.

We stood back to let Jamal answer, guttural debate resulted before he moved out of the line of the door-keeper's sight and waved a hand in our direction. The reaction was immediate, locks were thrown back, chains rattled and the door opened to reveal a long dark corridor with bright lights in the distance. Music, singing and shouting greeted us – it sounded like a lot of people having a jolly good time.

We filed in wearing grins, except Swift of course, who was determined to remain a wet blanket. We tried to persuade Jamal to join us, but he refused and went off into the darkness.

A happy hour later, one of the ladies was shimmying her navel before our boggle-eyed gaze as we sat on low couches, sipping some sort of paint-stripper. Actually not all of us were drinking, Bing had been threatened, on pain of being booted out, if he took so much as a sniff. He had a glass of honeyed camel milk, or some such concoction.

Dimly lit alcoves, like private booths, were arrayed around the dance floor. Ours, and all the others I could see, were furnished with couches, cushions and low tables. To one side of the smoke-filled room were musicians playing lutes, zithers, tambourines and a drum. They belted out frenzied notes while, in the centre, dancers quivered under sparkling chandeliers. The ladies dazzled in sequinned tops above bare midriffs and hip-hugging skirts of gaudy silk, which flared and flashed as they swayed to the rhythm of the beat.

We'd been mesmerised from the minute we sat down.

'What are we supposed to do now?' I hissed to Swift, whose bad temper had mostly melted in the intoxicating mix of belly dancers and strong liquor.

'Keep your eyes open, someone's bound to spot us.' He hissed back, under cover of the rowdy music.

I looked around at the various alcoves where the clientele lounged in robes of many hues. Most of them were imbibing merrily or smoking jars of bubbling liquid, with their eyes fixed firmly on the entertainment.

'Swift, we couldn't be more spottable if we were wearing flaming beacons.'

His reply was lost as another lady sprang into the centre of the dancing floor and started swaying faster and faster. Clapping began and we slapped our palms to the tempo as she shimmied across the floor. Then more ladies swirled out until there were over a dozen, jiggling their hips as everyone stamped and yelled.

'Is this the 'seven veils'?' Bing said loudly.

'The what?' 'I shouted back.

Dreadnaught laughed. 'Innocents abroad! I told you, Major, you are in need of broadening your education.'

'Yeah, you should come to Hollywood,' Vincent laughed. 'Now that's an education!'

The dancing reached a sizzling climax, then the ladies suddenly ran off through a doorway as waiters emerged with trays of delicacies. The music fell to a light melody, as a feast of small dishes was set before us. Not one of them featured sheep's eyes, which Tommy Jenkins had assured me was standard fair in these exotic parts.

'What's Hollywood like?' I asked, having had visions of woods with prickly leafed trees but now suspected that was an unlikely scenario.

'Booze, broads and big bands. It's a blast.' Vincent leaned in to heap a plate with pastries filled with minced lamb and mint. 'Parties every night, music and dancing, whatever you want, it's yours. And now that the dames are emancipated, they're letting their hair down and turnin' their hem-lines up.'

'There's a dance called the Charleston,' Bing joined in. 'And everybody goes wild with excitement. It's a ragtime jazz, you see. Totally new music and you just can't help but get up and jig to it.'

Dreadnaught had mellowed with the alcohol. 'We used to dance the waltz back in Bavaria in black-tails and bow ties. But, in Hollywood, I can wear whatever I like, dance however I want and talk to whomever I choose.'

'Why can't you talk with 'whomever' in Bavaria?' Swift asked sipping his glass of Arak. He was leaning back on a heap of colourful cushions with his trench coat cast aside, looking relaxed for a change.

'We are very stiff-necked in the upper classes,' Dreadnaught replied. 'One cannot bend to look below one's nose, you know.'

'No different than the English, then,' Swift rejoined.

'Ah, no. We Germans are very different. This is our strength and our weakness.' His handsome face fell serious. 'We are a communal people, you see, we act as one and we follow our leaders slavishly. And this is good, because like bees in a hive, each has his role to play and his work to do and it makes the hive productive. But, if we have bad leaders, like our vainglorious Kaiser, then still we follow without question, and it becomes dangerous. There is no room for dissent in our society, nor individualism. It can be stifling.'

'Hasn't the war changed things?' I asked, being very aware how our own class boundaries had begun to break down.

'A little.' Dreadnaught sipped his shot glass of clear spirits. 'But in Germany we merely rebuild our society back as it was. We look always to the past, to keep things as they were.'

'Or as you thought they should have been,' Swift threw in, which I thought rather perceptive.

'Ja.' Dreadnaught smiled. 'And so you find me in Hollywood, not in Hohenburg.'

'Yeah, Hollywood, there's no place like home.' Vincent laughed.

More drinks arrived and Vincent threw a handful of American dollars onto the table for the waiter. I noticed we were receiving furtive glances from several quarters.

'You're from the Bronx, Vincent.' Bing had left the food untouched and was still cradling his glass of milk.

'But I adopted Hollywood,' Vincent replied. 'I got pals in high places too.'

'Wouldn't be spies, would they?' I put in.

This made him laugh even harder. 'No, money men. Everybody wants to make the good times roll, and by that I means rolls of cash.'

'And you and Mammie are making it in the movie business?' Swift asked a leading question.

'Mammie! Boy has that woman been good for me.' Vincent suddenly softened. 'She's the best. A real pro. Wanted to be an actress but she ain't no beauty and her folks was strait-laced, didn't even want her to go out an' work. But Mammie don't let nothin' get in her way and she got hold of a camera and started making a few shorts for herself. Trouble is, she ain't technically minded, so someone told her to come and find me in the backlots of Hollywood. I was trying to scrape together enough dollars to buy my own camera when she turned up. She took me from bein' a hustler to a real movie director and we ain't never looked back.' He laughed again. 'And, to answer your question, yeah, movies make money. Hell, it's almost like printing it!'

'Well, you certainly saved my bacon, old man.' Bing raised his glass of milk in Vincent's direction.

'I ain't gonna save it for long if you don't give up on the booze, Bing,' Vincent's good humour died.

'Where are you from in England, Bing?' I changed the subject before the conversation soured.

'A scion of West Sussex, old bean.' Bing's smile drifted away. 'Raised by fusty old school masters from a tender age.'

We raised our brows in question, so he explained.

'I'm a by-blow. Ridiculous in this day and age, isn't it – that it should matter? Pa was heir to the Lordship of the Manor, Ma was a shop girl. They met, fell in love, followed the primrose path to happy conclusion and voila! I was the result.' He raised a wry grin. 'I'm afraid my appearance rather put a spoke in the romance. Marriage was vetoed, Pa was packed off to foreign parts, Ma married a publican and died of consumption.'

He sighed. 'I was catered for on the QT and eventually pushed into a position in the Foreign Office. Did my bit for King and Country and then fell along the slippery slope into Hollywood.' He laughed lightly. 'My face is my fortune, don't you know.'

'I do know and you'd better look after it,' Vincent growled.

'Your lawyer.' I decided to take a dig at Vincent. 'He's been dead for two days and you don't seem to give a damn.'

'He's not mine,' Vincent took a deeper draft of Arak. 'He was dumped on us by the spooks.'

'Spies, you mean?' Swift asked, leaning in.

'Mammie knows them from way back. Nothin' to do with me.' His eyes shifted away toward the quietly strumming musicians.

'Is Mammie an agent?' Swift asked outright.

'No, and she never was before you ask,' Vincent replied. 'She's no more than a messenger, she gets given stuff, she passes it on. That's it and that's all it's ever been. Midhurst was tagged onto us so he could go poking around out here. But neither of us is involved in all this sneaking about so you lay off her.' He suddenly stabbed a finger at Swift. 'Or you'll find I got a mean side you guys don't wanna mess with.'

The musicians ramped the beat back up again as waiters appeared in droves to clear the tables and we all leaned back in anticipation. Must admit to being a tad disappointed as a group of men came in wearing very long frock coats and began twirling on the spot. It was dizzying to watch, but as the music rose in tempo it wasn't long before the whole place was clapping and shouting.

'Whirling Dervishes,' Bing shouted above the noise.

The Dervishes whirled to a halt and were instantly replaced by a half dozen scantily clad ladies shaking their hips. They now bore tinkling bells, strung to the tops of their bottoms. The clapping abated as the gathered throng stared in rapture then suddenly exploded again when more ladies emerged and began to pull men onto the dance floor.

'It's the Dabke!' Bing announced and leapt to his feet to join in. Vincent followed in the kind of hopping gait only a short stocky chap from the Bronx can make.

Swift's hand was grabbed by a smiling lady, and protesting every step of the way, he was made to join the mob forming a circle in the centre, kicking their feet. Dreadnaught took no persuasion and I was just about to follow them when a hulking man with a bushy moustache cut across my path.

CHAPTER 17

There were a dozen moustachioed henchmen, all dressed in black with swords hanging from their belts. We were seated around a long table; six heavies on each side, me on a stool at one end and the tomb-robber at the other. He had greeted me in excellent English.

'I am Qarsan.'

'Greetings,' I offered. 'I'm…'

He cut me off. 'You are Major Lennox, and you are a fool. Do you not understand that your every movement is reported instantly to me?'

I had expected a ruffian in robes, but he wore an immaculate grey suit with a white shirt, dove-grey waistcoat and silk tie. His thick black hair held traces of silver and he smiled with perfect white teeth in a smooth, olive-hued face, pierced by darkly intelligent eyes. Vincent would have cast him as a noble sheik in a movie.

I had been escorted along a lantern lit corridor to a room adorned with panels of richly tinted tiles in brilliant blues, greens and reds, with flecks of gold worked into the ceramic. Oil lamps flickered above our heads to cast disquieting shadows across the ceiling.

I leaned back before remembering I was sitting on a stool and jerked upright again.

'In that case, you know why I'm here,' I replied.

'The reason you are here, Major Lennox, is because I had you brought here,' he spoke precise English with barely an accent. 'You have the medallion. Please pass it to me.'

'No.'

'Would you prefer it be taken from you?'

'Erm, no… Look, you're supposed to tell me where to find the house of Hanno, or draw a map or something first,' I stuttered, never having negotiated with a tomb-robber before.

He appeared amused. 'As you say, Major.' He regarded me, his manicured hands resting lightly on the polished wooden arms of his throne-like chair. 'But you are in my domain – among my men. My orders are merely a snap of the finger away.'

He went as if to click finger and thumb together and each of his men reached for the hilts of their swords. He slowly lowered his hand as cold sweat formed on the back of my neck.

My reply was as measured as I could manage. 'Not until I see the map, or whatever you have. You've given your word to Charles Langton, and you must know that I am here in his stead.' I didn't know that for a fact, but it seemed like a good riposte.

'Ah, the unfortunate Mr Langton. Colonel Fontaine has incarcerated your friend — rather bad sport, don't you think?'

'He's not my friend,' I retaliated, 'but, yes, it's bloody bad sport and I've been dragged all the way from England for this.'

He laughed drily, then demanded, 'Who killed the lady?'

That took me aback. 'I... erm... why would you want to know that?'

'I ask the questions, Major Lennox,' he reminded me coldly. 'You and your friend pretend to be British detectives. I suggest you detect the lady's killer if you wish to leave this city.'

I stared back mutely, wondering what his interest in Josephine Belvoir was.

He returned to the matter in hand. 'Do you know what the house of Hanno represents?'

'Erm... no.'

'Or the medallion?' he asked.

'It's some sort of antique,' I replied. 'Like a treasure map. It's Phoenician.'

'Ahh, very good. And what do you know of these people, Major Lennox?'

'They were ancient sea-traders, erm, during Roman times.'

He smiled, as though mildly amused. 'Let me enlighten you further.' He relaxed, leaning back. 'Phoenician history is mostly legend, but they have left their traces to those who choose to look, and I do look, Major Lennox. I search very hard for their artefacts, because I am one of them. One of the few who can be sure that the old blood still runs through heart and veins. Does this surprise you, my friend?'

I tried to appear impressed but didn't entirely succeed, although I noted the word 'friend' and hoped it was a good omen. I wondered briefly what Swift and the others were doing and if they were searching for me.

He clapped his hands suddenly and a waiter scurried in with a tray of shot glasses brimming with clear liquid, which I assumed to be the local Arak.

Qarsan picked up his glass with an elegant movement, emptied it and replaced it on the table. The henchmen all knocked back theirs and returned to staring at me. I took a sip. It was a great deal more potent than the stuff in the dance rooms; it smelled like aviation fuel and tasted much the same.

'You do not possess the talent of dissembling, Major Lennox.' Qarsan flashed white teeth and continued his tale. 'The Phoenicians were a maritime race of trad-ers — the most successful of their world. This was the world where east met west. Where the desire to exchange ideas and luxuries, and some necessities of course, was compelling.'

He warmed to the subject. 'While the Egyptians were building their pyramids, and the Greeks were making way for the Romans, my people sailed from their city ports of Tyre, Byblos and Sidon and spread their towns and cities along the southern coast of the Mediterranean all the way to Carthage and beyond. Gold, silver, and metals were carried by Phoenicians on their ships from as far away as your English lands. And do you know where they took these marvels to be bartered?'

He paused to watch as I shook my head. 'Damascus!' he exclaimed. 'Here in this wondrous city, these goods were traded for silk, weapons and gems from the East. Merchandise that had travelled the Great Silk Road from as far away as China. Damascus was the very epicentre of the great trade routes. And so when Hanno finished his explorations he came here to spend the remainder of his days. He built a house and a water garden and he gathered all his knowledge of the ancient world and put it in a map, which he placed within the walls of his property.' He nodded and smiled as though waiting for enlightenment to dawn upon me.

'Ah, and everyone wants to find the house because of the map,' I said.

'Yes…' he seemed to be waiting for me to add something more, but as I couldn't, I didn't.

The smile faded from Qarsan's face. 'You really do not know what this is about, do you, Major Lennox?'

'No,' I admitted. 'But you could explain.'

His smile returned but he shook his head. 'The medallion, if you please,' he held out his hand.

I sighed in defeat, rummaged in my pocket and pulled it out with a dog biscuit I'd been saving for Fogg. I placed it on the table, the medallion that is, not the dog biscuit.

The bright shiny brass glinted in the light from the lamp overhead. The nearest henchman snatched it up and passed it down to Qarsan. I was sorry to see it go.

'You have cleaned it?' Qarsan frowned.

'Yes,' I smiled. 'It was covered with grime.'

'That is age, Major Lennox. It takes many hundreds of years to acquire a rich patina.'

'Ah,' I gathered he wasn't too pleased. 'Anyway, if I could have the directions to Hanno's house, I'll be off.'

He placed a hand in his jacket pocket and extracted a rolled up sheet of thick paper, tied with a ribbon and sealed in red wax. The henchmen passed it along in my direction. I took it, exceedingly relieved that I'd been given something, and slid a finger under the seal to break it.

Qarsan held up a hand. 'You can study your prize later, English Major.' He stood up. All of his men instantly rose to their feet.

'Fine. If you insist,' I agreed warily.

He fixed me with dark eyes. 'I am an honourable man. And I assure you, you have what you came for.'

'Right…' I would have said more but I was marched out of the room by one of the huge henchmen. I was returned to the club and left there.

The dance floor was now a tumult of music, shouting and frenetic women and men in varying states of inebriation.

'Lennox,' Swift shouted from beyond the crowd of revellers.

'Wait,' I yelled back over the din and wove my way through the throng to join him.

'Rather fun, isn't it?' he was pink in the face and clutching a glass of Arak.

'What?'

'The Dabke. It's like Irish stomping. Look at Vincent and Dreadnaught.' He nodded his head towards the crowd. Our companions were holding hands with ladies in a line of people. They were circling around, kicking their feet up and stamping them down to the music, clearly having a marvellous time.

'Swift,' I said.

'What?'

'Didn't you see me leave?'

'No,' he frowned.

'Well, I did and it's a damn good thing I didn't need any support.'

That made his eyes open. 'You mean you've seen the tomb-robber?'

'Yes, he's called Qarsan.'

'Qarsan?'

'Yes!' I shouted again. 'And I've got it.'

'The map?'

'Yes! And I want to go back to the hotel now.'

'Right.' He looked rather nonplussed. 'Um... Well done, Lennox, and um, sorry about the dancing and all that. Got a bit carried away.'

I shook my head. I could have said a great deal more, but I felt as though I'd been through the wringer and wanted somewhere to lie down quietly, preferably where there weren't any moustachioed henchmen or dead bodies.

He put his glass down. 'I'll get the others, shall I?'

We found Bing under one of the tables. He'd snaffled the unattended Arak while the others were cavorting. I made for the door, while my compatriots dragged him to his feet and carried him out.

He collapsed again when we reached the fresh night air and grinned inanely at the starlit sky far above, then started humming loudly.

'I ain't carrying him,' Vincent scowled.

'Wait, I have a solution,' Dreadnaught declared, his voice thick from the liquor. He went off down the alleyway and came back moments later leading a donkey.

'Come along, Bing, old fellow. You can ride home.' Dreadnaught dragged Harry to his feet, draped him across the donkey's back and led him off.

Vincent stalked behind, muttering under his breath. I had a feeling Bing's days as a Hollywood star could be reaching its nadir and couldn't help but think he'd brought it upon himself.

'You've really got the map?' Swift hissed at me, as we lagged behind the small procession.

'Yes, I told you.'

'What was he like?' Swift sounded contrite.

'He thinks he's the last of the Phoenicians.'

He looked askance so I told him what happened, including the part about Josephine.

'Why does he want us to find the murderer?'

'I have no idea,' I replied.

'Oh!' He looked thoughtful then gave a shrug. 'What does the map look like?'

'I don't know.'

'You haven't seen it?'

'No.'

'No!' He stopped in his tracks. 'Lennox, he could have given you a damn shopping list for all you know.'

'Well, it might be, but what the devil do you think I could do about it,' I retorted. 'Anyway, we need to show it to Persi, it probably won't mean a thing to either of us.'

Which proved entirely true.

We managed to sneak up the back stairs and slid along the wall in the darkness without being seen by the guard. I entered Persi's rooms first and met her coming out of the bathroom, clutching a towel about her damp figure. She almost dropped it in surprise which set my pulse racing and she stifled a laugh when she saw the look on my face.

'Go and sit down, I'll put on a robe,' she smiled.

'You don't have to…'

'What?' Swift came in on my heels.

'Oh, never mind, come on.'

I led the way to the couches by the window which were now shuttered against the night and lit by a table lamp. Swift sat opposite as I started to break the seal, but then stopped.

'Look!'

'What?' He came to lean over my shoulder. 'The sign on the bracelet!' He exclaimed.

We stared at the imprint of ship, sail and horse's head.

'Qarsan must have been her wealthy lover.' It was my turn to state the obvious.

'How did they meet?'

'Swift, I don't know any more than you do.'

'Sorry, stupid question. Better open the roll, see if it throws light on anything.'

I untied the sheet of thick paper and flattened it out on the low table between us. It was written in strange hieroglyphs, drawn within a spiralling coil. There were upside down 7s, a cross, a dash in a circle, a backwards K, a hook and so on. It looked a bit like Greek, although it could have been double-dutch for all I knew.

Persi reappeared and came to sit next to me on the sofa, she was enveloped in a fluffy white bath robe, she smelled of soap and perfume and… 'What?'

'I said 'it's fascinating, isn't it',' she repeated, leaning in to study the curious design.

'That image in the centre looks awfully like the dead camel that was on the medallion.' I placed a finger on it.

'It's not a dead camel, Heathcliff,' Persi replied. 'That's the house of Hanno.'

'Umm, not Heathcliff, old thing,' I reminded her.

'Really, darling, does it matter?' She was staring at the map as she spoke. I was a bit nonplussed, no-one had called me darling before. Perhaps I should use it too? Or should I think of something of my own? Like dearest, or sweetheart, or…? 'What?'

'I said, 'I've never seen anything like this before',' she repeated.

My heart sank. 'Do you mean you don't know what it says?'

'Oh yes, I can decipher it. It's written in ancient Phoenician, but the way it's written in this spiral form is so very peculiar.'

'Why?' Swift asked. 'Is it something to do with snakes?'

She laughed. 'No, not at all, it's because this map is a series of instructions that lead below ground.'

'What!' Swift and I exclaimed.

'It's the levels, you see.'

We didn't see.

'Oh dear.' She sighed. 'This city, is terribly old. Thousands of years old, actually, and it's been built and rebuilt many times by different peoples. The last time was by the Romans. You may have noticed that some of the streets are quite straight and form a grid pattern, whereas the older parts of the city were built in the usual hodge-podge way ordinary people do.'

She looked from one to the other of us with her lovely blue eyes and I had to snap myself out of a trance and pay attention. 'Below the streets are layer upon layer of rubble and stone from earlier civilisations. Quite a few remnants survive almost intact because the Romans used them as foundations. Look here,' she pointed again to the dead camel. 'Hanno's house is just beyond the Temple of Jupiter.'

I suddenly realised I may have seen it. 'Is it the place with stone columns?'

'Yes,' she replied. 'The Temple was rebuilt on an existing religious site constructed by the Arameans, who you must have heard of.'

'I've read about the Romans.' I offered.

'So have I,' Swift added. 'But not very much about the people of Aram.'

'Well, it doesn't matter. I'm going to make a copy and then translate it into English.'

I noticed the lamplight caught her hair, turning damp tendrils gold, her face pink with the warmth of the bath she had just left. Her… 'What?'

'I said will you concentrate, Lennox!' Swift reminded me.

'Look, I'm tired,' I bristled. 'And if we're discussing concentration, you should have been watching me rather than dancing…'

'Do be quiet, please,' Persi interrupted. 'This is terribly complicated.' She put the paper down. 'If we're going to hand a translation over to Lady Maitland in the morning, I will have to work most of the night.'

'Right,' I said.

'Right,' Swift said.

'Goodnight,' she said, without looking up.

We were dismissed.

CHAPTER 18

Swift arrived with the dawn. He didn't knock; he just marched in wearing his trench coat and a determined air.

I had barely donned my freshly pressed linen suit.

'Come on, we'll make some real progress today,' he announced, tightened the belt of his coat and exited.

'Swift…' I called out too late. He'd marched off down the stairs so I followed him, in some irritation, to the courtyard with Foggy at my heels.

'We need to distract Hamid,' Swift announced.

'No, we don't.' I said. 'Fogg needs a walk and then breakfast, in that order.' I crossed the courtyard in the direction of the garden and terrace.

'Lennox,' he called, but I carried on.

Fogg gambolled about, chasing birds and imaginary squirrels under leafy trees and flower-burdened shrubs. It was an oasis of peace in a city jostling with humanity beyond the high stone walls. I strolled across the lawn behind my little dog. Dew drops darkened the tan leather of my shoes and rose petals stuck to my soles.

Swift arrived at my side.

'Lennox…' he started.

'Swift, will you stop being so damned hasty?' I turned on him.

He was pointing a thumb over his shoulder toward the terrace.

'We have company,' he said.

'Ah,' I gave up my leisurely amble and followed him to join Lady Maitland and Genevieve, who were seated at a table on the terrace.

'Major Lennox. Chief Inspector Swift,' Lady Maitland greeted us. 'Sit down.'

Genevieve wore a cream dress with a fetching straw hat over her chestnut curls. She smiled warmly while we took our seats, then straightened her face as her aunt tapped her fingers on the table.

Pots of tea were served.

'Did you execute the exchange?' Lady Maitland demanded.

I opened my mouth to speak but was cut off as she raised a hand.

'I must warn you not to say a word if there is anyone in earshot. Do I make myself clear?'

Swift and I scanned around, then nodded.

'Sausages,' I said.

'Pardon?'

'For my dog.'

'Ah,' her Ladyship broke into a smile as she shifted in her wicker chair to gaze down at Foggy. 'Well, you had better order some.'

I did, along with the usual pastries, fruit with sour cream, dishes of doughnut balls and whatnots of the like. We all ate, slipping titbits to Foggy, and waited until the terrace cleared of waiters.

'So, gentlemen?' Lady Maitland drilled a cold eye while poised over a tea cup.

Swift glanced at me.

'Right,' I replied. 'But in exchange, we'd like some answers.'

'I will consider it, but first I wish to be informed of last evening's events.'

I told her about Qarsan and the exchange, but didn't mention the bracelet, or the demand to detect the murderer – or the dancing for that matter.

'And the paper giving directions to the house?' Lady Maitland held her hand out.

'Yes, but first I'd like to know...' I began, then stuttered to a halt because there were so many questions, 'Look, would you just tell us what you're allowed to tell us? Please.'

I received another appraising look, then she gave the briefest of nods.

'Very well, gentlemen. I am attached to the Foreign Office, Charles Langton is one of my agents and answers directly to me.' She glanced briefly at the silent Genevieve, who presumably was her right-hand woman. 'Charles was instructed to make his way to Damascus and contact the tomb-robber.'

'Qarsan,' I interjected.

'Yes, Qarsan. Please resist pointless interruptions, Major,' she replied. 'Langton's next course of action was to exchange the medallion for the location of the house of Hanno, make a copy of the map within its walls and return with the information to me in London.'

'I thought you said you were en route back from India?' I said.

She glared at me. I decided to shut up.

'What information?' Swift asked. 'What does everyone want?'

'That is on a 'need-to-know basis' Inspector.'

Why the hell were they all so damn secretive? I thought. Actually, they were all spies, I answered my own question – they were bound to be secretive!

Genevieve poured more tea. Bright sunlight dappled through the leafy canopy to light the table and glint off her chestnut hair.

I broke the silence. 'Why did Qarsan want the medallion so much?'

'Did you not ask him?' she shot back.

Damn it, it was like drawing blood from a stone. 'Yes, he said he's one of the last Phoenician's and he collects Phoenician artefacts.'

'He was telling the truth,' she replied. 'There is a society of them, although there are only a few remaining; they are similar to the Knight's Templar but of greater antiquity. One of his men discovered the whereabouts of the house of Hanno some weeks ago. Qarsan let it be known that the location was available at a price.'

'And his price was the medallion?' Swift put in.

'It was,' she replied.

'If he's so keen on Phoenician whatnots, why would he let Langton or anyone else in it?' I asked.

'It's hardly going to suffer any damage, Major,' she replied as if talking to a ten year old. 'One is simply going to observe the information it contains.'

I restrained a curse and carried on. 'Well, if Qarsan's men are swiping artefacts all the time, why didn't they get the medallion for him?'

'This country has an abundance of ancient artefacts, Major, but the medallion happened to be held by the British Museum and that is considerably beyond Qarsan's reach.'

'The British Museum?' Swift repeated in astonishment.

'You stole it from the British Museum?' I asked, imagining Lady Maitland holding the curator at gunpoint.

She found that amusing. 'It is quite unnecessary to commit theft, gentlemen. The Foreign Office simply placed pressure on the trustees to return it to its place of origin and eventually they agreed.'

'Good Lord,' I muttered, though rather pleased that at least one mystery was solved.

Swift leaned in with a question. 'But Britain is not the only power interested in Hanno's map, is it?'

'Considering the presence of foreign agents in this building, I think that is self-evident, Inspector,' Lady Maitland replied witheringly.

'But…' I raised a hand. 'How did they know? The foreign agents, I mean, Josephine and the rest?'

'Please do pay attention, Major Lennox,' she retorted.
'I have already said that Qarsan let it be known what
he had discovered in the house. He engendered a price
war between the national powers to see what they were
willing to bid. There was considerable jockeying to offer
up treasures, but we knew he was primarily interested in
Phoenician artefacts. As we held the medallion, we won.'

I digested this for a moment. Whatever was in Hanno's house must be of enormous value, although, quite
frankly, I couldn't imagine what on earth it could be.

'So.' Swift's mind was moving more quickly than mine.
'Josephine set up Langton by falsely accusing him of
attempted murder and Fontaine locked him up to try to
force him to hand over either the medallion or the location?'

'Yes, as you say.' She stood up and held out her hand.
'Now, Major Lennox, the paper?'

'Is with Miss Carruthers,' I gave her my best smile – it
fell on stoney ground.

She snapped a retort. 'Gentlemen, if you impede this
mission, I will see to it that you share Langton's plight.
And there won't be any ridiculous Gallahads coming to
rescue you from your folly.'

She stalked off, Genevieve cast us a wry grin and
followed.

Swift and I looked at each other.

'Better wait until the coast is clear before we try to see
Persi,' I suggested.

'Hum,' came the reply, as Swift leaned back in his seat
with his hand over his eyes.

'What's wrong?'

'Hangover.'

'Serves you right!'

'Lennox, I am merely…' he was interrupted by a cast shadow.

'Ah. Good morning, sir,' Greggs appeared at my side.

'Greetings, Greggs!' I was rather pleased to see my old retainer.

'Mrs Vincent has informed me we will be departing within the hour for a day of filming.'

'So you're off once more into the burning desert, where shifting sands, roving bandits and scorpions await you.'

'Scorpions, sir?'

'And snakes.'

'Snakes!'

'And crocodiles,' Swift chipped in.

Greggs stared round eyed, then frowned. 'I believe you are pulling my leg.' He sucked in his paunch with mild affront.

We laughed good-heartedly.

'I assume you would like to take Fogg on your adventures, old chap?'

'If you permit it, sir.'

'Fine, but no pink ribbons, Greggs,' I warned. 'He was thoroughly embarrassed, you know.'

'As you say, sir.' He reached down to retrieve Foggy, who was sitting at my feet watching us with cocked ears and bright spaniel eyes. 'I wish you good day.'

'And you,' I replied.

'Oh and, Greggs…'

'Yes, sir?'

'You don't happen to have a spare toothbrush do you?'

'I'm afraid not, sir.'

He went off, smartly turned out in a freshly spruced tailcoat and tie with Foggy in his arms, who was looking rather doubtful about the day's adventure.

Silence fell as Gregg's footsteps receded. I dug out my fob watch, noted the hour and addressed Swift.

'Swift.'

'No, I don't.'

'Don't what?'

'Have a spare toothbrush.'

'That wasn't what I was going to say.'

'What then?' He was again leaning back in his chair.

'The murder of Josephine…'

He sat up. 'Yes?'

I had been thinking about Sherlock Holmes, and the art of deduction. 'There are two possible motives.'

'The betrayal of Beatrice, or the secret of Hanno's house,' he replied.

'Exactly,' I refrained from using the word *elementary.* 'But whatever the motive, it could only be one of the Vincents or Bing, or Dreadnaught, because of the missing gun.'

'Or Persi, because she needs to find the secret in order to release Langton. And she hated Josephine.'

'Swift, it wasn't Persi.'

'Lennox, it's about logic.'

I decided I needed to read more of Sherlock Holmes's
dictums. I sighed and said. 'Do you think the coast will
be clear and we can see Persi now?'

He didn't reply because Mammie arrived at that
moment.

We rose to our feet to welcome the lady.

She was bright and chirpy. 'Good morning to you
both! Major Lennox, I really must commend you on your
butler! Such a dear man, and the doggy too.'

I thanked her and helped her settle in a chair between
us.

A waiter appeared, she informed him loudly that she
never took breakfast, so he returned with more tea.

'I hear you are setting off to make movies, Mrs Vincent,' Swift continued.

'Oh my, yes. But we will film within the walls today.
We were almost overrun with hoodlums yesterday,' she
rattled on. 'And we must leave as soon as Pappie is able to
rise from his bed. You kept him out very late last evening,
you naughty boys.'

'Well, he didn't have to come,' I remarked.

Swift frowned.

I switched tack. 'Mrs Vincent... Mammie.'

'Yes?' She twinkled.

'Do you know who gave Josephine a gold and diamond bracelet?' I was certain it was Qarsan, but thought
I'd start softly.

She laughed delightedly. 'Oh, it was so romantic.'

'Really, what happened...?' I uttered encouragement.

'Wellll…it was all such a secret. She was very fond of secrets, but she's gone now, so…' she gave a small shrug. 'We had a day's break from filming, it can become quite tense, you know, and Josephine announced she was going to the souk. Dear Harry offered to escort her, but she was determined to go alone. And when she returned, I could see she was very pleased with herself. The very next day a huge bouquet of flowers arrived – the perfume was simply divine. Gardenias, roses, jasmine – simply beautiful,' she added in a fulsome tone. 'After filming that day, she slipped off again, this time in the Rolls Royce. I teased her when she came back, in a kindly sort of way, but she wouldn't say a word.' She laughed again. 'I just knew she had a new amour – she positively glowed!'

'And the bracelet?' I cut in, before we had any more romantic nonsense.

'That arrived two days later. Well, I was agog to hear the details, after all, who could have possibly sent it? She wouldn't tell me, but then I just happened to mention it to Mr Midhurst and he knew!' she exclaimed in triumph.

'Who was it?' Swift asked before I did.

'The Sheik, the real Sheik. The Chief of Chiefs! Just like in the film. Can you imagine anything more romantic? And after that, she saw him most days until… well, until she was…' Her voice trailed off.

'How did Midhurst find out about this?' Swift had pulled out his book and was making rapid notes.

'Oh, it was his job to discover things, poor man,' her voice faltered for a moment, then she continued.

'Josephine really was quite extraordinarily beautiful. I know you didn't meet her while she was alive but she could captivate even the most hardened of hearts.'

'Talking of Midhurst...' Swift began, but Mammie put up her hand to stop him.

'Colonel Fontaine has interrogated me to exhaustion on that subject. Please dear boy, I really can't bear to talk about it again.'

Swift wasn't ready to give up. 'You knew Josephine well though. Could she have killed Midhurst?'

'As I said, Inspector, she could captivate even the hardest of hearts, and she could do that because she didn't have one. Yes, I believe she could have killed him and I think you know why.'

I was about to blurt out 'Hanno' when Swift kicked me under the table.

'Well.' She gathered herself together. 'If you will excuse me, dear boys, I simply must go and wake Pappie.'

'Just one more question,' I had a number of questions, actually. 'You told Dreadnaught that Josephine Belvoir betrayed Beatrice Langton, didn't you?'

Her face froze. 'I... I, really, Major, how insensitive.'

'But *how* did you know?' Swift enjoined.

She shifted uncomfortably. 'Because she told me herself.'

'Why?' I asked.

'It was after Langton arrived here, she became frightened and,' she stuttered. '...And she confided in me.'

'Did she say why she did it?' Swift asked, his pen poised.

'She said it was by accident. One of the people in Beatrice's group was a traitor and Josephine denounced that person, but somehow it led to them all being captured. She didn't learn what had happened until a long time later.'

'Did you believe her?' I asked.

'I don't know. Really, Major Lennox, I am most upset at your questioning, these are unpleasant memories and I do not know why you must drag them up.'

I must say I felt a bit of a heel.

Swift was made of sterner stuff. 'Can you prove any of this?'

'No, and why should I?' Her mouth quivered and she stood up suddenly. 'Now, I refuse to stay any longer. The Colonel was very unpleasant about Mr Midhurst and now you have interrogated me about Josephine. I bid you good day, gentlemen.' She walked off.

We watched her go.

'Do you believe her?' I asked.

He looked down at the notes he'd just made. 'I have no idea, it sounds plausible on the face of it.' He bit his lip. 'Qarsan isn't just the head of a bunch of tomb robbers, is he? He actually is a real Sheik and he's probably a very powerful one.'

Having met him, this didn't come as much of a surprise to me.

Swift swore. 'Hell and damnation! Every time I think we're getting a grip on this, it spins further away.'

CHAPTER 19

Vincent arrived. He was unshaven and looking a great deal the worse for the late night revels. He growled a greeting.

'Lennox, payday.' He tossed a bundle of notes in my direction.

I muttered a quiet thank you in return, feeling rather churlish for the way we'd treated his wife.

'You seen Mammie?' he asked.

'Just missed her. And, erm, I rather think we've upset her, old chap,' I confessed.

'Yeah, well she's mad at me too. That lawyer's dead, the French are plaguing her with questions and she don't like me going out drinkin' and dancin' without her.' He shambled off before we could explain.

'The ladies will have spoken to Persi by now. I suppose they'll be going to find the house shortly,' I remarked.

Swift had returned to making notes and didn't bother to look up from his writing. 'It doesn't make any sense. It must be thousands of years old, how can it possibly be standing?'

'I doubt it's standing at all,' I replied. 'Persi said it was underground, so it must be the remains of his house.'

'Well, the ladies were hardly dressed for digging,' he responded tersely.

I assume his hangover was still bothering him.

I stood up. 'I'm going to follow them.'

'Who?'

'Lady Maitland and Genevieve.'

'What?' He finally looked at me. 'Don't be ridiculous, she'll pull a gun. And there's much more to this than we understand, you could jeopardise everything.'

'I'll be careful. I do go stalking you know, I'm not entirely useless.'

'Shooting game in the woods is a world away from following practiced spies through the streets of Damascus!' he countered. 'For heaven's sake, Lennox, don't be so naive.'

'Nonsense.'

'Damn it!' He put his pen down. 'I'll have to come with you.'

Now it was my turn to argue.

'No, you should go and see Persi. Ask her what this secret is about, and the murder, and – well all those questions you've been writing down.'

'I don't think…' He was set for an argument, so I cut him short.

'Swift, someone has to be here. Fontaine will have eyes and ears everywhere, he's bound to know what's going on and he may try to use Persi as a bargaining point.'

'Considering he has her under lock and key, that won't be difficult,' he countered.

'Um, yes.' I hadn't thought of that. 'Well, find a way to smuggle her out.'

'How?'

'I'm sure you'll think of something,' I remarked and strode off to track down the lady spies. I got as far as the bar where Harry Bing was sampling a liquid brunch.

'What ho, old chap,' he called from his stool. 'I've been sacked, you know. Vincent didn't seem to think my lapse was terribly amusing.'

'He's right, it's not funny,' I told him. I declined a drink from the ever attentive bartender. 'Bing?' I leaned over. 'Haven't seen Lady Maitland and Genevieve have you?'

'Upstairs,' he pointed with his thumb. 'Are you sleuthing?'

'Yes, but don't tell anyone.'

Swift had pocketed his notebook and followed me, ready to continue the argument. 'Lennox, I really think you should wait until we've spoken to Persi.'

'No... look, old chap, we agreed.'

'You mean you did.' He sighed in irritation and turned to Harry. 'Bing?'

'What ho, Mr Policeman!' Bing grinned, waving a glass of whisky in Swift's direction.

'Would you go upstairs and distract the guard again.'

'Again? Ha, marvellous! You fellows do know how to have fun, don't you.' He eyed a bowl of fruit over on a marble-topped side table. 'I'm jolly good at juggling you know, as well as miming and acting, not that I'll be doing that any more. I might join a circus.' He wobbled off to gather up some pomegranates from the bowl, and came back with an armful. 'Right. Ready when you are, old bean.'

I spotted the ladies coming down the stairs, they had changed into robust looking loose pants and shirts, although Genevieve still wore the same straw hat. I ducked down into the surrounding jungle of potted plants. Harry followed me into the undergrowth, dropping a pomegranate en route.

'I say, you're taking this very seriously,' he whispered.

'Bing, try to be quiet, would you.'

'Right oh.' He popped up to see what was happening. 'All clear. They've gone.'

I stood up brushing my knees. 'Swift, I'm off,' I told him and aimed for the gateway. I didn't get very far, I was intercepted by Jamal who emerged from a recess.

'Effendi,' he bowed in my path.

'Busy, Jamal.' I tried to sidestep past him.

'Widow number two is here, effendi.' He waved in the direction of the shadows where I could just about make out a figure, draped in black. She looked to be the exact same proportions as yesterday's widow.

'I must apologise for my temerity, effendi. I merely try to honour the wishes you proclaimed.'

'Right, yes, sorry.' I thrust a hand into my pocket, placed a bundle of bills in his fist and escaped into the sunlit streets.

I spotted Genevieve's straw hat through the melee. They were quite a way ahead and I was about to break into a trot when I noticed someone else was on their trail. It was the French sergeant, he was smartly uniformed as usual and peering around a corner with his back to me. I didn't think much of his snooping skills, he stood out like a sore thumb and was gathering curious glances from the local passers-by. I followed in stealthier style.

I hung back a bit, stepping behind pillars and posts, and even a camel at one point, without losing sight of them. We came to the milling throng in the souk where it became much more difficult and I almost lost them. I wove this way and that before glimpsing Genevieve's hat some way off.

They turned a corner with the sergeant still on their trail. I dodged a donkey cart and saw them enter into a lofty archway.

I had to put in a smart stride to catch up, I turned the corner and stopped. Fontaine must have been lying in wait with four gendarmes. The sergeant arrived to join them, just as Fontaine held his hand out for Lady Maitland's gun. I could see her reluctance to part with it and it took even more threats before she handed him the rolled up paper I'd given Persi the night before. Fontaine wasn't stupid, he awaited the delivery of another page, which I guessed was the translation into English.

Hell! I swore under my breath, now what?

There was nothing to be done except report back to Swift.

As I retraced my steps through the souk, I realised I was being followed by the same beggar as yesterday – I thought he must be one of Qarsan's men. I'd read any number of novels where people are followed and the thing to do is move rapidly in one direction and then nip into a dark place, or doorway, and hide.

I put on a spurt and turned out of the market place into a winding street with higgledy-piggedly houses, then executed a nifty sidestep into a shady ginnel and nearly fell over a tethered goat. I peered around the crumbling stone wall to stare back from where I'd come but couldn't see a damn thing. The goat nibbled my jacket, I tried to shoo it off. I counted to one hundred then stepped out of the shadows to find the damn beggar leaning against the wall.

He grinned toothlessly, hopped in front of me and gabbled loudly, then he stuck his fist into his ragged robes and pulled out a bundle of filthy fur.

'No, thank you, old chap,' I politely refused and turned smartly about, but he was quick on the crutch and pivoted into my path again.

'No,' I shouted and shook my head firmly, with my hands up for emphasis.

He jabbered away then prodded the fur.

It squeaked.

That made me stop and stare.

The man was no fool and realised he'd got my attention. He almost stuffed it up my nose in enthusiasm. It squeaked again. I lifted a matted tuft of fluff from the top of the bundle and saw two bright eyes, a small black nose and a pink tongue. It was a puppy.

I let loose a sigh. It proved to be a five dollar puppy, which seemed a lot of money for such a tiny scrap of dog. The beggar was suddenly miraculously cured of most of his afflictions and raced off jabbering and gesticulating in apparent delight – well, at least I'd brought cheer to somebody's day.

It took me some time to retrace my route to the Hotel Al Shami and I re-entered the courtyard hot and sticky. Swift was just coming down the staircase.

'Lennox,' he called.

I didn't reply, just went and handed him the tiny puppy. 'Here, hold this for a moment.'

'What the...?' he began, but I was already on my way to the bar.

Bing was slumped over the mahogany counter singing. 'Good-bye-ee, Good-bye-ee, wipe the tear, baby dear, from your eye-ee'. I grabbed the glass from his grasp, handed it to the bartender and hauled Bing off his stool by the collar. He protested all the way to the fountain and then yelled loudly as I tossed him in.

He caused a tremendous splash. A bevy of shocked servants arrived and formed a small crowd to gaze at him as he flailed in the water. He stopped floundering and sat up, chest-deep in the pool, to stare at me.

'What the devil did you do that for?'

'Because you need to get a grip, Bing,' I told him. 'And you have to stop pandering to your idiotic infatuation for Josephine. She's dead and she was never, ever, worth it.'

He clambered to his knees as the spray from the fountain sprinkled over his head, then, with sodden jacket and trousers, clambered over the wall to stand and face me.

'Lennox.' A puddle formed at his feet as water ran in small rivulets from his hair and clothes. 'Lennox,' he said again and pointed a dripping finger at me. 'If you ever do that again, I promise I will shoot you.'

Swift was still clasping the puppy, a smile playing on his lips.

I took the little tyke from him and held it out to Bing. 'This is yours.'

A waiter arrived with a mop and began swabbing the tiles at his feet.

Bing swayed as he brought the ragged ball of fur into focus. 'What is it?'

It barked a small woof.

He lifted a knot of fluff and raised his brows.

'It's a dog.'

'Yes.'

He leaned in to peer more closely. 'For me?'

'Yes.'

He touched the filthy fur. It tried to lick his hand.

'I've never had a dog before.' He reached out and stroked the matted knots away from its head. 'What should I do with it?' He asked gazing into its bright little eyes.

'You will bathe it, feed it, care for it, and teach it the basics.' I told him. 'And if you touch one more drop of liquor I will remove it from you and render the wrath of Heaven down upon your bloody head.'

'Right o,' he agreed and took the bundle very gently from my grasp and clasped it to his soggy chest. 'Thank you.'

He shuffled off, closely followed by the waiter with the mop.

Swift came to stand next to me and we watched Bing climb the stairs with his new charge.

'Lennox,' he said.

'What?'

'Come on, you deserve a drink.'

'Make it a large one,' I said, and grinned.

The barman placed two tall gin and tonics on the counter almost as we said it. He really was an excellent chap.

'What happened?' Swift said.

'They've been arrested, or detained anyway.' I told him what I'd seen.

'Bloody hell,' he swore quietly.

'What about Persi?' I asked.

'They've put two guards on duty, one at each end of the corridor.' He sipped his drink. 'I opened the door from the inner stairs and came face to face with the new man. He raised his sword and almost cleaved the door in two as I made a quick exit.' He gave a grim smile.

'Oh.' I took a draught of my drink, savouring it.

Swift continued, 'I saw you with Jamal. I had a word with him after you left.'

'About what?' I asked.

'The widows or rather one of them. I've got an idea.' He finished his drink, stood up, tightened the belt of his trench coat and marched off. 'I told Jamal to meet me in the roof garden.'

I downed my drink and followed.

Jamal was awaiting us with today's black clad widow hovering at a distance. I could hear her puffing in the heat.

'Jamal,' Swift began and then explained in unnecessarily lengthy detail that the lady must go to Persi's room, hand over the veils, and allow her to escape. Jamal translated. I lost interest and went to stare over the city rooftops. The fat chap in white was on the neighbouring roof, he sat up in his day bed when he saw me and watched in anticipation for whatever I may do next. I waved, he raised a hand back, then I returned to join Swift in his negotiations.

'The lady has agreed to do it!' Swift told me in triumph.

'Hum,' I replied, looking down at the widow's sandals just visible below the hemline. She wore socks, one of which had a hole in the toe. I can't say I am noted for my skills of observation, but to my mind, very few ladies have hairy feet. I stepped forward and ripped the veil from her head.

'Argh,' the bath-draw boy gasped in guilty horror.

'You!' Jamal stepped back, pointing an accusing finger. 'You are not dead!' he yelled in English then reverted to his mother tongue and let all hell loose.

There was a lot of shouting, probably some swearing, and plenty of drama. I noticed the fat man on the other roof had clambered to his feet to stare in our direction.

'Enough!' Swift eventually shouted. 'Jamal, you can deal with this later.' He turned to the bath-draw boy, who had become very red in the face. 'I want some answers from you first.'

'Not now, Swift,' I told him. 'We must get Persi out.'

Swift swore. 'Right, damn it! Jamal make him go and exchange himself for Persi. And don't let him go until we get back.'

'He is not leaving anywhere, effendi. He will remain in Ladies Row.' Jamal raised a finger at the accused. 'And after that, you will know the wrath of our master!'

I handed the veil over, and Jamal made the bath-draw boy drape it back over his head. Hastened along by the furious factotum, he stomped, off muttering under his breath.

It took almost fifteen minutes. We were anxiously peering over the bannister when Jamal re-appeared at the top of the staircase, followed by an apparition in black. A slim hand reached up to pull the veil away. It was Persi, she gave a huge grin. I picked her up and hugged her.

We laughed, even Jamal cheered up and we sent him off with hearty thanks. I didn't even remind him about getting my dollars back.

'She, or rather he, came in and pushed a pile of towels into my hands.' Persi related. 'Then he started struggling with his robes and I couldn't understand what on earth was happening.' She laughed again. 'And as he dragged the robes higher, I caught a sight of his underwear! I was about to shout for the guard when he wiggled out of the frock and I realised it was that funny little man.'

'Bandy legs and all!' I laughed and put my arm around her shoulders.

'Exactly and a far clearer view than I needed!' She exclaimed. 'Then he told me to put the dress on and come up here. I thought it must be your idea, I couldn't imagine anyone else thinking of such a harebrained idea!'

We found it all very amusing, but then we told her about Fontaine's ambush, which wasn't amusing at all.

'Do you have the directions, Persi?' I asked.

'Yes, I made my own copy,' she pulled a rolled up piece of paper and showed us. It didn't make much more sense than the Phoenician squiggles.

'We'll have to go,' I said. 'If the Colonel finds it first, we won't have anything to negotiate with.'

'You must take me with you, darling.'

'No,' Swift interjected. 'It could be dangerous and you will be breaking your terms of arrest. I insist you remain here.'

'Oh nonsense. You won't find it without me,' she told him. 'Even with the translation.'

'Why?'

'I made a mistake.'

'What sort of mistake?' Swift asked.

'It was the name of the fountain. I've sent them to the wrong place.'

'You mean, you've given Lady Maitland the wrong location?' I asked.

'Yes, that's what I just said!'

'Ha!' I kissed her on the cheek. 'Well done, old stick! I mean, dearest... erm...sweet... thing.'

'Wait, it's not...' Swift began then stopped. 'Oh, very well – lead the way, Persi.'

She laughed delightedly, then pulled the veil back over her head. 'Come on.'

Swift tightened the belt of his trench coat and we headed for the stairs.

CHAPTER 20

'The locals are watching us,' Swift hissed to me as we followed the black swathed form of Persi through the crowds.

'Swift, they are always watching us,' I told him.

'But everyone will know where we go,' he whispered.

I didn't bother to reply because they probably knew where we were going before we did.

Finding the Temple of Jupiter wasn't terribly difficult. I'd passed through its remnants on my travels to the souk, although I hadn't realised it at the time.

The huge entrance supported an arch and some perilously perched stones. The roof had long been demolished and the temple resembled a colonnaded market place – it even housed stalls between the rows of pillars. I looked up to spot the remains of delicate mosaics clinging to some of the highest stonework. The capitals topping each of the columns were intricately carved with leafy fronds, eroded fruit and curling tendrils. Many of them were cracked and broken in places.

'Hurry up, Lennox,' Swift called. 'Persi's gone through there.'

I strode to catch up as he pulled open a low door and ducked into it.

I blinked. We were in a cavelike chamber lit by two flaming torches held in iron cradles, driven into mouldering walls. A snarling carved lion's head splattered water into a stone basin. The room was filled with a mist of fine droplets which settled on our hair and clothes. The vaulted ceiling ran with condensation; green algae and moss clung to the stones and plasterwork – the place smelled like the bottom of a well. We had to raise our voices over the racket of the streaming torrent to be heard.

'This is it!' Persi threw off the black robes to reveal her archaeologists' garb of cream shirt and dull green trousers beneath. 'This is where the directions in the spiral start.' Her eyes shone with excitement.

'So, where did you instruct Lady Maitland to go?' Swift spoke above the noise.

'The Roman Lion fountain,' she replied.

'And this is…?' I asked.

'The font of the Roman lion,' she answered. 'But I think Fontaine will be able to work it out before long.'

'Are there many Roman fountains in the city?' I asked.

'Enough,' she laughed. 'Now, according to the directions, we go this way.' She stepped through an opening on the other side of the fountain, then halted again. 'Oh, I'm such an idiot! I forgot to bring a flashlight.'

'I have one,' I told her and fumbled in my pocket to give it to her.

'So do I, but I think it's best to keep them for later.' Swift said. 'Here, we'll take these.' He pulled the flaming torches from their sconces, handed one to her and the other to me.

Persi led the way along an unlit passage. The walls were formed from rough stones, slick, wet and slimy with the all-pervading smell of damp. The corridor ended at a set of uneven steps, which wound tightly downwards. I could hear scuttling somewhere below and swore to myself because I really hated rats.

'Down here,' she whispered, holding up the burning torch. We followed tentatively.

'Hell!' I let out a yell as a snake slithered out of a cranny next to me. I stepped back smartly as it plopped onto the steps to wind its way between our feet and down into the darkness beyond.

'Persi?' Swift had stopped. 'That snake wasn't poisonous was it?'

'It was a blunt-nosed viper and it's quite deadly,' she replied without breaking tread. 'But if you don't bother them, they will usually leave you alone.'

We went more slowly after that, keeping close together and nearly bumping into Persi when she came to a stop.

'In here,' she said quietly and entered a cave-like hollow. 'It's the Chamber of Tears.'

She raised her torch to illuminate the roof. A needle-like crystal protruded from the dark-red rock forming the ceiling.

'The water dripping from the needlepoint falls into this hollow below,' she moved the torch toward our feet where we could see a round hole in the sodden rock. 'It never fills up, the water has been falling for so many centuries that it has eroded its way through the stone and into the ruins below.'

'Have you been here before, Persi?' I asked, forgetting to call her dearest, or darling or some such.

'No, but I have read papers by archaeologists who've explored these tunnels.'

'But they didn't find Hanno's house?' I asked.

'If they had, we wouldn't be here,' she laughed.

I gazed upward once again, then looked down to realise she had vanished.

I froze. 'Where is she?'

'She's through here,' Swift hissed then scrambled under a hole, hacked out near the base of the wall. I crawled after him.

It was almost beyond words. Persi was standing some way ahead, her flaming torch creating a halo of light within the cavernous dark. She was standing amidst row upon row of sarcophagi. I gasped, then moved to take a closer look. The ancient coffins were carved from pale limestone, rectangular in shape and about six feet by three wide and the same in height. They were all covered with closed lids.

We were in what appeared to be a huge underground cave, supported by columns of chipped rock rising to a ceiling lost somewhere in the blackness. None of us breathed a word, we just absorbed the sight.

'They're tombs.' Swift broke the silence, his voice echoing away into the stillness.

'Yes, Roman tombs.' Persi strode over to the group nearest us. 'This quarry lies beneath the old city, it would have provided building stone until it was exhausted and abandoned. The Romans turned it into catacombs for the dead.'

'I thought they usually buried their dead outside their cities?' Swift said.

'They did,' Persi replied. 'But as the power of the Empire waned it became too dangerous to go beyond the walls and they used what space they had underground.'

'Look at these,' Swift had walked over to the far wall where hollows had been carved into the rock like sets of pigeon holes. Names were carved on plaques in precise Roman lettering.

'They would have held ashes in urns, but it looks like they've been stolen,' Persi informed him.

'Tomb-robbers,' I remarked.

'I'm afraid so,' she nodded. 'Oh dear, I'm not sure where to go from here.' She pulled out her sheet of paper and tried to study it one-handed.

Swift came to take her flaming torch and we huddled together to stare at the translation she had made.

'What does it say?' Swift asked.

'Descend the tomb of the revellers,' she showed us with a finger on the paper. It was about a third of the way into the spiral.

I heard the doubt in her voice.

'You are sure it says 'descend the tomb', old stick?'

'No, not entirely, darling. I think we should search for

a carving depicting feasting or something.' She and Swift set off to examine the outsides of the sarcophagi.

'Right o. Erm... dearest,' I called out, but too late because she was moving rapidly along the line of tombs.

I paused to regard a figure on horseback, he was finely dressed in toga and sandals which fascinated me because they were exquisitely detailed. So was the horse's bridle but the chap had neither saddle nor stirrups, which must have been jolly uncomfortable. A light layer of dust lay over the whole and I stroked some off, feeling the smooth cold stone through my fingers.

'Lennox, what are you doing?' Swift called back at me.

I ignored him. They were both quite a long way ahead, but I had another trail to follow. The floor was covered with a thick layer of dust, too powdery to define our footsteps into anything more than undulating dents. But I could tell that someone had been in here with a stick because the point had left a distinct dotted track in the fine residue. I thought it was probably one of the tomb-robbers and I'd have carried a stick too if I'd known about the snakes. I followed the track to the very tomb we were looking for.

The carving was indeed a mass of revellers having a marvellous time – some of them had even kept their clothes on. Goblets of wine, trays of delicacies and bowls of whatnots were held in hands or at the feet of the cavorting figures. There were depictions of amphora, laden tables, draped beds and couches too; I imagined the departed resident had been fond of good times.

I took a look around, no dust had been disturbed on the stone figures but it was evident the top had been moved. I swivelled it aside to open a gap.

'Over here,' I called to the others then peered into its dark interior before stepping smartly backwards. Something was moving inside, I could just make out writhing shadows in the light of my torch.

'Scorpions,' Persi muttered as she arrived to shine her own flame down onto a mass of shiny brown bodies with scrabbling legs and tails curled in threat.

'I was expecting bones,' I said as we stared at the creatures, some of them almost three inches long.

'So was I,' Persi replied. 'Someone must have put the scorpions in there.'

'Qarsan, or one of his men,' I guessed.

'Look,' Persi pointed her torch downwards.

We looked. As the scorpions moved away from the flames they exposed a rope attached to an iron ring.

'It's a trap door,' Swift said. 'But it's impossible to reach. We need a hook, or a lever.'

'Even if we could open it, what about the scorpions?' I asked.

'Perhaps they'll fall down into whatever is beneath the tomb?' Persi replied.

I tried pushing the sarcophagus, it didn't move.

'Shh,' Swift hissed suddenly. 'Voices.'

'French,' Persi said quietly.

'Fontaine,' I whispered.

I doubled over the side of the tomb and set the flames

of my torch onto the scorpions. They scrambled around in panic as I chased them with the fire. First one, then the rest, found a small crack in the stone work and they each scuttled through and away into the darkness.

'Well done!' Swift whispered.

Persi reached down and yanked up the trap door up by the rope.

'Come on.' She climbed in and went straight into the black hole below. I must say she was a very plucky lady.

Swift went next. I climbed inside and bent double to manoeuvre the lid of the tomb back into place. I hoped it would give us a march on the French.

A steep ladder, wet and slimy to the touch, led downwards. Persi and Swift were already some way ahead and I paused to listen, hearing the echo of dripping water from somewhere far away. Apart from my torch and Persi's in the distance, it was as black as night and the surrounding darkness felt like a smothering shroud closing around me. My heart sank. Swift and I had been trapped in a dungeon not long ago and the horror had not left me.

'Come on, Heathcliff,' Persi called from a distance. I could see her torch light and hastened to catch up.

'We're in an older level of the quarry,' Persi said as we followed a muddy path. Clear footprints ahead proved someone else had passed this way not too long before.

I held my own torch above my head, the flames picked out dim shapes of massive stone blocks. There were scratching noises, but I ignored them.

'I think this was abandoned when there was an earth-quake.' Persi led on.

'Earthquake?' Swift and I stopped in our tracks.

'Yes, there was a description of a terrible one centuries ago which killed thousands and brought down hundreds of houses,' she replied matter of factly, then pointed. 'Look there's an opening!'

It was a wide gateway, formed from white stone quoins, fixed with the rusted remains of hinges, the wooden doors long since rotted away. We followed the footsteps in the mud and came out onto a stone jetty, overhanging a canal, which gave us pause to stare.

We were in a tunnel formed from dark red bricks. They were around two inches in depth and held in place with crumbling mortar. Even I could recognise Roman construction when faced with it.

'I'm so thankful this is here.' Persi knelt on the cold stones of the jetty to pull in a raft of half-rotted logs, lashed together with thick rope. It was tied to a verdigris corroded brass ring by a line which looked fairly new – unlike the rickety raft.

'Didn't you know it would be here?' I asked.

'No, I thought we'd have to swim,' she replied.

I shone my flaming torch in an arc and realised there was no path or any means to walk beside the watercourse, the canal simply lapped up to the base of the brick walls. I looked into the water, it was difficult to say what depth it was, but by the sluggish flow of murk, I'd say at least a man's height.

'Did she mean that?' Swift whispered.

I shrugged, thankful that we didn't have to find out.

The structure held my fascination. The arching top of the tunnel was some fifteen or more feet above our heads and slicked with slime and moisture. In some places, the brickwork gave way to dressed stone walls; they looked like the remains of houses. There were rusted iron pulley systems trailing lengths of perished rope fixed above unglazed windows cut neatly into the stone; I half expected someone to poke their head out to see what the noise was about. I assumed the Roman engineers had simply incorporated them into the underground canal.

'Is it an aqueduct?' Swift's voice echoed along the tunnel and into the distance.

'Yes, but its origins aren't Roman,' Persi replied while pushing a finger into the rotted wood of the raft to test it. 'The Arabs made tunnels called Qanats all over Persia, they were built to bring water from the oasis outside the cities to feed wells and fountains. They're truly ancient.' She looked around. 'This one must have been rebuilt many times.'

A loud plop sounded and we looked over at the water's surface where rings rippled outwards. A rat swam downstream, away from us. A snake uncurled itself from a hollow in the opposite wall and slid into the flow in leisurely pursuit.

'What are those buildings?' Swift had taken his battery-powered torch from his pocket and shone the beam onto the wall opposite.

'Cool rooms or laundries,' Persi replied. 'They would have been basements belonging to the houses which once stood above here.' She clambered onto the raft, it swayed alarmingly.

'Look at that, Lennox,' Swift was still aiming his hand torch around.

I looked. There was a mosaic on the wall of a blue pool with green crocodiles showing large teeth in gaping jaws.

'That'll teach us to frighten Greggs with tales of scorpions, snakes and crocodiles,' I remarked.

We laughed then swung around as we heard shouting in the quarry behind us. Damn it! It was Fontaine and his men.

CHAPTER 21

'Quickly,' Persi waved for us to get aboard.

Swift and I hesitated.

'Come on,' she urged.

The voices in the quarry grew louder and we scrambled on, the blasted boat almost overturned as we shifted to balance. It was barely wide enough for us all kneeling one closely behind the other like three little Indians.

Persi untied the rope from its mooring and began paddling with her hands to propel us in the direction the rat and snake had gone.

'Just a minute, Persi,' I told her. There was something stuck under the logs, I yanked it out, it looked like a flattened cricket bat. 'Found an oar.'

Swift held both the flaming torches while I provided propulsion at the rear. We made quite a few yards before Fontaine raced onto the jetty followed by more men armed with lanterns and guns.

'Arretez!' He yelled, pulled out his revolver and aimed it at us.

I paddled like fury as Persi peered round at him. He

fired a shot over our heads making us duck and causing a reverberating racket to rattle through the tunnel. We rowed hell for leather around a bend and out of his range and laughed because we'd flummoxed the bloody French.

'Where are we going?' Swift asked as we passed beneath a miasma of old cobwebs strung from mildewed bricks.

'The house of Hanno,' Persi replied with a note of glee. 'Look for the sign of the ship with the horse's head.'

We paddled on as the smell of mould and decay enveloped us. Cold water dripped onto our heads from the roof and our flames sent shadows writhing along the walls beside us. The only sound we could hear was the oar dipping in and out of the water and the occasional scuffle and splash of creatures in the dark. We followed the canal past more basements, some had been reduced to ruin, others were more or less intact, it was like a subterranean Venice, but long since abandoned.

'There, look!' Persi broke into the silence and pointed upwards.

It was a faded blue mural of the image I'd seen on the back of the medallion, only larger and more easily defined. The ship had been painted with two rudders, a single billowing sail and a cresting horse's head on the prow.

I stopped paddling and sat back to drift to the foot of the building. It was in better condition than most, with neatly dressed stones fashioned with enough skill to stand the test of millennia.

There were two window openings set high in the wall above us.

'I can't see a handhold or cleat,' I said as the raft bumped against the building's base.

'I think I can reach...' Persi stood up, wobbling the boat again as she did. She tried to jump and grab the sill of the nearest window, but missed and nearly threw us all into the water.

'Persi!' Swift shouted. 'Sit down. Please, let me do it.'

She was about to argue, but he shoved the torches into her hands, knelt upright, tightened the belt of his trench coat and started giving out orders.

'Lennox, paddle close to the wall, then when I say 'brace', you must brace.'

'Swift...' I began to protest but he was having none of it.

'Just row!' he said.

I rowed.

'Brace!' he yelled.

We prepared ourselves as he clambered to his feet and made a leap for the window ledge. His sudden propulsion caused the raft to shoot to the other side of the canal, despite my furious paddling. Persi twisted round to stare as we lurched perilously on the rotten logs.

'I said brace!' Swift dangled with arms fully extended and feet floundering some way above the water line.

I cursed under my breath while rowing back to the wall. How the hell did he expect us to brace on a bloody raft!

I steered underneath him. He managed to put a foot on my shoulder and kick upwards to clamber in through the window. The force of his leap sent us and the raft back across the damn canal again.

I paddled back.

'Hand me the torches, please, Persi,' Swift leaned as far as he could from the window.

She passed them up, almost on her tiptoes to reach. He took them and tossed them somewhere inside, then came back and extended an arm down.

'Come on Persi, grab my hands.'

She prepared to jump.

Swift shouted, 'Brace, Lennox.'

'Swift, will you stop telling me to brace!'

'Ready,' Persi said and stepped onto my shoulder. Her boots dug into my neck then she leapt upwards, causing the raft, and me, to shoot back to the other side of the bloody canal again. I hit the wall on the opposite bank with a thud and swore, then I paddled back in the bloody dark because they had both the torches and the lanterns.

'Lennox,' Swift shouted again. 'Come on.'

'Oh, it's simply marvellous!' I heard Persi exclaim from within the room.

'Pass the rope,' Swift ordered.

'Wait a damn minute, will you.' I had to fish about to find it and drag it out of the water where it had fallen, fortunately it was still tied to one of the logs. 'It's too short to throw and there's nowhere to tether it.'

He stared down at me, his face silhouetted from the torchlight behind him.

'If you stand up and throw yourself at the window ledge you should be able to make it.'

I didn't reply, I was judging the distance. It was beyond my reach but, if I made a good jump...

I stood up, took a deep breath, wobbled, leapt with all my might, almost reached Swift's hand then fell with an almighty splash into the water.

I was right, it was deeper than a man's height, absolutely bloody freezing and as black as death. My feet touched mud on the bottom and for a moment I felt as though it were sucking me down. I kicked back, swept my arms forward and rose to the surface gasping for breath.

'Lennox,' Swift was yelling. 'Grab the rope.'

'What?' I spluttered. I couldn't see a damn thing for water running down my face and the raft had disappeared somewhere into the darkness.

'Heathcliff, I found a rope, can you reach it?' Persi called. She had extended her arm out of the window while holding a torch. Swift was clutching one end of a thick knotted line which he dangled out of the window. I swam for it, and grasped it in my hands. Water poured from my hair into my eyes and mouth – it tasted foul and stank like a London sewer.

Hell and damnation! I cursed as I slowly pulled myself up the rope to clamber and fall over the sill and into the room.

Persi smiled delightedly as I lay in a thick layer of sand, trying to catch my breath. 'Well done, darling!'

'You've lost the raft,' Swift said.

'Swift,' I panted, then stumbled to my feet, intent on giving him a piece of my mind – then I caught sight of the walls.

'Good Lord,' I muttered.

'It's the house, darling. Hanno's house, isn't it extraordinary.' Persi had turned to stare at the images painted on the walls as I dripped puddles onto the sand.

She was right, it was breathtaking. From floor to ceiling, on each of the four walls, there were paintings in bright colours of people going about their daily tasks. Men in little more than loincloths were carrying crates and barrels in a procession to waiting ships. Ladies strolled along under stylised parasols, followed by musicians playing instruments. I could make out flutes, lyres, bells and even castanets. A number of scantily clad women wore elaborate head-dresses and carried fans of feathers while another group bore jugs upon their heads. I joined Swift and Persi to stare more closely at the details.

'You would think it was made yesterday,' Swift remarked, his arms folded while he gazed at hunters on horseback, hounds racing along at their feet. One man held a hawk on his wrist while a splendidly robed fellow held a leopard on a leash.

'What does it mean, Persi… um dear?' I asked.

She shrugged. 'Life. The life of the Phoenicians of the time, and their trade. Here.' She raised a finger to indicate a ship piled high with amphora and bales of wrapped cloth. 'This is their cargo and on this dock here…' She moved her finger to what appeared to be a wooden jetty. '...they're unloading baskets of rocks which look like silver and tin. And this man here is weighing something against gold coins on a balance.'

I leaned in for a better view of the details, the coins had indeed been gilded with gold. In fact, all the figures were delicately picked out with intricate detail in red, white, green, purple, blue, silver and all the usual hues. It must have taken months, if not years, to complete the fresco. Each figure held a different feature or expression.

'And here,' she moved her finger to a picture of workers painting black tar onto upturned boats. 'Look at how they're mending their ships.'

'Persi?' I asked.

'Yes?'

'This is extraordinary, but I still don't understand why everyone is so keen to find this house.'

'Don't you see?'

'No,' Swift and I answered as one.

She smiled then spun around, as a loud thud suddenly reverberated from the ceiling.

'What...?' I began and stepped backwards, pulling Persi with me against the far wall.

There was a squared off area in the ceiling, I assume it had once given onto an opening above, but had been sealed off. A crack ran across its plastered surface as another thud fell, more heavily this time, causing chunks of whitewashed stucco to fall to the floor. The next one broke a hole in the centre of the square, followed by a beam of light and then clouds of dust which set us choking.

'Encore.' It was Fontaine, he was ordering another strike of a huge mallet.

Another blow opened a gap large enough for the men above to peer through. As the dust and debris fell I could see the face of the Colonel staring down.

'And so,' he said as he lowered himself to the ground, his feet falling softly in the sand. 'We find the English here.' He almost smiled. 'Vennez,' he called up to his men.

I heard them scrambling to line up ready to descend.

'Fontaine…' I began.

'You really are most persistent, Major.' He nodded his head toward me, then turned to Swift. 'Inspector, and of course, the charmante Mademoiselle Carruthers.' He made a neat bow in her direction.

I ran fingers through my hair to try to dislodge the dust but that made it worse because it was stickily wet from my dunking in the canal.

'Fontaine…' I began again but didn't get very far.

'Charles!' Persi shouted in shock.

A tall, slim man had lowered himself through the hole in the ceiling. He wore a near immaculate linen suit with a pale tie and a blue silk handkerchief folded precisely in the top pocket. He smiled, strode two steps to Persi and picked her up in his arms to swing her around, laughing as he did.

Langton! And he didn't look to be anywhere near death's door.

'But… but Charles,' she stuttered, 'you're fine. I thought you were in prison. They said you were held in the cells below the citadel. They said you were terribly ill and weakening by the day.'

Langton frowned. 'Rather an exaggeration by the Frogs, darling girl. I think they were pulling your strings.'

'But where have you been?' she almost wailed, aghast at his perfectly fit appearance and the realisation she had been duped.

'Held at Fontaine's leisure in the old Embassy building. Impossible to get any word out; he had me under lock and key.' He smiled at her with perfect teeth in a smooth handsome face. He had dark eyes under thick black hair, only lightly layered by the dust now settling around us.

'You damned…' I growled and took a step toward him.

'No,' Persi rushed forward to hold me back.

'Lennox,' Swift warned.

'Ah, you must be Persi's hero, the fabulous flying Major. Fontaine's told me all about you.' Langton made an extravagant bow. 'Well done, old chap! Bravo.'

I couldn't tell if he was mocking me or not and I glowered at him while water dripped down my face.

Persi looked up at me with pleading eyes. 'I'm so dreadfully sorry. I never would have called Swift had I known. Oh, and you've come such a long way…' Her lips trembled as she bit back a sob.

I put a hand out to gather her to me but her temper suddenly flared and she spun around to confront Langton.

'What are you doing here, Charles? Are you helping them?' Her eyes flashed in fury.

'Mademoiselle,' Fontaine addressed her, 'we have brought Monsieur Langton here because the instructions from Lady Maitland were incomprehensible. He only agreed to help when we informed him we were holding you under arrest.'

'Yes, exactly, darling.' Langton took a step closer to her. 'He unlocked my room, told me to get a move on. He said I had to co-operate or he'd prosecute you and I for conspiracy to murder. Then he handed me a paper written in Phoenician'

'I don't believe a damn word of it.' I growled.

Persi cut in. 'It's true, Charles is an archaeologist too, Lennox. That's how we met, it was before the war.' Her eyes flicked between Langton and me.

She called me Lennox. I watched her and my heart sank.

'Right, well damn it!' I would have sworn a lot worse if Persi hadn't been present. 'Come on, Swift. We may as well go.'

'One moment,' Fontaine held up his gloved hand. 'I'm afraid we cannot allow anyone to leave until we have the map.'

'What map?' I demanded.

'The map of Hanno the Navigator, of course,' Fontaine replied. 'Where is it?'

Silence fell as we realised there wasn't an image of a map anywhere in the room.

'I was assured it would be here,' Fontaine frowned, a note of warning in his voice.

'Fontaine,' I said. 'I will tell you where it is, if you give your word to drop all charges against Miss Carruthers and let us leave.'

All attention switched to me as a hush fell.

Fontaine came over, his leather boots scuffing the sand. 'You know the whereabouts of the map, Major?'

'Your word, Fontaine,' I demanded.

'If you provide the map, then yes,' he replied. 'But, I will not allow a murderer to go free.'

'Nor will I,' I said. 'Do I have your word?'

'You have my word of honour,' he agreed.

'Very well,' I said and scraped my shoe to push the clumps of wet sand away from under my feet. 'It's here.'

He looked down. As the water had dripped from my clothes and boots into the sand I had caught a glimpse of colour and thought it could be a mosaic floor. I had gambled it was his map.

Swift laughed quietly as Fontaine rapped out orders in French. Two more men dropped through the hole in the ceiling armed with small collapsible spades. They began shovelling the sand and depositing it out of the windows.

Swift came to stand beside me. 'Well done, Lennox.' He gave me a grin.

'I still don't understand why they are all so keen on it,' I replied, watching the men at work.

'We'd better ask Persi.' He looked in her direction, she was pushing sand aside with her hands to reveal a section of detailed map. I could make out red and black lines crossing blue seas and green coloured coasts decorated with palm trees. As Persi and the men shovelled, more images appeared; there were towers and castles representing ancient towns and cities. Ports appeared illustrated with tiny ships and even lighthouses. It was as fascinating as the images on the walls and almost as detailed.

'Persi,' I called.

She stopped. 'Oh, I am sorry.' She stood up and came to join us. 'Everything seems to be happening so quickly it's all quite confusing.'

'Persi, will you please tell us why this map is so important.' I asked.

She looked up at me and smiled. 'It's quite simple, darling. It's oil.'

CHAPTER 22

'What!' I exclaimed.

Persi laughed. 'The Phoenicians traded oil, or rather asphaltum, as it was called. They bought it from desert tribes who gathered it from tar seeps.'

'Petroleum!' Swift exclaimed. 'So that's it! Good God, of course! The governments want to find the source of the asphaltum because there could be oil fields in the desert.'

'Ah,' I said, realising the importance at last, then thinking how remarkable it was that a map over two thousand years old could hold such valuable knowledge.

'Ici,' Fontaine was shouting at his men, shovelling the sand away as quickly as possible. He was pointing at the floor in the centre of the room.

I raised my brows in question to Persi, as we watched the frantic activity.

'It's the part of the map covering Syria,' she half whispered. 'They're looking for reserves in territory under French control.'

Langton had gone to another part of the room and was pushing sand aside with his shoes.

'And he's looking in British territory?' I said.

'Yes,' she laughed. 'Neither of them seem to be having much luck.'

'What do you think the oil seeps will look like?' Swift asked her, watching as carefully as we were.

'Like the black stones in the medallion,' Persi replied.

'Oh, so that's what they were!' I realised. 'Good Lord, it's all rather clever.'

Persi smiled. 'It is, isn't it.'

I turned my gaze from the men shifting sand to regard her, and wondered just how much she already knew.

'Erm, Persi,' Swift began. 'Perhaps you could explain the lines and symbols?' He had tugged his notebook out of his pocket and was poised with pen, ready to make notes.

'Of course,' her face lit up, she was delighted to discuss ancient history. 'Hanno was an explorer and he made this map showing all the countries known to the Phoenician people. He also included the origins of the traded goods and the routes along which they passed. Look – that's Damascus.' She pointed to where Fontaine was standing, I could see an image in the mosaic similar to the 'dead camel' on the medallion. 'And the red line running west is the trade route from Damascus to the Phoenician ports of Tyre, Byblos and Sidon. From there they would have crossed the Mediterranean to Rome, Greece and Europe, which we should see once the sand has been removed from those areas.'

She stepped across to the other side of the room away from the shovelling French. 'Now, if you follow the red line travelling east...' She pointed to the bright mosaic tiles leaving Damascus. '...it leads to Babylon – which is this collection of towers here.'

She knelt and placed a finger on the spot, then began brushing sand away where it still lay untouched. 'Babylon was the terminus of the Silk Road. You can see how the red line continues eastwards, it would have gone all the way to China. But, what is more important is...' She leaned forward, strands of blonde hair escaping her bun as she swept more sand aside with her hands, '... this black line running south out of Babylon and down to the Persian Gulf. You can see here how the route is shown running through the Gulf, which would be the track taken by trading ships, as they went from one port to another. This is Kuwait and, if you look further south, there's a port called Gerrah.' She pointed to a city motif on the West coast, then continued, 'It's a fabled city, said to be one of the richest of antiquity.'

She was still pushing sand away from the bright stones set in the floor. 'Ha, look, these are the oil seeps!' She suddenly laughed, pointing to a large number of black spots just inland from Gerrah.

'Where?' Langton had been listening and strode over. 'Show me.'

Fontaine spun around too.

'Isn't that Bahrain?' Swift asked, pointing to an island just off Gerrah.

'Damn it!' Langton swore.

'Merde,' Fontaine followed suit.

I deduced that the area was outside both British and French influence.

'There are more here.' Persi had gone back to sweep sand aside from the route of the black line. 'Look at Basra, west of Kuwait – see!' She showed us more black stones. 'That proves it. Oil has already been discovered around Basra.'

Swift stood back to make rapid sketches of the area and locations in his notebook.

'What about the south-west coast, opposite Bahrain?' I asked.

'They are all Arabian,' Persi told me. 'They're controlled by the local tribes and there are wars in many of these areas.'

'Must be rather a disappointment,' I remarked, noting the two men's scowls.

'Perhaps for their ambitions,' she replied. 'But this room is still a marvel of antiquity.' She flashed another smile. 'I couldn't be more thrilled.'

I was about to put an arm around her shoulder and give her a hug when bloody Langton came back over.

'What a colossal waste of time and effort!' He complained. 'It will take years of negotiating with the Arabs to gain access to these sites.'

Fontaine was scowling down at the black stones set in the mosaic. 'And they will continue their game of playing one nation off against another.'

'What about the gold?' Langton said scanning the mosaic, now half-cleared by the gendarmes.

'Here,' Persi pointed to an area in the mosaic where a small square of gold had been implanted next to a much larger one of copper. 'It's the mines in the Timna Valley, South of the Dead Sea. But they have already been explored, Charles, there's nothing left there. The ancients valued them as highly as we do; they were dug to exhaustion a long time ago.'

'Leave now,' Fontaine turned on us.

'But…,' Persi began to argue.

Fontaine snapped something in French to his sergeant, who had been supervising the installation of a ladder under the hole in the ceiling.

The sergeant came over, his hand on his gun holster.

'Fontaine there is really no need…' I protested.

'Colonel, please,' Persi pleaded. 'May I remain to examine the walls? It may be the only chance I ever have.'

His stern expression softened a touch. 'Very well. You may remain, Mademoiselle. And your Monsieur Langton will stay too. But, you…' He indicated to Swift and me. 'Allez.'

'No, I'm not leaving Miss Carruthers,' I argued. 'You've already kidnapped Lady Maitland and Genevieve, and held Persi under false pretences. I don't trust you a damned inch, Fontaine.'

'The English ladies have been released and, as you can see, your Mademoiselle has not been marched back to captivity. She has been allowed her liberty, despite the charge of murder against her.'

'Are you going to arrest her again?' I demanded.

237

'I will keep my word, Major, but you must leave now,' Fontaine sounded suddenly weary and nodded to the sergeant who took a step closer.

'Lennox,' Swift pushed his notebook into his trench coat pocket. 'We need to get back.'

I turned to Persi.

'I'll be fine,' she said. 'I will see you at the hotel, darling.' She came to me and stood on tiptoe to kiss my cheek.

'Right,' I beamed. I ignored Langton's scowl, gave her a farewell wave and followed Swift to climb the ladder through the hole in the ceiling.

We traced the route of destruction made by the French. It was evident they had simply knocked their way through ancient walls and rooms until they had found us. We were led by lantern light back to the Roman fountain and left to make our own way to the Al Shami. I was still wet, my shoes squelched and I hadn't had lunch.

'What ho, Swift, and you too, Lennox,' Bing hailed us as we trailed into the hotel courtyard. 'Ha, did someone throw you in a fountain too?' He laughed at my soggy appearance.

I muttered under my breath.

'Look.' He came over, opened his bulging jacket and carefully extracted the puppy. 'I've given him a haircut!'

The puppy had indeed had a haircut, or rather had chunks of fluff snipped from him. His white fur was very short in parts and overlong in others. Swift and I both laughed at the raggedy appearance as the pup peered at us below unevenly cut brows. He had small ears, one up, one down. His brown eyes shone bright with excitement and he had a little whip of a tail, which wagged furiously.

'What did you trim him with, sheep shears?' I asked, as I ruffled tufts of fur on his head.

'Or nail scissors?' Swift added, smiling and tickling the little dog under its chin.

'Ha! Well deduced, Inspector,' Bing laughed. 'It was all I had and it was jolly difficult snipping the knots. I was terrified I was going to cut him, poor little mite. I'm just off to take him for a stroll around the garden.' He took a length of curtain cord from his pocket, looped it gently around the pup's neck and put him on the floor.

'Does he have a name yet?' I asked, pleased to see the care Bing was taking.

'Napoleon.' Bing grinned.

'A big name for a little dog,' Swift replied.

Bing laughed. 'He's my antidote to Josephine.'

'Oh, my goodness, look Auntie M!' Genevieve appeared from the direction of the stairs. 'What an adorable little doggie! Oh, Mr Bing may I see him?' She came over, her cheeks flushed with genuine delight.

She was full of questions and shot them at a proud Bing as she bent over to make a fuss of little Napoleon. The puppy jumped about on its hind legs, squeaking with joy.

Lady Maitland joined us.

'I see Fontaine has let you out,' I remarked to her.

'Evidently, Major Lennox,' she replied coolly. 'I gather by your appearance that you have had an adventurous day.'

'Yes,' Swift replied.

'You have found it?'

Swift nodded. 'And the French have released Langton and Miss Carruthers.'

'Ah,' her brows arched. 'Then you have indeed met with success. Very well, gentlemen, I must ask you to come and answer some questions.'

'No,' I refused. 'I'm going to have a shower and lunch, in that order.'

'Major Lennox, I insist.' She gave me a sharp stare.

'I'll come,' Swift said. 'Lennox, I'll see you later.'

'Isn't this little tyke adorable, Auntie?' Genevieve was still playing with Napoleon.

'He's mine,' Bing said with pride. 'I've never had a dog before.'

'Mr Bing, that is not a dog, it is a knot on a piece of string,' Lady Maitland remarked and sailed off in the direction of the terrace.

Swift laughed quietly and followed.

Bing offered his arm to Genevieve and they headed toward the garden with Napoleon cavorting between them, leaving me free to squelch off up the stairs.

A long, hot shower eased my muscles, cleaned the stink from my body and sharpened my mind. I went back over Fontaine's words. He would release Persi from captivity, but as long as the murder was unsolved, I didn't think he'd allow her to leave the city. I sighed – at least now that the secret was revealed we could finally investigate properly.

Jamal was in my room when I emerged in a thick white dressing gown.

'Ah effendi,' he bowed and waved toward a tray arrayed with a feast of local delicacies. 'Your meal awaits.'

I tucked in while he poured a generous glass of red wine and offered advice on which dishes of succulent meat went with which vegetable, piquant sauce or spicy sour cream side. I was almost full when he revealed a honeyed dessert. I finished every last morsel of the mushed nuts and flaked-pastry deliciousness and felt human again.

'May I serve coffee, effendi?'

'Yes, please, Jamal. And...the bath-draw boy?'

'Ah, a shameful deceit. He has been made to repay his ill-gotten dollars.'

'Oh, really?' That was a bit of a turn up!

'Indeed, effendi and I was ordered to donate them to his illustrious and innocent wives, who have suffered indignity upon their family reputation.'

'Ah,' Not such good news then. 'But surely he'll just swipe the dollars from them?'

'The owner of this esteemed hotel has made the order. The guilty one will not dare defy our master.'

'Yes, but Jamal, they were my dollars!'

He looked up with nut brown eyes in a mournful face. 'Would you deny the ladies their due, effendi.'

'No, of course not,' I gave it up and asked a question that had been rather tickling my imagination. 'Anyway, what exactly do bathing ladies do?'

'Ah, it is a most delightful and beneficial process.' He smiled. 'First, they ensure a sheet is wrapped entirely around the personage and draped about the bath, to build steam. This leaves the head free and then they wash the hair, effendi, and massage the scalp.' He ended with a solemn nod of the head.

'Is that it?'

'Indeed, it is a most noble tradition.'

Must say, it didn't really live up to expectation. 'Right, so I assume the bath-draw boy has been sacked?'

'He has not, effendi, but he will suffer punishment for his acts.'

'Not jail, surely?'

'No. This foolish man is the third cousin of the wife of the nephew of the owner of Hotel Al Shami, effendi. His is to be no longer the bath-draw boy. Now, he is boot-boy.'

'Oh.' I wondered momentarily if there was any lower he could go, then thought I'd better ask some proper questions. 'When he was the guard on Ladies Row, did he really see the man who tried to murder Josephine Belvoir? The first time, I mean.'

'He swore he did, effendi. He said the man wore the wrong shoes.'

'What?'

'The shoes were too large. They were not his shoes.'

'Really? I think you'd better bring him back up here so I can question him properly.'

'He is being asked questions at this moment, effendi. By the high lady and your friend.'

I laughed. 'Ah, well that will be punishment enough.'

A smile broke his plump features and he crossed to my bedside table to return with a slim cedar-wood box. 'I believe there is a gift awaiting your attention, effendi.'

I raised my brows and the lid of the box and laughed. It was a toothbrush lying in thinly sliced wood shavings. I picked it up, it too was carved from cedar, I could smell it. The bristles were made from peeled twiglets set into the wood with resin. It was a work of art, if a rather unusual one.

'There is more, effendi,' Jamal said. 'On the other side.'

I turned the toothbrush over. Someone had carefully carved a tiny ship with a billowing sail and cresting horse's head into the handle.

'Who sent this, Jamal?' I asked, checking the box for a message or tag.

'The Sheik, effendi. It is a mark of honour.' He bowed as he said this.

'And who is this Sheik?' I asked, although I already knew.

'The owner of this establishment, effendi.'

Qarsan, I thought and smiled wryly. 'And what else does he own in Damascus?'

'Many things, effendi, he is everywhere. And he knows everything.'

CHAPTER 23

Fogg came bounding in and greeted me ecstatically; I must say I was very pleased to see my little dog again. Greggs followed at a stately pace, clutching a large brown envelope.

'Good day, sir,' he uttered. 'We are returned.'

'Yes, Greggs. So I can see.'

He was exceptionally well turned-out. Butlering togs pressed and starched, hair carefully brushed and I'd swear he was wearing face cream. I hoped this movie making wasn't going to his head.

'How went it?' I asked.

'Delilah of the Desert is in the can, sir,' he proclaimed.

'What?'

'It is a movie term, sir. It means the film is complete and ready for production.'

'Well, you could have just said so.'

He stifled a sigh as though I were being difficult.

'I have photographs, sir. I thought you might like to see them.' He opened the envelope and withdrew a number of large glossy photos. 'Mr Bruce, the camera man, insists upon taking portraits of the stars of each movie.'

I regarded the first image. 'Fogg is wearing a ribbon on top of his head.'

'Indeed, sir, and Mr Bruce has made a notation on the base.' He pointed to the type-written text which read, "Delilah of the Desert. Damascus."

He showed me another photograph. It was of him, seated with his back straight, chins raised, a smile on his face and hair neatly combed over. It was well done, the lighting had been set to smooth away his more wrinkled features – he looked rather suave, actually, and had signed the base of the photo with a flourish.

'I thought you said Bruce only photographed the stars in the movies?'

'Ah, but I am in the movie, sir. At the very end, when the young Prince has returned to his father and the shepherd boy becomes his best friend, a telegram arrives. It informs the Sheik that Delilah's family have sent their trusty butler from England to bring her home to the Countess's castle.'

'Really?' I replied dryly. 'And you were the 'trusty butler'.'

'Indeed, sir. I was filmed with Mr Fogg in my arms and a carpetbag at my feet.'

'Greggs,' I was about to make a retort but noticed he was beaming, so changed my tone. 'I hope you enjoyed yourself.'

'Thank you, sir, it was rather a commendable experience,' he fidgeted with the envelope. 'And I have been invited out this evening by Mr Bruce.'

'Have you?'

'You did say I should treat this trip as a holiday, sir.'

'Well, you've certainly done that, Greggs'

He coughed discreetly. 'May I remind you that you are holding my fees...'

'Ah, yes, just a minute.' I nipped back to the bathroom where I'd left the soggy dollars in the sink. They'd been in my pocket when I'd tumbled into the filthy water.

'Here.' I handed them over.

He looked unimpressed. 'Sir?'

'You can count them while I get dressed.'

I left him to it, while I donned proper tweeds with a shirt and waistcoat.

'Where are you going?' I asked, as I peered into the wardrobe in search of a tie.

'There was talk of a club, sir, with dancing ladies. Mr Bruce is certain he knows the whereabouts.'

'Umm,' I mumbled as I picked out a natty green and brown specimen.

He gave a discreet cough. 'I believe your dark red tie was packed, sir. It would be more appropriate.'

'But this is my favourite, Greggs.'

'It may be suitable for a winter's day in England, sir. But we are in Damascus.'

'Yes, I do know that, Greggs.'

His taste in attire tended toward the avant-garde and he was always trying to update my wardrobe. He rifled through the various whatnots.

'Here it is, sir.' He held it up.

'Oh, very well, Greggs!' I slipped it around my neck. 'Is Vincent going to the club with you?'

'It was his intention, and he did speak very highly of it, but alas, Mrs Vincent overheard the conversation.'

'She's confined him to base, has she?' I grinned.

'I'm afraid so, sir.'

'Well, keep your eyes peeled in the city, old chap. There are dangers in the dark.'

'Would that be the snakes, scorpions and crocodiles you mentioned this morning?' He raised his brows.

'Something like that, Greggs.'

'Somewhat exaggerated, I thought, sir,' he uttered and went off clutching his envelope.

I looked down at my little dog who returned my gaze, eyes bright, ears cocked, head slightly to one side.

'Come on, Foggy.' I picked him up, gave him a much needed hug and headed for the rooftop.

We arrived to the sound of a single voice, singing out the call to evening prayer, the mournful tone rippled across the sun-soaked stones to die in the desert. A bird warbled a trill of notes as if in echo and a bell tolled from a distant tower. It felt eternal, a city of a hundred thousand yesterdays and tomorrow was just another dawn, treading the path of time.

I sank into a chair and gazed at the horizon. Fogg jumped onto my lap and we watched the sun sink in florid glory. My mind revolved around death, or rather murder, and why it was that Josephine had to die.

Qarsan was part of the mystery. I smiled at the thought of the gift he'd sent me – a toothbrush – it was a nice touch and proved he really did know everything down to the detail. So how much of this was by his design? All of it I would say, or almost all, anyway.

He must have been highly amused by our efforts to discover the house of Hanno, after all, he'd orchestrated the whole thing. He'd enticed the allies with the lure of oil and set them against each other. Then he'd sat back while they offered their most precious treasures in exchange for a prize almost beyond price. And, finally, today he'd revealed that none of them had actually won it.

Soon, reality would dawn among the western powers that they would have to negotiate with all the diverse tribes in Arabia. I had no doubt Qarsan would be in the centre of it all, acting as chief mediator – the spider in the web. An ingenious plan and he'd played it like a master.

But, I mused, he'd fallen in love with Josephine; there was a twist of fate he'd never expected, perhaps never even experienced before. What had come of this unlikely love story? Had she fallen for him? Unlikely given her past history; I was certain she knew the power he wielded and decided to make use of him. So did he arrange her death in revenge? No, he had made it plain he wanted her killer found. Was she an obstacle in someone else's way? That was more likely, given what was at stake. Or perhaps the reason really did lay in the past?

I watched a small bird flit across the rooftop opposite. The fat man must have retired because his day bed was empty. My thoughts drifted toward Persi, and Langton and I shook them away, preferring to consider the complexities of murder to the mysteries of tender emotions.

'Heathcliff, there you are!' Persi broke into my musings.

'Greetings' I bounded to my feet and kissed her cheek. By the delectable fragrance I'd say she'd bathed in rose water and dabbed on a very classy perfume.

'Erm, not Heathcliff, old stick... I mean dearest. Well, you can call me whatever you..., it's just... I'm not keen.' I coughed to cease my babbling and tried again. 'You look nice. The dress is... is,' I ran out of words because she looked absolutely sparkling. She'd let her blonde hair fall loose and it rippled in waves around her shoulders. There were traces of pink on her lips and she wore a long silk frock in pale green, shimmering in the half light, with a sort of wrap around her shoulders made of gauzy translucent stuff which was floaty and... 'What?'

She laughed. 'I said, 'isn't it beautiful up here'?'

'Yes, yes. It's a garden of sorts. There are plants in pots, flowers, palms and... and that sort of thing...' I trailed away. I wanted to kiss her properly, but the thorny subject of Langton was still waiting to be excised.

'I know,' she replied. 'I used to come up here before Colonel Fontaine placed me under lock and key.' She smiled. 'I'm so relieved it's over.'

'Apart from the matter of murder,' I said, then wished I hadn't as the smile faded from her lips.

'Persi.' I gazed at her. 'I... I... Can I get you anything? A gin and tonic or...'

'Jamal told me you were here and offered to bring a tray up.' She said just as our loyal servant arrived, puffing with exertion and carrying a clinking tray.

We were duly served with tall glasses, a jug full of iced G and T and a couple of dishes of nuts and dates. He busied himself lighting lamps about the place before returning to the courtyard, or wherever he went.

The moon showed full in the deep-blue sky glittering with stars; an enchanted evening charged with the breath of romance.

We clinked glasses.

'To Hanno.'

'And his map.' I smiled.

'It was utterly extraordinary,' she told me, warmth returning to her tone. 'The images on the murals provide more information about Phoenician life than anything we have discovered so far. And the map extended right around the coast into Africa.'

'You'll be telling me they discovered America next,' I teased.

That made her laugh. 'Who knows! The world is more complex and extraordinary than we'll ever comprehend.'

'And the oil? Do you think there will be much of it?'

'I really have no idea. It's of no interest to me outside the use they made of it in antiquity.' Her face fell sombre.

I didn't want to dampen the mood again. I watched her expression and suddenly realised that, more than anything, I wanted to get to know her. All the little things; what she liked and read and thought about and... well everything.

'Persi, can I ask you something?'

'Of course, darling.'

'What's your favourite book?'

That caused her to smile. 'I thought you were going to ask about the murder.'

'Oh. Did you do it?'

'No.'

'Do you know who did it?'

'No.'

'Right. So, what's your favourite book?'

She thought about it. 'I'd say *Pride and Prejudice*, but... Can I have two?'

'Erm...yes.' I poured another drink for each of us.

'*King Solomon's Mines*!'

'Ha!' I exclaimed. 'That would be mine too.'

'Really? What's your other favourite?'

'Ah,' I realised I'd painted myself into a corner. 'You won't laugh will you?'

'Probably,' she replied, her eyes dancing with delight. 'You have to tell me now.'

'It's...' I paused. '*The Wind in the Willows*.'

She did laugh and so did I. It was intoxicating, I reached for her hand and she wove her fingers through mine.

'I like *Treasure Island* too,' I added.

'That's three,' she said. 'Mystery and adventure!'

'Apart from Mr Toad.' I sipped my drink. 'It's history and adventure in your case, isn't it?'

She nodded and leaned closer to me. 'You're a hunter, aren't you?'

I regarded her. 'So are you.'

'I suppose so,' she became thoughtful. 'I watched you and Swift while we were at Braeburn Castle.'

'Uum?'

'He's the trained tracker, isn't he? The professional detective, following clues and uncovering evidence. Rather as I do, really. But, you're just...' She let the sentence hang.

'What?'

'Chaos! You disorientate your quarry by disrupting all their careful plans and then you begin to unravel them. You operate on instinct.'

'Is that another way of saying I blunder about brainlessly?'

She laughed again. 'No, my darling. I'm saying you have a knack for it, even if it is rather erratic.'

'Persi... I...' I put my drink down and turned to her.

'Heathcliff, wait,' the laughter died on her lips. 'I came to tell you something. I'm leaving tomorrow, darling.'

That threw me. 'Why?'

'Because I must. Fontaine's playing games, he's already manipulated me, making me believe Charles was dying and then arresting me. I won't stay here and be dragged back into everything.'

'But...' I sighed, not wanting to spoil the moment by explaining that she wouldn't be able to simply walk away from a charge of murder. I switched tack. 'Persi, how did you come to be here in the first place?'

She pushed hair away from her face with long fingers. 'I was due back in Byblos. Do you remember I told you I'd been working there before I met you in Scotland?'

I nodded. I hadn't taken much notice at the time, not having known where Byblos was.

'I had intended returning there, but then… then I met you and had second thoughts.' She paused to bite her lip. 'Out of the blue, I had a telegram from Charles telling me he had to go to Damascus. He said he wanted to stop by in Byblos, to see me.' She picked up her glass and held it. 'Of course, he didn't know I wasn't there at the time, actually I was surprised he knew I'd been there at all. Anyway, the telegram had been redirected to me at my parent's home in Sussex.'

'When was the last time you saw him?' I asked.

She let loose a long sigh. 'We haven't seen each other or spoken since the end of the war. Actually it was Christmas of 1918. That was when he wrote to me about what he had done. He was in a terrible mess. Beatrice had been declared dead and he'd become mixed up with Josephine. He admitted he had betrayed me and asked if he should do the decent thing and cry off.' She glanced from her glass to me. 'It broke my heart. I couldn't bear to speak to him, or see him, so I never gave him an answer.'

I remained silent, letting her recover from the tumult of emotions I could see crossing her face.

'And so when he contacted me again, I didn't know what to do. I had a ticket for Byblos already paid for and if it weren't for meeting you, I wouldn't have hesitated to use it. But…' She gave me a tight smile. 'I really didn't know what my feelings were. I thought I should hear Charles out and I knew my colleagues were hoping I'd rejoin them – we were always shorthanded.' She sighed. 'So I went to Byblos.'

I gave her hand a squeeze. Foggy must have noticed her anguish and jumped up to give her a lick. She stroked his fur absentmindedly.

'Just after I arrived a letter came. Charles wrote that he had already gone on to Damascus and encountered the movie crew. He explained that he'd had no idea Josephine was going to be there, but that she was involved in the same 'hunt' he was. He claimed she made a false accusation of attempted murder against him.'

'I assume the medallion was included in the letter?' I asked.

She nodded. Her hair fell forward and she swept it back again. 'Yes, it was wrapped in the note I slipped to you. Jamal brought the package with Charles's letter. I had never met him before but Charles trusted him.' She turned her blue eyes to me. 'Anyway, Charles instructed me to find the tomb robber and give him the medallion. Whatever information I received was to be used to negotiate his freedom from jail.'

'So you came to Damascus and Fontaine told you Langton was in the Citadel and near to death?' I said.

'Yes, it was a terrible shock. I'd assumed he was simply being detained, but Fontaine made it sound as though Charles was failing by the day.' She bit her lip. 'I contacted Swift because I was sure he would know what to do.'

'Why not me?' I asked the question that had gnawed at me.

'You must know why – how could I ask you to help me release my fiancé? It was nonsensical and...' She paused. 'And I didn't want to put you to the test. Your feelings for me may not have been terribly deep, so why would you help me? Swift, on the other hand was with Scotland Yard, I thought he'd at least know the right people to alert. It just made sense.'

I took her hand again. 'What was his reply?'

'He said he would go to London, talk to the Foreign Office and do whatever he could.' She shrugged.

It was my turn to fall silent. Swift hadn't told me he'd been to London. I mused upon that for a moment, then asked, 'Have you talked things out with Langton?'

She shook her head. 'No, but I believe I must.'

'Well, when you do, you won't forget about me, will you, old girl. Because... because... I...'

'Yes, darling?' she turned to gaze into my eyes.

I was about to rise and take her up in my arms when...

'Oh, there you are,' Langton broke in.

CHAPTER 24

He strolled across the terrace, dressed in an immaculate pale blue suit with hand-made loafers, a club tie and a perfectly folded handkerchief in his top pocket. He glanced at his watch. 'We'll be late darling. I've told the restaurant we would be there at seven thirty and it's close to that now.'

'Charles!' She jumped to her feet, a flush rising to her cheeks.

'Damn it!' I swore quietly.

I didn't move, merely held out my hand to her as she smoothed her dress down. She touched her fingers lightly onto my palm, bent to place a kiss on my cheek and went to join him. I didn't watch them go, I stared into the night sky, seeing nothing.

Fogg glanced up at me in sympathy then jumped into my lap. I smoothed the fur on his head.

'Oh, there you are, Lennox!' Swift came in with a light step, his trench coat undone, hands stuffed in pockets. He dropped into the chair vacated by Persi.

'Pretty bloody obvious, Swift,' I retorted.

'Oh, do buck up, man!' he sounded almost jolly. 'Fontaine has admitted to Lady Maitland that he's convinced Josephine killed the lawyer.'

'Did he say why?'

'Midhurst was here on behalf of the American Government. He was preparing to offer Qarsan a blank cheque – providing all negotiations with rival nations were cut off. That would have thrown a significant spanner in the works, so he thinks Josephine removed him.'

'Hum,' I mumbled, not surprised to hear the motive for his murder was the oil. 'Does he know who murdered Josephine?'

'Not as far as I'm aware.' He fidgeted in his seat. 'Do you have any idea?'

I shook my head. 'Did Lady Maitland tell you anything else?'

'Not really, she's a lady who plays her cards very close to her chest. I gave her the outline of today's events, but she'll receive a full briefing from Langton.' He paused to glance at me. 'Look, Fontaine has released Langton – we've achieved what we came here to do, Lennox.'

'We still have to clear Persi's name.'

'Yes.' He paused. 'I saw her leave with Langton. You shouldn't let it bother you. I doubt there's anything in it.'

I can't say I wanted to discuss that or anything else, but I knew he was trying his best.

'They needed to talk, or that's what she told me.'

'Well, it's understandable,' he replied.

'You didn't tell me you'd been to London, Swift,' I threw in.

His face fell sombre. 'I assume Persi told you. It's true. I did go to Scotland Yard but they dismissed me entirely – told me I was no longer with the force, and to keep my nose out of police business.' He sighed quietly. 'Anyway, I wasn't prepared to give up, so, I scouted around and managed to find one of my old colleagues. He agreed to pass a message to the Foreign Office. He didn't think anything would come of it, but I assume he achieved something because Lady Maitland turned up here.'

'Why didn't you tell me?' I demanded.

He shrugged. 'I was embarrassed, Lennox. They told me I should clear off back to my castle now that I was one of the nobs.'

That must have stung, and it was unfair. 'I'm sorry, Swift.'

'Hum.' It was his turn for a touch of the doldrums.

I turned the subject. 'Did you talk to the bath-draw boy?'

That brought him round. 'Ha! Yes, the bloody fool. He had been asleep on the job and had only woken up when he'd heard the shot and Josephine shout out. He saw the figure of a man race past him and go down the stairs. He said the man was wearing Langton's coat and hat, but the only thing he really noticed was the shoes.'

'I heard the same,' I said. 'Does it mean the coat fitted whoever it was?'

'Possibly, but it may be that the clothes were western style and it didn't mean much to him.'

I nodded, thinking that was plausible.

Swift continued. 'We'll have to measure Langton's feet.'

'He's almost the same size as me,' I told him. 'I noticed his footwear when he came for Persi.'

Swift leaned down to regard my shoes. 'Vincent and Bing are quite short, I imagine they'll be smaller than you.'

'Um,' I agreed. 'What about Dreadnaught?'

'I don't know, we'll take a look.' He stood up suddenly and clapped his hands together. 'Right, come on. Dinner will be on the table shortly and I missed lunch. You can brood later.'

I didn't want to move, but Foggy jumped down from my lap because he understood 'dinner' and a spaniel's mind is very singular. I sighed, gave up and followed Swift and my dog downstairs.

Foggy hadn't met Napoleon before but he took to him in an instant. There was much barking, tail wagging and then they hared around the garden as we settled on the terrace to watch their antics with the assembled guests.

Harry Bing left his lemonade to throw sticks, but the dogs were too busy frolicking to notice. Genevieve went to join in and I saw him quietly take her hand and they wandered off together, away from the colourful lights and the collective gaze of the guests.

'I think you have lost your assistant, Lady Maitland.' Mammie smiled archly. She was dressed in another florid frock of yellow and red with a string of glossy pearls around her neck.

'Thought she was your niece,' I said. We were gathered

around a couple of circular tables, under the leafy rafters of the terrace. It was still warm from the heat of the day and softly lit by hanging lanterns.

'I think that was another little subterfuge,' Mammie remarked while Lady Maitland retained a frozen disdain.

'The frogs took my camera,' Vincent complained in what may have been an attempt to change the subject. 'I need that camera, it's the best. They better bring it back or I'll have the lawyer onto them.'

'He's dead,' Swift chimed in, sipping from a tall glass of gin and tonic.

'Oh yeah.' Togged out in his customary checked shirt and braces, Vincent was puffing on a large cigar. I noticed Swift had taken a look at the various shoes on show.

Dreadnaught strolled in. 'Ah, good evening, ladies and gentlemen. Please do not get up.'

'We wasn't going to,' Vincent replied, he was in an obnoxious mood.

I looked at Dreadnaught's feet, he was almost my size, but I didn't think that ruled him out.

'Ladies, Gentlemen,' he clicked his heels with a bow.

'Hello, dear boy,' Mammie gushed. 'Do come and sit by me.'

Dreadnaught turned his handsome profile in her direction 'Are we leaving tomorrow?'

'We most certainly are.' Mammie patted his hand as he took a chair next to her. 'Back to Hollywood and we will have our new film to promote. It will be such a hit, I'm absolutely certain of it!'

'But surely without the leading lady it will not be possible?' Dreadnaught's brow furrowed.

'Nah,' Vincent replied. 'We'll make it like a tragic accident, the public will love it. Bing can be the heartbroken dupe who shot her with the wrong gun. You wait till I start feeding this to the papers. It will make the front page.' He laughed. 'And the publicity will all be free.'

'So you are keeping Bing on?' I asked, unimpressed by Vincent's tasteless scheme.

'We are, Major Lennox. I insisted, didn't I, Pappie?' Mammie smiled again. 'He has promised he will behave and now that he has that darling little dog, I know he will be just fine.'

'And it seems he has a new romance,' Dreadnaught remarked, nodding in the direction of the garden where Bing and Genevieve could be seen playing with the two dogs.

'Perhaps she could become your new leading lady?' I suggested.

'Did you hear that, Lady Maitland?' Vincent laughed. 'How'd you like that, hey?'

He received no response.

'Now, Pappie,' Mammie offered the mildest scold. 'Lady Maitland does not like your teasing. And I've already told you, it's the blonde one we need.'

That caused me to sit up. 'Persi?'

'Yes, dear boy, but we'll have to change her name. Why, I can't even pronounce it myself.' She laughed. 'The camera will adore her.'

Vincent leaned forward. 'I persuaded her to take some stills before that frog stole my camera. She's a real beauty. I'm gonna make her a star!'

'I am not a 'frog', Monsieur Vincent.' Fontaine had entered quietly from the shadows. 'And I am here to return your camera, so you may not call me a thief either.' He stared coldly, then nodded to the sergeant, who came forward to place Vincent's camera on the table in front of him.

'Yeah, whatever.' Vincent blew cigar smoke in Fontaine's direction.

Lady Maitland addressed Fontaine. 'I assume you will be returning our passports, too?'

'What?' I asked.

'Colonel Fontaine has confiscated our passports,' Lady Maitland delivered the news.

That caused an uproar and everyone started shouting at once, including me.

'Silence!' Fontaine ordered. 'Sit down.' He waited until we were sat down. 'Your passports will be returned.'

'So hand 'em over,' Vincent demanded.

Fontaine looked down his thin nose. 'When the murderer of Josephine Belvoir reveals himself, you will receive your passports,' he said, then turned on his heel and left.

More shouting followed, but I'd had enough and sought to escape. I went into the garden to call Fogg, both he and Napoleon came running over. Napoleon was tiny, no more than eight inches from paws to shoulder and I doubt he'd grow to half Foggy's size. He was a sparky little chap though, bouncing around on hind paws, tufted white fur, pink tongue beneath a black nose and eyes as bright as buttons.

'Lennox,' Swift had come to join me. 'We'll put our heads together after dinner.'

'Yes,' I threw a small stick for the dogs. Fogg reached it first and Napoleon grabbed the other end to tug it away.

We all sat down in the mahogany-lined dining room, under glittering chandeliers. It began as a noisy argumentative affair and faded into suspicious silence as we watched each other, wondering who'd done it. As we were about to be served dessert, the accusations started flying.

'Bing shot her,' Vincent declared, pointing a cake fork at Harry who turned pale. 'I'm gonna tell Fontaine he can keep him and then we can leave.'

'You unutterable cad!' Genevieve retaliated on Bing's behalf. 'Harry is a gentle soul. He could never have harmed that woman, however much she deserved it.'

'How would you know?' Vincent argued back. 'You only arrived the day before! And he did shoot her, we all saw him do it.'

'That's…' Bing tried to protest, but Mammie cut him off.

'Pappie is quite right. But, my dear,' she turned to the ashen Bing, 'I don't think you are the guilty party. It could have been almost anyone.'

'No, it couldn't because the other gun disappeared before we or the ladies arrived,' I replied.

'Oh my,' Mammie said. 'I had entirely forgotten that.'

'But we don't know when you really arrived, do we,' Vincent turned on Lady Maitland. 'I don't believe you came here from India.'

Lady Maitland didn't have a reply to that, because it was actually true.

Genevieve rounded on him. 'You really are insufferable.'

I must say, I found her far more interesting now that she'd dropped the dizzy 'flapper' act.

'Well, we need to leave, so someone must be given up,' Dreadnaught said.

'Yes, the murderer,' Swift cut in.

'Or whoever,' Vincent replied through a mouthful of baklava. 'They've arrested the blonde, they can keep her.'

'Right,' I threw my napkin on the table as mayhem broke out again. 'That's it!'

Foggy was at my feet and he followed me as I stalked out without having touched a mouthful of my pudding.

'Lennox.' Swift came behind me. 'Wait, this doesn't help.'

I slowed my steps to let him catch up.

He continued. 'Look, why don't we order a pot of coffee and go to my room. We can go over the evidence.'

'Hum, right,' I agreed. 'With baklava.'

'Yes, yes, come on.'

'And brandy.'

He didn't reply, he just led the way up to his rooms.

Baklava and bitter-sweet coffee are the best combination imaginable, followed by a snifter. I felt a great deal better by the time I'd partaken and was sitting in a chair, warming my brandy with Fogg by my feet and Swift seated opposite.

He'd taken all his notebooks out of the drawer, along with some papers he'd used to write down thoughts on everyone and his sketch of the map from Hanno's house – which was quite good actually.

He placed the map in the middle of the table. 'This is what brought them all here. Oil.' He patted a hand on the black spots near Bahrain and Kuwait, then picked up a sheaf of loose papers. He spread each page out in a circle, like the hours of a clock around the map in the centre. 'I've written each person's name on a single sheet as well as their activities as we know them.'

I regarded it. 'We don't actually have any evidence, do we Swift?'

'No, Fontaine has what little there is.'

'Why the hell doesn't he solve it then?' I was exasperated.

'Because he's a peace keeper, not a detective, Lennox. It's down to us, so just concentrate, will you.'

I did and it didn't help.

We went through everything we knew, including Qarsan's oil scheme, the death of the lawyer, the disappearance of one gun, the planting of the Kongsberg-Colt and the bullets that killed Josephine, Fontaine's subterfuge and our thoughts on Langton.

'It's the motive,' Swift complained. 'I cannot fix the damn motive.' He slammed a hand down on the papers.

We were both weary.

'Swift, I'll see you at breakfast,' I told him. 'Sleeping on it may help.'

'No.'

'What?'

'I mean, yes. Oh, hell. Goodnight, Lennox.'

I bid him the same, suspecting that he wasn't going to sleep much at all. I made my way with my little dog at my heels and my mind on Persi, wondering whether she had returned with Langton and what she had decided.

'Ah, there you are, Major Lennox,' a voice in the darkness greeted me as I entered my room. 'I have been waiting.'

CHAPTER 25

Foggy growled, gave a short, not very brave woof, then hid under the bed.

It was Qarsan, dressed entirely in black; black robes, black head-dress, black scarf and a large curved sword hanging from his waist in a black scabbard. He was silhouetted against the window, one foot up on a stool and emanating an air of disquieting danger in the unlit room.

'Sit down,' he ordered as though he owned the place – which, as I recalled, he did.

I sat.

'You, Major Lennox, and your detective friend Inspector Swift,' he began.

'Actually, he's left Scot...' I trailed off, because explanations probably weren't a good idea. I shifted in my seat and asked. 'What do you want?'

'I want you to leave. All of you. It is necessary.'

'To your plan to play off the governments?' I replied.

He laughed and ignored the remark. 'The French Colonel is restraining you because of the killing.'

He had a habit of speaking in statements.

'I assume you want Swift and me to solve the murder of Josephine?'

'I remind you, I have given you this task. See that it is completed by midnight tomorrow.'

How the hell were we supposed to do that? I almost uttered but stopped myself because babbling wouldn't help.

I switched tack. 'You loved her, didn't you?'

He stiffened, I sensed his sudden unease.

'She was beautiful, but one doesn't love women. They are playthings. Ornaments.'

'You wanted her for your harem,' I said into the semi-darkness.

He laughed again; a throaty laugh, deep in the chest. 'This is not the Middle Ages, Major, we do not have harems.'

'Just a number of wives?'

'It is our duty. A wealthy man should support as many women and children as our culture allows.'

I was about to deviate into the keeping of numerous wives and my personal thoughts on the subject, but decided it wasn't advisable in the circumstances.

'Did Josephine agree to be a 'wife'?' I asked.

'She did not disagree,' he replied. I noted the uncertainty in his voice.

'Did you tell her the secret of the oil?' I asked.

He laughed without humour. 'Women have no place in men's business.'

I deduced that meant no.

'Why wait for us to reveal the killer? I thought you knew everything that happened in this city?'

'Spies and assassins are adept at hiding their deeds. My men have failed to watch as closely as they should. They have paid for their failings.'

'Ah.' That gave me pause. 'You do know that Josephine murdered the lawyer?'

'Enough. You have your orders, Major Lennox. Do not fail me.' He stepped out of the window, which considering we were two stories up, stopped me in mid-breath.

I strode over to the wide-open frame to see him being lowered to the ground by a rope with a foot-loop tied at the end. I leaned out and looked up. There were men in black on the roof. They were holding the rope and, even as I watched, tossed it down to Qarsan, then disappeared into the night.

I closed the windows with a bang, followed by the shutters and dropped the latch to secure them. Why on earth didn't he just come through the door? He owned the place after all. I suppose he preferred to keep to the shadows, or some such.

'Fogg,' I called. He came out and I gave him a reassuring hug, lit the lamps, then sat on the bed. Now what?

Something in the back of my mind had been bothering me all evening, but the question over Persi and Langton had distracted me. I went to the ornate table I'd been using as my desk and took out my notebook. I hadn't written very much in it, unlike Swift, who'd almost constructed a novel.

I moved aside the photos Greggs had given me, then paused and put them back in the centre of the table.

Despite the ribbon, it was a very flattering photograph of Foggy, probably the best I had, actually. I turned it over, Bruce had stamped his name on the back in black ink. I looked more closely at the images.

That was it, the photographs!

It didn't take long to run up to the room being used by the Vincents, I knocked on the door – nothing. I put my ear to the door – still nothing. I decided they were probably downstairs. It was locked, but I had my lock picks, which had survived my drenching in the canal. I was listening carefully for that quiet 'clunk' of the cylinder when someone hissed in my ear.

'Sir, sir, you must desist.'

'Greggs, what the devil are you doing?'

'This is not your room, sir.' He swayed.

'I know,' I turned around to hiss back. 'Have you been drinking?'

'A sssmidgeon, sir. It was strong liquor.' He giggled. 'But most excellent and to be highly recommended.' He started noisily humming some sort of tune.

'Greggs, I'm busy. Go to bed, there's a good chap.'

'I'd like to thank you, sir, for my very, very, very… um.' He paused to cudgel his addled brain. 'Very good holiday, sir.' He swayed some more. He was quite dishevelled actually, bow-tie askew, shirt front escaping and stiff collar wilted.

'Glad you enjoyed it, now go away,' I whispered more firmly.

'There were dancing girls, sir. We danced too, with the

girls, you know, and they had veils. And they took them off slowly, while…' He suddenly raised his arms above his head and did a slow, unsteady twirl.

I paused to watch. 'Greggs.'

'Yes, sir?' He stopped in mid-twirl.

'If you would just wait here for one minute, I'll take you to your room.'

He carried on humming under his breath. 'Very well, sir.'

I unlocked the door as he recommenced his unsteady pirouette. It was hardly a surreptitious break-in.

It didn't take a minute to grab the photographs I'd seen in Vincent's briefcase and I exited with them tucked into my inside pocket. Greggs was lying flat on his back, snoring on the floor. Damn.

I stepped over him, thinking to leave him where he was, then had second thoughts and grabbed him. He was a hell of a weight, I had to drag him under the arms. I was barely able to catch a breath by the time I got him as far as the stairs.

'Lennox! Good God, is Greggs hurt?' Swift emerged from the darkness.

'Of course not. He's just drunk.'

'Greggs is drunk?'

'Swift, will you stop making pointless statements and help?'

'Right.' He took Greggs under one shoulder while I hoisted him by the other and we manhandled him to his room. He was singing by the time we rolled him, fully

clothed, onto the bed. We shut the door and left him to
it.

'What are you doing out here, Swift?' I asked him once
I'd got my breath back.

'Couldn't sleep,' he replied. 'It's been going over and
over in my mind – there's something we've missed, but I
can't put my finger on it.'

'Come on,' I said.

'You know?' He stood staring after me.

'Yes.' I headed in the direction of my room.

'Right.' He tightened the belt of his trench coat and
followed.

'Here, see.' I spread the glossy photographs across the
ornate table. There were half a dozen or more photographs of each person and I placed them so that everyone
of relevance was represented; Dreadnaught, Josephine,
Bing, Beatrice.

He picked them up one at a time before turning them
over. 'There are more of Beatrice than the others.'

'Yes.' I nodded.

'Who took the photographs of her?'

'It wasn't Bruce. He wasn't with them during the war.'

'So Vincent took them,' he stated.

'I believe so,' I replied.

'What do you think happened?'

I told him. It took quite a lot of telling so I opened
the brandy and we discussed the hows and whys into the
early hours. When he finally departed to bed, I fell into
mine with my little dog snuffling gently beside me.

Thin lines of sunlight filtered through the shutters the next morning. The ceiling fan whirled slowly in rhythmic circles, making my head hurt. Actually my eyes hurt too. Fogg was sitting on the pillow next to me, wagging his tail and watching me with expectation.

I'm giving up alcohol.

I showered and dressed.

'Come on, Foggy,' I called and we trotted down to the garden while avoiding any human contact, then ran back upstairs again. Jamal was exiting my room as I entered, having deposited a sumptuous tray of breakfast. He bowed, I nodded and we parted without a word. The man was a paragon among factotums.

'Sir.' Greggs wobbled in just as Fogg and I finished the last eggy toast.

'Aspirin – next to my bed.'

'Sir, I... I...'

'Serves you right, Greggs, for taking this holiday nonsense too literally.'

'Yes, sir.' He was dressed in bowtie and tails but all yesterday's spiffiness was gone. He looked as though he'd been through the wringer. He swallowed a handful of tablets, washed them down with water and tottered back toward the door. 'I apologise, sir, for my untoward behaviour.'

'Accepted, old chap, and we are abroad, after all.'

'Indeed.' He wilted. 'Can we go home now, sir?'

'Yes, Greggs, I think we can.'

He closed the door as I turned my mind to contemplate the murderer. The problem was the utter lack of hard evidence. There was nothing that would convict the culprit, so there was only one solution – we had to flush them out. But I didn't have the faintest idea how.

'Ready?' Swift walked in without knocking.

'No.'

'Well, you'll have to work something out, because I've told them to gather on the terrace.'

'Swift, I've only just had breakfast!'

'So has everyone else.' He eyed me with his hawkish gaze. 'Are you sure about this, Lennox?'

'Well…' I was ready to prevaricate.

'Look, if we don't catch the aeroplane this afternoon we'll be stuck here for another three days at least.'

'Oh, in that case…' I stood up.

'Come on,' he tightened the belt of his trench coat and led the way.

Colonel Fontaine was waiting in the courtyard with his sergeant and a number of gendarmes. They followed us through to the terrace and lined up at the back.

The Vincents had taken centre stage, or the centre of the group anyway. They sat next to one another in wicker chairs on the terrace. Dreadnaught was on one side and Harry Bing, clutching Napoleon, on the other. Genevieve sat close to him, with a very stiff-backed Lady Maitland beside her.

Langton was seated next to Dreadnaught, making for an interesting contrast between the blond German and the dark-haired Englishman. Persi was nearest to Langton, she gave me a hesitant smile as I arrived, which I returned with as much confidence as I could muster. I hadn't had time to reflect on our discussions of last evening, but they weren't far from my mind.

I realised there were a number of hostile stares directed at me.

'Greetings,' I hailed them through the mists of my hangover.

'Major Lennox,' Lady Maitland pierced me with a steely eye. 'Inspector Swift has informed us that you are about to reveal the murderer of Josephine Belvoir. I find the idea ridiculous.'

'Laughable, more like,' Langton sniped.

'Nonsense,' Persi cut in, 'I've seen Heathcliff unveil a murderer before. He has a talent for it. Don't be so disparaging, Charles.'

All eyes turned to her, she blushed but held her chin up in defiance. I grinned, the day had suddenly taken on a rosy glow and I didn't even mind her calling me Heathcliff.

'Sir.' Greggs doddered in, still the worse for wear. 'You left these on your desk. I thought you may require them.' He held out the photographs Swift and I had been poring over last night.

'Thank you, old chap.'

He went to sit at the rear.

I smiled at Persi again, she smiled back. I stumbled over a low table that some idiot had left in the way, righted it and placed the photographs on its surface.

Swift hissed. 'Lennox, get on with it. We'll miss the damn plane at this rate.'

'Right,' I straightened up.

They looked at me, I looked at them. Fogg went to sit at Bing's feet from where he could touch noses with Napoleon.

'Right,' I said again. 'One of you killed Josephine Belvoir.'

'Yeah, it was Bing, we saw him do it,' Vincent growled. 'And if you don't…'

Genevieve instantly interrupted. 'That doesn't mean anything. Someone switched the guns.'

'No, it was not so,' Fontaine joined in, in his cool manner. 'It was the magazines that were switched, not the guns.'

'You are both right.' I paused to put my thoughts in order. 'But, that was later, much later. Because this is a story about love and betrayal, and a loss that could not be borne.'

CHAPTER 26

'Dear boy, could you refrain from these dramatics,' Mammie said in her soft southern accent. 'I have sent Bruce to pack our equipment, but I simply must be there to help.'

'Yeah, we got a plane to catch and we all know Bing did it,' Vincent interrupted again. I held up my hand to stop him.

'Let's start at the beginning, shall we? Josephine Belvoir was murdered with Charles Langton's gun.' I strolled in front of them, turned about then wandered back. 'An attempt had already been made on her life. Someone dressed in Langton's clothes, slipped on his shoes and took a clumsy shot at Josephine. They missed.'

'Who says it wasn't Langton?' Vincent disputed.

'It was Langton,' Dreadnaught cut in. 'The bath-draw boy said he saw him.'

'No, it was the guard,' Mammie interrupted.

'The bath-draw boy was the guard before he was demoted,' I said.

'Ah, yes, this is so, but he did see Langton,' Dreadnaught argued.

'The bath-draw boy is an entirely unreliable witness,' Swift countered. 'He saw someone pretending to be Langton.'

'I am here, you know,' Langton spoke in exasperated tone.

Fontaine joined in from the rear. 'You lied about being at the souk at the time of the attempt.'

'I was searching for the tomb-robber,' Langton said. 'I could hardly admit that to you.'

'You have no proof of that,' Fontaine replied.

'According to Persi's flying Major, he's going to provide it.' Langton sat back and folded his arms.

'Right.' It was tempting to just pin it on bloody Langton and go home, but I carried on. 'We know the murderer stole Langton's gun because it was used to shoot and kill Josephine.'

'Are you saying Harry did it because…' Genevieve entered the fray.

'No, I'm not, will you all stop interrupting!' I shouted.

'Lennox, will you get a move on,' Swift hissed.

'I'm doing it!' I replied then took a breath to slow down and explain. 'The original gun was a Colt 45, it was hidden and replaced with Langton's Kongsberg-Colt some days later – I assume this was to cause confusion. Langton's gun was then used to murder Josephine. We know how it was done, but not why?' I said. 'A question that has been almost impossible to answer because everything has been shrouded with mystery and lies.'

'Sir?' Greggs handed me a glass of water with a dash of bicarbonate.

'Thank you, Greggs.' He really was a most excellent chap. I took a sip and continued. 'The mystery was caused by the quest for oil, or rather its whereabouts. That is the reason you are all here, not to make movies. The film crew was a cover for Midhurst to negotiate with Qarsan, isn't that right, Mammie?'

'I think you know this, dear boy.' She smiled, she seemed to be enjoying the show. 'And we did make the film!'

I nodded and carried on. 'The American Government sent you, just as they had during the war. But the war is over and old allegiances have changed. Josephine was here on behalf of the French Government, and she had her own plans.' I turned toward Fontaine. 'I imagine her reward for finding the map in Hanno's house was almost unlimited. She persuaded you to work with her, didn't she Colonel, to make sure that reward was secured.'

'Are you pretending I killed the woman to gain this 'reward' for myself?' Fontaine's brow creased in a frown.

'It's possible,' I suggested. 'If you had killed her, the secret to the oil would be yours.'

'This idea is risible. My work here is to keep the peace.'

'But you helped Josephine? She asked you to introduce her to Qarsan,' I conjectured.

'Yes, that is true,' he finally admitted. 'I was forced to enter this playground, but the situation is not quite as simple as you think, Major. We French took control of this region only eighteen months ago. Even then, there were rumours of oil in the desert. Men were sent out to

Arabia to search for these 'tar seeps' as they were called. They never returned.' He paused, nobody moved as we waited for him to continue.

'The man who held this post before me was a hard, ambitious man. He subdued this city by harsh means until there was no more cooperation, no-one willing to collaborate or to inform. We French had become tyrants and the citizens hated us. So I was sent here to form a new order.' He paused as though unwilling to divulge information. 'Sheik Qarsan was the key to peace. I knew this and, little by little, he and I began to understand each other. But then there was the oil and I realised this man was playing his own game, not only with us, but the British and their allies, the Americans, too.'

'He made us compete,' Lady Maitland interrupted.

'He wanted the medallion,' I added.

Fontaine nodded. 'Yes, my government offered riches, gold even, but he wanted his Phoenician history and it was held by the British. Even Josephine couldn't entice him from his desire.'

Lady Maitland suddenly laughed, which caused everyone gaze at her. 'He will have it all in the end.'

'Hum,' I turned back to Fontaine. 'Langton had the medallion and Josephine needed it. Did you collaborate with her to have him jailed?'

'Non, and there was no need. He attempted to kill her and I interned him in the Embassy.'

'Langton?' I turned to him.

'Utter rot. She set me up and he locked me up.'

'Non, you lie!' Fontaine snapped in anger. 'She swore you tried to kill her and I believed it. And I continue to believe it.'

Langton regarded him, intelligence in his eyes. 'Are you saying someone really did try to kill Josephine that day?'

'Yes, obviously he is,' Swift chipped in. 'He's been saying that since we started.'

'He doesn't know what the hell he's talking about!' Langton was dismissive.

'If it had been a set-up,' I replied. 'Fontaine would have been close at hand to detain you before you had time to hide the medallion. The fact that he wasn't means he and Josephine weren't involved.'

He opened his mouth to argue, hesitated and then shut it again.

I let him digest that leap of logic while I took another sip of water.

Fontaine broke the silence. 'May I ask a question of Mademoiselle Carruthers?'

'Yes.' Persi looked at him with some surprise.

'When I detained you, Mademoiselle, we searched your person and your rooms. But we did not discover the medallion. I was certain you had it, but where was it?'

She laughed and ran fingers through her loose hair. 'Tucked inside my hair, Colonel – my bun to be precise.'

He had the grace to smile.

I took up again. 'When Langton was placed under lock and key, Josephine must have thought he would cave in to the pressure and hand over the medallion, but then Persi arrived.' I turned to face Langton. 'You'd written to her.'

He nodded. 'She was in Byblos. I sent her the medallion and instructions. I knew she'd find the house, she's a plucky girl.' He offered her a smile, which she didn't return.

I stepped back in. 'It must have been a surprise when Persi arrived here and threw Josephine's plan awry. But Josephine was well practiced in deceit and she concocted the lie that you, Langton, was at death's door, thinking that Persi would exchange the medallion for your freedom.'

'I never would have,' Persi broke in.

I smiled at her. 'No, you contacted Swift and that resulted in us arriving here.'

'And us,' Genevieve added.

'Exactly,' I agreed. 'But before that happened, Josephine had made plans of her own. She'd made a conquest of Qarsan and she'd murdered Midhurst.' I paused. 'But there was something else she did, and that's what led to her murder.'

'Well, what was it?' Lady Maitland demanded.

I regarded their faces, knowing that if I didn't lead them along the right track I'd never get the confession we needed.

'It all goes back to the war and the betrayal of Beatrice Langton,' I answered.

There were murmurs of surprise.

'Josephine knew who was responsible for betraying Beatrice,' I revealed.

Another gasp of shock rippled around the terrace.

'Who was it?' Langton shifted forward in his seat.

'Wait,' Swift ordered him.

'This is not making sense,' Dreadnaught rejoined. 'It was Josephine who betrayed Beatrice.'

'How do you know?' I asked Dreadnaught quietly.

'Because Mammie...' He broke off and looked toward her.

Mammie's face had turned to stone. 'It's true. Josephine told me so herself.'

The murmuring grew louder.

'She should have been shot,' Lady Maitland uttered in a freezing tone.

'She was,' Swift replied.

I continued questioning Mammie. 'Why did Josephine wait all this time to reveal such a devastating secret and then expose it when you all came here?'

'She... she...' Mammie struggled for words. 'I told you, she was frightened. She was certain Langton had come to kill her.'

I turned toward Langton at the same moment everyone else did.

'Is that true?' I asked him.

'No, I was sent here to exchange the medallion for the oil. I didn't know Josephine was here until I arrived.' His tone was coldly controlled.

'None of this is proof, Major,' Fontaine broke in.

I nodded in agreement. 'Josephine is dead and we cannot know what she did, or said or did not say – it has all been conjecture. Neither do we know what happened during the war, there are no records left.' I turned around to pick up the photographs lying on the table. 'Except for these.' I held them up to general puzzlement.

'Bruce took those, they're our stills,' Vincent said.

'Not all of them, did he, Vincent?' I shuffled through the glossy photographs of smiling faces until I came to the images of Beatrice. 'You took these, didn't you?'

His face fell. 'We didn't have Bruce then, so yeah, I took them. I was a photographer and cameraman when I started. I'm good at it.'

'Look at these photographs,' I ordered. I held up two images, one a smiling portrait of Josephine, showing her dazzling beauty, the other of Beatrice. Her eyes were softened with love as she stared into the camera, or rather, as she stared at the person behind the camera.

'She loved you,' I directed my words to Vincent.

He didn't reply.

'You were going to leave your wife, weren't you?' I continued.

'I...' Vincent stuttered to a halt.

'No, he wasn't. He would never leave me.' Mammie put her hand over his. 'Would you Pappie?'

'He was going to leave you,' I repeated.

'No. Without me, there wouldn't be any movies.' Her voice hardened.

'Oh yes there would,' I told her. 'He wouldn't have to give up making films, he has the knowledge and the talent. You, on the other hand, only have money and that can be replaced.' I stepped forward. 'That's why you were so terrified of losing him. Not just for the love you undoubtably hold for him, but because without him, your whole world would collapse. Your world of movies and travel and glamour and all the excitement that goes with it. He represented your life-time's ambition.'

Mammie almost screamed. 'That's not so. How could you say that! He was never going to leave me.'

'It was you, Mammie.' I wound up the pressure. 'You asked Josephine to betray Beatrice, didn't you? And she did, because she knew that, one day, that act of betrayal could be very valuable to her. When you all came here to find the secret of the oil, she decided it was time to make use of that fact. Josephine knew that the information would flow through you, just as it had during the war. And to get it, all she had to do was blackmail you. And she did, didn't she?'

Mammie panted heavily, staring round-eyed at me. Then she pulled herself together and sat upright in her wicker chair. 'No, I didn't do anything. Josephine did it. I told you yesterday what happened.'

'Yesterday, you said she did it by accident,' I reminded her. 'That was another lie. You said Josephine had learned of a traitor within Beatrice's group and only the traitor was supposed to be denounced, and then it spiralled out of control. But how can you denounce a traitor to the Germans? They were the very enemy the so-called traitor would be working for!'

'I...I was only repeating what she told me.' Her voice shook.

'Beatrice loved your husband,' I needled her. 'Didn't she? And he loved her.'

'She was a trollop,' Mammie suddenly shrieked in fury. 'She was just like the rest of them, those scheming tarts, throwing themselves at him because they wanted to be movie stars. They wanted what I had.' Her face distorted with rage.

Vincent stared at her, horror slowly gripping his face. 'Mammie, I never touched one of them, never. It was just an act, you know that, you know…'

'None of them except Beatrice. She was different, wasn't she Vincent?' I pressured him.

'She was… loving.' Vincent's voice lost its harshness. 'Nobody really cared for me before. Not like that.'

Mammie opened her mouth to protest, but I turned on her. 'You were going to lose everything, weren't you? The movie making, the man you loved – it was all about to be taken away from you. But you knew how easy it would be to stop it. You only had to ask Josephine to drop the word in the right ears and it would be over. So that's exactly what you did.'

The atmosphere froze as everyone stared at Mammie.

'You sent her to her death?' Vincent's voice faltered as he stared at his wife. 'She was tortured.'

Langton made to move, but Swift quelled him with an out-thrust hand.

'How can you say such a thing? I didn't send her any-where.' Her voice became shrill.

Vincent leaned away from her, loathing growing in his

eyes. 'She was innocent; she was just a girl. She had more humanity in her little finger than you have in the whole of your sick being.'

'Don't you say that,' Mammie exploded with rage. 'Don't you talk to me like that. I made you, I paid for it all. You are my husband. How could you look at another woman? Why did you do it? I gave you everything and you were going to leave me with nothing. Nothing!' she screamed at him and suddenly lashed out, pummelling him with her fists.

He raised his arms but didn't retaliate, I could see tears running down his face, all semblance to the brash movie man vanished.

'You did it, didn't you?' I repeated the accusation to Mammie.

She slumped down in her chair, her eyes glazed and unseeing. I don't think she heard my words, the shock of her exposure was too great.

'You caused the death of Beatrice.' Lady Maitland had leaned forward in her chair to fix Mammie with a look of steel. 'She was an innocent girl. Her life had barely begun. She risked her life for her country and you betrayed her?' Cold, deadly anger was growing in her voice.

'Margaret,' Genevieve turned to Lady Maitland. 'Don't.'

Her warning arrived too late. A shot rang out, loud and shocking in the confines of the terrace and garden. We watched in silent horror as red blood seeped onto Mammie's dress. She clasped her hands over the wound, panting with terror. 'Pappie, Pappie,' she cried out.

He didn't speak, his eyes widened, his mouth dropped open in silent horror and he watched his wife gasp for breath and die.

CHAPTER 27

Lady Maitland put the gun back in her handbag and stared at Fontaine, defying him to act.

He didn't move and neither did anyone else. Until, suddenly, they did. The gendarmes lined up behind Lady Maitland, hands to their revolver butts, ready to arrest, or possibly shoot her.

She turned to Fontaine and said simply. 'I claim diplomatic immunity, Colonel.'

Bing went to Vincent and put a hand on his arm, leaning over him to talk quietly. Genevieve joined Bing to gently take Napoleon from his grasp as Vincent began to sob noisily. Persi looked on as though stunned, while Langton slumped in his seat.

Swift came to stand beside me.

'Rather chaotic, Lennox,' he said. I've no idea if he meant my efforts at unveiling the killer or the aftermath.

'Um,' I sat down in a wicker chair and sighed, my headache suddenly returning with a feeling of utter weariness.

'Sir?' Greggs came over from a shady corner.

I looked up at him, his hang-doggedness even more pronounced, his shoulders slumped and dejected. Poor chap, adventuring in foreign fields was too much for him. I've no doubt that witnessing a cold-blooded execution hadn't helped either.

'Why don't you go and pack, Greggs?' I told him.

'Very good, sir.' He trudged off, shell-shocked.

Swift went to Fontaine and they formed a huddle away from the rest of us. I could see there was an animated discussion taking place.

I glanced over at Persi, breaking her trance-like state as she watched the actions around us. She came over and sat in the chair next to me.

'Heathcliff,' she began. 'Lennox, I mean. That was… well, it was rather shocking, darling.'

'Um,' I murmured, then held my hand out to place it in hers.

'Look, Charles needs to get away from here.' She paused to fix her blue eyes on mine. 'He's not as immune as he thinks. I know him, his sister's death almost destroyed him and now…' She looked about. 'And now this.'

She squeezed my hand then returned to Langton's side. She took his arm gently and persuaded him to rise to his feet before leading him away. My heart sank.

Swift came to my side as Fontaine suddenly snapped out orders. His men moved forward to surround the body, then started to push people toward the door, back into the courtyard.

'He's going to detain Lady Maitland,' Swift said. 'Everyone else can leave.'

He waited for me to reply but I didn't.

'Including us,' he added. 'Lennox, are you listening to me?'

'Yes,' I muttered.

'Right.' He waited while I gathered up my little dog and slowly followed him out.

Fontaine came to my rooms some time later as I sat by the window staring out.

'Felicitations, Major, I had not expected you to uncover the culprit.' He made a short bow.

I nodded in return, wondering what he wanted.

'You were correct that Langton did not make the attempt to murder Mademoiselle Belvoir.' He sat down on a hard chair, his back and shoulders rigid. I imagined it must be difficult for him to admit he was wrong. 'Madame Vincent stole Langton's gun and donned his coat and hat. I suspect she filled the overlarge shoes with socks or stockings to try to make them fit her.'

'Unsuccessfully,' I replied. 'Didn't you question the bath-draw boy about it?'

'As your friend Swift remarked, he was an unreliable witness, and,' he added an aside with a brief smile, 'an unreliable guard too.'

'And it suited your purpose to use his garbled account as an excuse to accuse Langton and lock him up.' I threw at him.

He shrugged. 'I have done worse.'

I looked again at the hard lines around his eyes and nodded. I'm sure he had done worse, he would consider it his duty, although I still liked to believe he was a fair man beneath the tough exterior.

He continued. 'Mademoiselle Carruthers has been officially cleared, I have expunged her records.'

'They should never have existed.' I retorted.

'No, in this you are wrong,' he made as if to argue, but paused and moderated his tone. 'But, I have not come to dispute with you, I came here to thank you for your work.'

I nodded an acknowledgment. 'I suppose peace keeping must be a difficult job.'

'It is,' his face returned to stone. 'And these events have not made it any easier. Bon voyage, Major.' He rose to leave and I got up and walked to the door with him.

Once over the threshold he paused and gave a brief salute, I returned it, watched him descend the stairs, then went back to my room with a heavy heart.

Bing turned up some time later, holding Napoleon.

'Hello, old bean.'

'Bing,' I replied from the sofa.

'We're running away together.' Bing grinned.

'You and Napoleon?'

He put the little dog down and he and Foggy gambolled about the room.

He laughed. 'No, Genevieve and I. Napoleon too, of course. We're off to the bright lights.'

'Hollywood?'

'And movies, if they'll have us.'

'You're going to make Napoleon a star?' I asked reaching down to stroke the little dog's head as he came to jump up at me.

'Who knows.' His laughter died. 'Thank you, Lennox, for putting an end to the misery. I don't think anyone truly realised what Beatrice's death had meant to us. Or how much frisson Josephine caused amongst us in the crew – and to me, of course.'

I nodded mutely, I was rather touched actually.

'Well, come along little doggy,' he picked up Napoleon and left with a cheery wave.

Swift arrived almost on his heels, wearing his trench coat unbelted and loose.

'Fontaine's holding Lady Maitland, but she insists he'll have to let her go and I think he will.'

Greggs had gone off to order coffee and biscuits.

'It was cold-blooded murder, Swift.' We sat by the window, sun streaming in to light the room with bright warmth.

He shrugged glumly. 'Perhaps that's what spies do. You said it yourself, assassination.'

'What time are we leaving?' I asked, having had enough of murder and death.

'In about an hour, Jamal will come and tell us. The place is in a bit of an uproar, actually.' He explained. 'They're arranging to remove the body and Vincent's a mess. I said I'd go and help.'

'Good of you,' I remarked.

He nodded, patted Foggy again and left quietly.

Greggs arrived with a tray of coffee and goodies, then went off again. He's a stalwart old soldier in a crisis, even if it wasn't really our crisis.

I felt a bit better after the coffee and whatnots. Dreadnaught came in just as I finished the last confection. I would have locked the damn door but I had been hoping Persi would walk through it.

'He is a nice dog,' Dreadnaught remarked as Foggy greeted him.

'What did you want Dreadnaught?' I asked.

'A copy of the map,' he replied.

'What?'

'I think you heard…'

'Yes,' I cut across him. 'Why?'

He laughed. 'I want to go home, Major.'

'Really?' I said, wondering what he was talking about and wishing he'd clear off.

'I need the map. The location of the oil, I know you have it.'

'Ah,' I nodded. 'And this will help you return home – assuming you mean home to Germany?'

'Ja, Germany. The new government would welcome such information. And if I brought it to them, then I believe they will forgive me. After all, they profess that they did not support the Kaiser's plan any more than me. Although they did not try stop him.'

'And you did?'

'I tried what little I could. And now I am exiled for it.'

'You realise I'd be committing treason if I gave you a copy.'

'Germany is not allowed to make any overseas explorations. Nothing will come of it, Major, but it will persuade them of my good intention and my loyalty to my country.'

'Hum,' I wasn't prepared to make any commitments. 'I thought you said it was stifling, or words to that effect. And that's why you were in Hollywood rather than Hohenburg.'

'But, it is still my home and I miss it. And my family.' He paused. 'Maybe I can help bring change – I would like to try.'

'I don't actually have a copy, old chap.'

'But you can find one?' he asked.

'I'll consider it. But there's something I'd like in exchange.'

'What?'

I told him, he laughed, agreed and left.

Greggs returned to tell me he was going to supervise Jamal and the Rolls Royce, then he went off again.

Persi came in last of all, just as I finished tucking my notebook and the photographs into my carpet bag.

'Hello.' She raised her eyes to mine.

'Hello, old stick.' I tried a smile.

'Lennox, I...'

I wanted to pull her into my arms but she kept her distance. 'You can call me Heathcliff if you like.'

She laughed. 'Then you'll really hate me.'

'I'll never hate you, Persi.'

'Darling,' she began again. 'I'm going back to Byblos.'

'With Langton?'

'No, although I do need to make sure he returns to England. I think Lady Maitland will help him once she's released. But, Darling…'

'Persi,' I stepped closer, took a deep breath and said, 'Persi, I love you.'

Her eyes shot up. 'I love you too,' she said.

I moved to draw her into my arms, but she held up her hand to stop me. 'But…I need some time, Lennox.'

I stifled a sigh. 'Why? What is stopping us both getting on the aeroplane now? You don't need to work, Persi. I have enough for us both.' Actually, that may have been an exaggeration, but it was said in the hope of being true.

'It's not about my work, darling. It's about being sure.' Her voice trembled. 'Charles and I had been inseparable before the war. We promised no-one else would ever come between us – that we'd be together forever, if we survived. And then… he betrayed me.' She paused, holding back tears. 'So I fled. I buried myself in my work and I thought I had got over him. But, you see, I don't know if I have and that's why… that's why…' Tears began to run down her cheeks and I held out my arms as she crushed her face against my chest.

I tugged a handkerchief out of my pocket to put into her hand and she sobbed into it then blew her nose. I decided to let her keep it.

'You could think about it in England, my love. You don't have to stay out here,' I tried to persuade her.

She attempted a teary smile. 'It's for the best, darling, really it is. I will write.' She dropped her arms from mine.

'Persi, as soon as you have made a decision I will come to you. Just send word. Do you promise me?'

She nodded, her blonde hair catching the sunlight streaming in from the windows. 'Yes, I promise.'

I pulled her toward me to gaze down into her eyes. I wanted to absorb every detail of her face, before I pulled her into my arms and kissed her.

CHAPTER 28

Dust and sand swirled up from the runway. I was holding my carpet bag in one hand and Greggs' suitcase in the other. He was clutching Foggy and they both had cotton wool stuffed in their ears and scarves tied around their heads. I had told him it was pointless, but he refused to listen.

The Bleriot-Spad started up with a spluttering roar and the propeller sent more sand whirling into the air. Swift was fidgeting to be allowed aboard but they hadn't even wheeled up the steps yet.

Dreadnaught was behind me, he had far too much luggage. I've no idea how he thought they'd let him take it, but then he was a movie star and a German Baron, so perhaps they would. He had a copy of Hanno's map in his pocket – it wasn't an exact copy. Actually, I'd drawn out a map of the Persian gulf, put a couple of random crosses on the west coast and given it to him. He seemed quite happy with it.

Just as a group of airport staff began pushing the steps toward the rumbling aeroplane, everyone turned to look in the opposite direction. I frowned, and shifted slowly around. A group of men on camels had approached. There were five of them, four dressed in robes of black and the chap in front entirely in flowing white. They stopped a few yards away.

Jamal had been standing beside the Rolls in which he'd transported us, but at the faintest nod from the man in white, he ran over to the group. The man leaned from his camel to pass a small package down to him and give him a curt instruction. Jamal nodded, bowed, then turned to trot in our direction, his hand holding his turban in place against the growing power of the propeller's blast.

'Effendi, a gift from the Sheik himself.' He shouted to me as he held out a small cedar wood box, delicately carved and etched.

I took it, lifted up the box and gave a deep bow in the direction of the sheik.

Qarsan nodded and then nudged his camel to turn about and they went off, back to the desert, or wherever they'd come from.

'Was that him?' Swift came over.

'Yes.' I had dropped my bags to take the gift.

Greggs came over to stare in mute silence – actually, he might have said something but it was lost amongst the scarves and muffler.

'What is it?' Dreadnaught joined us.

I opened the lid. A gold ring caught the light and glinted in the sun dropping low in the amber-hued dusk. It was a signet ring, set with a black stone which had been delicately engraved with a ship, a single billowing sail and a cresting horse's head on the bow. I slipped it on, it was a perfect fit.

'Phoenician,' Swift remarked.

I nodded.

'So, are you now an ancient mariner?' Dreadnaught laughed.

We looked at him. 'Very amusing,' I muttered.

EPILOGUE

Tommy thought the blazon on the ring was marvellous and insisted on making a drawing of it to show to all his school friends.

My library had been polished and spruced in my absence and I sat in comfort, with my feet up in front of a blazing fire and a hot toddy at my side. It had taken almost a week to recover from the appalling flight and the malady that had developed as soon as I stepped off the damn plane.

Swift had caught it too, but struggled on to Braeburn where Florence would be anxiously waiting.

Tommy was rattling on. 'Now that you ain't dying, sir, can you tell me all about Damascus, and the camels and your adventures? And the movie-making!'

'I wasn't dying Tommy. I had flu and possibly pneumonia.' I coughed. 'And bronchitis.'

'Auntie said you only had a bad cold.'

'Nonsense.' I coughed again and reached for my toddy. 'Just because I managed to fight it off, doesn't mean it wasn't serious.'

'Did you bring any autographs, sir? Of the stars?'
Tommy asked.

'Possibly. They were in my carpet bag. You had better
ask Greggs where they are.'

'He put a big thick envelope up on the shelf, sir.'
Tommy pointed, then jumped onto a stool to reach. 'It's
here.' He handed them to me and stood at the side of my
chair, almost hopping with excitement.

I pulled out the contents and leafed through them.
'Here,' I held one up.

The boy's face fell. 'That's Mr Gregg's, sir.'

'Yes, he's in a short movie. It's called Delilah of the
Desert.' I held up another one of Foggy in his top knot.

'That's Mr Fogg, sir. He looks like a girl.' He didn't
sound terribly impressed.

'Right,' I passed him a different photo.

'Who's that, sir?'

'Harry Bing, he's second lead. Well, he was, I'm not
sure if he's still treading the boards, or whatever it is they
do.'

'Oh,' his face fell. 'I don't think he's really a star, 'cause
I've never heard of him.'

'Hum,' I showed him the next one out. 'How about
this?'

The boy gasped. 'Oh, sir. It's Josephine Belvoir. She's
famous! Did you get her autograph?'

'Erm, no. Bad news I'm afraid, she… erm, well, she
had an unfortunate accident.'

'You mean…?'

'Yes, dead. But it's a jolly good photograph.' I gave it to him, she wore an elegant chiffon gown with a diamond necklace and looked stunning.

'Thank you, sir.' He stared at it dubiously. 'Do you think it matters if she's dead?'

'No, in fact, it might even make it more impressive, because there won't be any more!' I said with encouragement.

'Yes, it's jolly super, sir!' He broke into a big smile.

'Here,' I said, 'I saved the best for last. He autographed it especially for you.'

Scrawled across a corner was written – '*To Tommy Jenkins, with best wishes, Dick Dreadnaught.*'

'Oh, sir! Dick Dreadnaught! He's a huge star. I saw him in a movie last summer, The Lost Sailor of Nanking. He was ever so good.' He bounced on the spot with glee.

'I'm pleased you like it Tommy, although he's actually given up movies. Gone back to Germany, apparently.' With a map, I thought to myself, which held as little value as the signed photograph he'd exchanged it for.

'So he's not a movie star any more, neither? That's terrific that is, now nobody will have anything like it' He sounded positively gleeful. 'These are going be the best collection of autographs ever, sir!' He bounded off toward the kitchen clutching the photographs.

'Tell Greggs that tea and cakes wouldn't go amiss,' I called after him but I don't know if he heard. He came back twenty minutes later. I was reading by the fire, 'The

Hound of The Baskervilles' a marvellous book, full of
adventure and some excellent tips for sleuthing.

'There's a letter come, sir.' He announced, then jumped
into the chair opposite.

'Oh,' I closed my book. I'd been hoping for news from
foreign shores. 'Where is it?'

'It is here, sir.' Greggs arrived with a laden tray and
a pale blue envelope propped on a tea cup. Foggy came
in with him, straight from the garden. He was covered
in snow and paused to shake it off over my legs before
he climbed into his basket. I lifted Tubbs off my lap to
place him next to the little dog and they both snuggled
up together.

'What does it say?'

'Ah, one moment, sir.' Greggs poured tea for me and
served a hot buttered scone on a plate. It was fresh out
of the oven and jolly good. Tommy snaffled one too and
Tubbs gave up his spot by the fire to jump onto the table
and await a saucer of cream, which had become a new
habit when tea was served.

Greggs straightened his back, pulled out a pair of pince-
nez he'd recently acquired and placed them on the end of
his nose. He peered at the letter, bringing it closer to his
face, then moved it away. 'It is from Inspector Swift, sir.'

'Oh.' My hopes wilted. 'Very good. Read it out, would
you?'

He cleared his throat.

*'Home and all are well. Florence is blooming, she has been
supervising the rebuilding works with Donald MacDonald.*

I had a bit of a cold but it soon passed. My old friend at Scotland Yard has sent word – Bing and Miss Genevieve are in Hollywood, so is Vincent. He plans to continue making movies. The death of Mrs Vincent has been announced, it is said she suffered sudden heart failure.' Greggs paused and looked at me with raised brows.

'Well, it's true Greggs, they just failed to explain the actual cause of her heart failing.' Such as a bullet, I thought, but didn't say because we didn't want Tommy to hear.

Greggs recommenced reading. *'Lady Maitland has returned to the Foreign Office, Langton flew back with her and is believed to be taking a sabbatical. Baron Grunberg has resumed residence in his ancestral home and has been offered a post with Royal Dutch Shell, an oil exploration company.'*

That raised my brows as images of Dutch chaps digging fruitlessly in the sand sprang to mind. I shook them off to listen, but there wasn't actually much more in the way of news, Swift went on about the castle and preparations for the baby and Christmas and whatnot. We heard him out and then I asked Greggs to place the missive on my desk.

'You haven't seen any more letters, have you old chap?' I asked him.

'I'm afraid not, sir. But may I remind you that you are leaving for Melrose Court tomorrow for Christmas.'

'Yes, I haven't forgotten, Greggs. I've been ill, not comatose.'

305

'As you say, sir.'

I finished my tea feeling a bit disconsolate, so I took a bite of hot scone and jam.

'I showed Auntie the photographs you gave me, sir,' Tommy piped up. 'She said that dead movie actress was in the papers.' He stared at the photograph of Josephine he'd brought back in with him. 'What's the name of the movie, sir? I'm goin' to go and watch it when it's on at the pictures.'

'Didn't I tell you, Tommy?'

'No, sir.'

'It's called 'Death in Damascus'.'

AUTHOR'S NOTES

Please don't read this until you've finished the book!

The film, 'The Sheik', did indeed hit the screens in 1921 and was a roaring success. It broke box office records and started a new fashion for exotic romance. The film was made in the deserts of California starring Rudolph Valentino and Agnes Ayres.

The world in 1921 was a very different place to today and far more complex than I have portrayed. The hunt for oil was fully underway in various parts of the globe. Oil had been discovered in Basra (which was then in Mesopotamia before it came under Iraqi control), but the general belief among the Western nations was that there was nothing worthwhile in the Arabian peninsula. This was despite rumours of oil seeps near Qatif on the south-west coast of the Persian Gulf.

It is true that men were sent out to search, but they rarely returned, and never with any news of discovery. One man changed that. In 1922 Emir Ibn Saud, the Arabian leader who eventually quelled the warring factions to found and rule Saudi Arabia, agreed to meet New Zealander, Major Frank Holmes. Holmes was an experienced mining engineer who had seen extensive action in the war and served with distinction. He was absolutely convinced there was oil in the region and he persuaded Ibn Saud to sign a concession to allow Holmes to begin his search. It took ten years to strike oil and by then American, British, Persian, French and Dutch oil companies had taken over the concessions. Holmes never struck it rich, but he was greatly respected by the Arabian leaders and they named him Abu Naft, or the 'Father of Oil'.

I'm afraid there was no Phoenician map to help them. The Phoenicians were an ancient maritime trading race who spanned hundreds of years before finally falling to the Romans. Our alphabet is said to have originated from the Phoenician's, and the Bible was so called because papyrus used by ancient scribes came from the Phoenician port of Gebal, which the Greeks knew as Byblos. And I suspect most folk know 'Phoenician' comes from the Greek word for the mollusc 'Phoinikes' used to provide the highly prized purple dye – the Royal Purple – which the Phoenicians produced and exported around the mediterranean world.

They did indeed use oil or 'asphaltum' to line their ships, it was also used as mortar and for just about anything that required waterproofing. Their ships are depicted with a single sail, two rowing oars and bows with cresting horse's heads.

The medallion is a figment of my imagination, as are

the ruins below Damascus, although the Romans certainly rebuilt a great deal of the city.

An account of the trading methods of the Phoenicians is to be found in a text by the Greek historian **Herodotus of Halicarnassus** 480–425 BC.

"*The Carthaginians (Phoenicians) tell us that they trade with a race of men who live in a part of Libya beyond the Pillars of Heracles. On reaching this country, they unload their goods, arrange them tidily along the beach, and then, returning to their boats, raise a smoke. Seeing the smoke, the natives come down to the beach, place on the ground a certain quantity of gold in exchange for the goods, and go off again to a distance. The Carthaginians then come ashore and take a look at the gold; and if they think it presents a fair price for their wares, they collect it and go away; if, on the other hand, it seems too little, they go back aboard and wait, and the natives come and add to the gold until they are satisfied. There is perfect honesty on both sides; the Carthaginians never touch the gold until it equals in value what they have offered for sale, and the natives never touch the goods until the gold has been taken away. Herodotus, Histories 4.196; tr. Aubrey de Selincourt.*"

Hanno the Navigator travelled all the way to the wilds of Africa and encountered Gorillas. Here's a brief account of his affairs by the Greek historian **Arrian of Nicomedia** c 92 AD–175 AD.

"Moreover, Hanno the Libyan started out from Carthage and passed the Pillars of Heracles and sailed into the outer Ocean, with Libya on his port side, and he sailed on towards the east, five-and-thirty days all told. But when at last he turned southward, he fell in with every sort of difficulty, want of water, blazing heat, and fiery streams running into the sea." —*Arrian of Nicomedia.*

And one by the Roman Encyclopedist **Pliny the Elder** written c 23 AD–79 AD.

"When the power of Carthage flourished, Hanno sailed round from Cádiz to the extremity of Arabia, and published a memoir of his voyage, as did Himilco when he was despatched at the same date to explore the outer coasts of Europe."

I am aware that the Islam forbids images and icons, but there are stone lions and ancient statues in Damascus museum and there may still be one or two quietly forgotten in backwaters within the city's ancient walls.

I do hope you enjoyed the book. I could happily expend hours upon history and its myriad complexities, but this is a story of murder, mystery and a smidgeon of adventure. The next book will take Lennox et al, to Yorkshire – that brooding county of stark moors, medieval monarchs and ancient monasteries.

I do hope you enjoyed this book. Would you like to take a look at the Heathcliff Lennox website? As a member of the Readers Club, you'll receive the FREE short story, 'Heathcliff Lennox – France 1918' and access to the 'World of Lennox' page, where you can view portraits of Lennox, Swift, Greggs, Foggy, Tubbs, Persi and Tommy Jenkins.

There are also 'inspirations' for the books, plus occasional newsletters with updates and free giveaways.

You can find the Heathcliff Lennox Readers Club, and more, at karenmenuhin.com

* * *

Here's the full Heathcliff Lennox series list. You can find each book on Amazon.

Book 1: Murder at Melrose Court
Book 2: The Black Cat Murders
Book 3: The Curse of Braeburn Castle
Book 4: Death in Damascus
Book 5: The Monks Hood Murders
Book 6: The Tomb of the Chatelaine
Book 7: The Mystery of Montague Morgan
Book 8: The Birdcage Murders – ready to pre-order now, previewed for release in Summer 2022

All the series can be found on Amazon and all good book stores.

And there are Audible versions read by Sam Dewhurst-Phillips, who is amazing, it's just like listening to a radio play. All of these can be found on Amazon, Audible and Apple Books.

A little about Karen Baugh Menuhin

1920s, Cozy crime, Traditional Detectives, Downton Abbey – I love them! Along with my family, my dog and my cat.

At 60 I decided to write, I don't know why but suddenly the stories came pouring out, along with the characters. Eccentric Uncles, stalwart butlers, idiosyncratic servants, machinating Countesses, and the hapless Major Heathcliff Lennox. A whole world built itself upon the page and I just followed along...

An itinerate traveller all my life. I grew up in the military, often on RAF bases but preferring to be in the countryside when we could. I adore whodunnits.

I have two amazing sons – Jonathan and Sam Baugh, and his wife, Wendy, and five grandchildren, Charlie, Joshua, Isabella-Rose, Scarlett and Hugo.

I am married to Krov, my wonderful husband, who is a retired film maker and eldest son of the violinist, Yehudi Menuhin. We live in the Cotswolds.

For more information my address is:
karenmenuhinauthor@littledogpublishing.com

Karen Baugh Menuhin is a member of
The Crime Writers Association

Made in the USA
Coppell, TX
07 June 2022

78547361R00175